Biblioasis International Translation Series
General Editor: Stephen Henighan

D0005745

THE MUSIC GAME

THE MUSIC GAME

STÉFANIE CLERMONT

TRANSLATED FROM THE FRENCH BY JC SUTCLIFFE

BIBLIOASIS
Windsor, Ontario

FIRST EDITION

Library and Archives Canada Cataloguing in Publication
Title: The music game / Stéfanie Clermont ; translated by JC Sutcliffe.
Other titles: Jeu de la musique. English
Names: Clermont, Stéfanie, 1988- author. | Sutcliffe, J. C., translator.
Series: Biblioasis international translation series ; 36.
Description: Series statement: Biblioasis international translation series ; 36
Translation of: Le jeu de la musique.
Identifiers: Canadiana (print) 20210318996 | Canadiana (ebook) 20210319011 |
ISBN 9781771963787 (softcover) | ISBN 9781771963794 (ebook)
Classification: LCC PS8605.L5415 J4813 2022 | DDC C843/.6—dc23

Edited by Stephen Henighan and Daniel Wells
Copyedited by John Sweet
Typeset by Vanessa Stauffer
Cover designed by Natalie Olsen

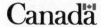

Published with the generous assistance of the Canada Council for the Arts, which last year invested $153 million to bring the arts to Canadians through-out the country, and the financial support of the Government of Canada. Biblioasis also acknowledges the support of the Ontario Arts Council (OAC), an agency of the Government of Ontario, which last year funded 1,709 indi-vidual artists and 1,078 organizations in 204 communities across Ontario, for a total of $52.1 million, and the contribution of the Government of Ontario through the Ontario Book Publishing Tax Credit and Ontario Creates.

PRINTED AND BOUND IN CANADA

Printed by Imprimerie Gauvin
Gatineau, Québec

CONTENTS

THE MUSIC GAME

PROLOGUE

THE PLACE WAS ALIVE

IT WAS A LIVING PLACE, without any responsibilities, where clean water (or at least water we liked to think was clean) had inexplicably found its way into the channels and filled up the big former reservoirs like little in-ground swimming pools where shoals of red-and-white fish lived, mysteriously, summer after summer. To get there, you had to go to the end of Rue Ontario, and then a bit farther, and then cross the railway tracks. The grass grew more than two metres high. There was no concrete except for a few islands of graffiti dotted around, and everywhere else was grass and spiky bushes and the tall trees whose leaves chattered loudly in summer. We swam in the reservoirs, even if the water irritated our skin every other year. At night we made fires with branches from the big trees. We napped in the long grass, sad and alone or surrounded by friends and drunk on sunshine. This was in Hochelaga. Right at the end of

Rue Ontario. You know where that is? On the other side of the tracks. Vincent loved that place. In August, he went there to kill himself. He hanged himself from a tree. The next summer there weren't many campfires there. This place without a name had become the place where a friend had died. I went back there one time and couldn't stop staring at the trees, as if the one that had helped him that day would somehow make its presence known to me. And then the seasons passed. I don't know if this place still exists. I don't know if the underground water (or was it rainwater?) still fills those pretend pools. I don't know if, as rumour had it, they put condos up there. I don't know if there are still fish living in the reservoirs and crazy people who swim there on the other side of the tracks right at the end of Rue Ontario.

There are barely any of these quiet places, places where you can live and die in peace. There are barely any left. And the fewer there are, the less we remember that other life, the one that begins in the stomach and explodes in the throat, in the eyes, between our legs, in our tongues that touch the sun.

PART 1

FIRST WITCH

When shall we three meet again
In thunder, lightning, or in rain?

SECOND WITCH

When the hurly burly's done
When the battle's lost and won

THIRD WITCH

That will be ere the set of sun

FIRST WITCH

Where the place?

—WILLIAM SHAKESPEARE, *Macbeth*

THE EMPLOYEE

IN A BRIEF LULL BETWEEN two customers, I headed over to the cash register and pressed the Feed button. I took the rectangle of white paper that spooled out of the printer and laid it on the metal work counter. Mrs Gélinas had gone off to get "a nice cup of coffee," and I, the employee, was now all by myself at the stall, desperate to get a few ideas down. I unclipped the pen from my apron, stuffed a handful of ground cherries into my mouth, and bent over the scrap of paper. In tiny writing I scrawled a list of things to do when I got home. Laundry. Push-ups, sit-ups. Read the news (thirty minutes). Research Quebec's colonial history. Submit a poem to a poetry review. When I'd filled the whole paper, I folded it in half, slipped it into the back pocket of my jean shorts, pulled out a fresh slip of register tape, and wrote a list of things I wanted to do before the end of the year. Join the Y. Finish writing poetry collection. Send at least three short stories to literary reviews. Learn Spanish. Save five hundred dollars (unrealistic?). Take driving test. Take first-aid course. Deepen connections with friends. Learn to identify local plants. Go camping (more than once). See Jess at least three times. For a split second, I forgot I was at work.

But the appearance of two customers dragged me quickly back to earth. It was a woman and a man, thirtyish, hunting for the perfect basket of strawberries to take to a family dinner. I spotted them out of the corner of my eye as they peered at the fruit. The guy wore a grey T-shirt that clung to his pecs and showed the first hint of a paunch; his hair was still wet from a recent shower; around his neck he wore a little cross on a gold chain that he probably hadn't taken off since his confirmation. The woman was wearing one of those synthetic tanks with a built-in bra, its criss-crossed straps forming the shape of a sun on her back; her hair was pulled back from her face with a pair of Dolce & Gabbana shades. The two of them gave off such a vibe of contented exhaustion, lullabies, soft words, and milky kisses that I was astonished—almost concerned—not to see a baby carrier on either of their shoulders.

"My mother loves strawberries," the man said, raising his eyes heavenwards to indicate that his mother was rather difficult.

"Should we get those? How about these ones, honey?" the woman said, tasting strawberries, moving away from her boyfriend but still holding his hand so she tugged him with her.

"Whatever you think, bae," said the man, in a tone that suggested his girlfriend was the one being difficult right then.

I took a couple of steps sideways and flashed them a friendly, unassuming smile. "It's your decision," my smile said. I noticed they were both wearing flip-flops, and the woman had painted her toenails white. While they were trying to decide, I went on thinking about my lists. Take jiu-jitsu classes. Discover good music. Go to the art house cinema. Do more dumpster diving. Make jam. Get my name on the waiting list for co-op housing. Register for university? No. I mentally put a line through that last item.

"Excuse me!" said the woman, her mouth full of strawberries. She took a moment to mime the ecstasy she was experiencing from the little red fruit and then asked, "Where are these strawberries from?"

"They're from the Île d'Orléans," I said, in precisely the same way I might have said, "They're from Wonderland."

"These are the ones! We have to get these ones!" said the woman, handing me her strawberry tops, which I tossed into the soggy cardboard box we used as a garbage can. "This is the winning basket of strawberries!"

She laughed and turned to her boyfriend, but his phone had started vibrating in his pocket and he was walking off to take the call.

"Yyyyeeeeello?" said the man, as the woman pulled out an enormous white leather wallet to pay.

I swaddled the basket in a plastic bag, held it out to the woman, and took one last look around to make sure the pair hadn't forgotten a stroller somewhere nearby. As I looked, I met the eyes of the Lebanese grocer, who was sweeping the floor in front of his stall. I said, "Have a nice day," to the customer, waved at the grocer, and went back to my list. Just then Mrs Gélinas arrived back at the stall with her coffee and a pastry.

"A nice cup of coffee to start the morning!" she said. She perched on a stool and bit into her Danish. I nodded in agreement, as if to say the boss certainly deserved such a treat before making a start on her workday. Silently, I was filled with disgust at myself.

I stuffed the list into my pocket, smoothed down my apron, and headed over to the walk-in fridge. I got out some crates of strawberries and raspberries and laid them on the work counter. I grabbed the all-purpose knife lying on the stainless steel surface and, forcing myself to repress the vivid images of bloody accidents parading through my head, I cut open some of the boxes and arranged them in rows on the fake-grass display. Mrs Gélinas had already had to abandon her breakfast to deal with a regular, an old guy wearing a canary-yellow suit. I opened a cupboard underneath the display and took out a variety of small, medium, and large baskets. An idea for a poem came to me (red fruit, canary-yellow suit, bloody workplace accident, grey souls) and I plunged my hand into my pocket to find some paper to scribble it down—but then I noticed a customer in his fifties wearing cycling gear waggling his chin at me, waving a basket of raspberries to get my attention. I wiped my hands on my apron and went over to serve him. When I was done with the cyclist, there was a young anglophone woman—tattooed arms, half-shaven head, red dress with white polka dots—then a gangly French guy in his twenties, then a retired Italian, and then half a dozen other early risers.

Whenever I had a spare moment, I got some more paper

and wrote more lists. Things to do every day: write, eat well, do more push-ups and sit-ups, study film or read (postmodern philosophy, Russian literary classics, and so on), write a letter to a friend or to someone in prison. Write to Jess. I drew a heart around Jess's name. I'd remember to write to Jess without putting it on the list, but I liked forming the letters of his name. A list of things I should stop putting into my body: alcohol, coffee, cigarettes, sugar. A list of friends I ought to write to more often. A list of books to read. A list of nice clothes I'd buy myself one day.

I yawned and glanced at the clock. Still only nine. On the other side of our displays of strawberries, raspberries, and rhubarb, a constant stream of customers had started pouring into the Jean Talon Market. The typical customer wandered around, latte in hand, eyes half-closed or hidden behind smoked glasses, a satisfied smile playing on their lips, delighted that spring had finally arrived. I remembered sadly that I too had once loved spring; that I too had once been a customer at this market, wandering around the stalls with a latte in my hand. But this year spring had left me cold. That wasn't quite accurate, though. It was more that I felt as though I'd become part of it myself, that I was simply another adorable bud on the verge of blooming, a young shoot engorged with sap, just one more detail among all the charming elements of the Jean Talon Market. I was ornamental. I'd now become something akin to the coffee they offer customers at a car dealership: a nice little touch.

Anka arrived at the stall pushing a cart. She didn't say hi, and I didn't say hi to her either. Anka made me nervous. She managed the second Gélinas Fruits stall, on the other side of the market, so I never got to work with her. Every morning when she arrived, I tried to do something interesting so she'd notice me. But what could I do other than sort strawberries and serve customers? How could I know what Anka was interested in since I'd never talked to her? I groped my way forward. Some days I directed tortured looks her way, others I smiled at her. Today, I pushed the sleeves of my T-shirt up to my shoulders and tried to ignore her.

"Hi, Lucille," Anka said. She'd been at Gélinas Fruits long enough to be on first-name terms with the boss. Her voice was husky, low, sweet.

"Hello, Anka," Mrs Gélinas said.

She put her bag in the cupboard (Right next to mine! I thought), disappeared into the walk-in fridge, and came back out with at least six crates, which she carried as though they weighed nothing. She piled them onto her cart and repeated the operation several more times. Then she came back over to her bag, took out a cap, which she put backwards on top of her curly hair, and went off pulling the cart like a calm warrior heading out to the battlefield. She was wearing a T-shirt with wide stripes and overall shorts that revealed long, muscular legs a basketball player would have been proud of. I sighed and closed my eyes, overwhelmed by desire, and then I tidied up the metal counter.

During my lunch break, when I spent ten dollars because yet again I'd forgotten to bring a sandwich, I got out my notebook and started writing a serious list: Staying in Montreal vs. Getting the fuck out to the country.

Points in Montreal's favour: It's a place where you never stop learning new things. So many stories mingle here. I like living in Montreal because there are books and music, readers and musicians. The people I know who've moved to the country hardly read at all anymore. The only things they read are Margaret Atwood or *The Big Mushroom Guide*. In Montreal, you have a lot more opportunities to meet people, to develop meaningful connections, to form groups with like-minded people (which is necessary for the struggle). I don't want to save *myself alone*, I don't want to be an individualist. You have to be strategic: there are more opportunities for the struggle in the city (at least for now).

What options would I have for a social life in the country? A) end up in a polyamorous collective, B) become the village hermit to the detriment of my mental health, C) try to integrate into village life, also to the detriment of my mental health. I wrote "alienating" in my journal, landing on the *mot juste*. If I leave here, I might never make another friend, never mind find comrades or lovers. When I reread, I noticed that I'd moved from listing to editorializing. I took a bite of my shawarma and a sip of Canada Dry. Then I picked up my pen again and wrote: Also (by this point I had greatly reduced the size of my handwriting), maybe one day I will publish books or find myself a job in journalism or something like that, and there are more potential contacts in Montreal. I sighed.

Points against the city: There is no life except for human life. There are no lakes, rivers, forests. There are no deer, clearings, fish. Just a few stars one night in ten. It fucking stinks. The tap water tastes of chlorine. I live on the third floor of a triplex on Saint-Denis with two other girls. I can barely get three tomatoes to grow on the balcony.

I have to buy, steal, or dumpster-dive for all my food. I can barely even get a job in a café because jobs are so scarce. You practically need ten years' experience just to get a minimum-wage job with decent conditions. If I stay here, I'll probably die without ever seeing a fox. Everything irritates me, everything makes me sick, the cars, the buses, the trucks, the police, the Metro, the jobs at the Jean Talon Market, my friends' careers, my friends' studies, my friends' alcoholism, my alcoholism, the Place des Arts, the Grand Prix, the Plateau Mont-Royal neighbourhood, the Petit Laurier neighbourhood, *Tout le monde en parle*, the cat grooming places, the twenty-dollar fish and chips, the Mile-Ex, the queer parties where everyone is too cool to talk to you, the men who call out "nice ass," the crooked bosses, the crooked landlords, the crooked friends of friends, Jarry Metro station, and the hundreds of people who every single day walk past old beggars and the homeless woman who sells the *Itinéraire* and the people who hand out the *24h* newspaper, staring at the ground and then buying themselves a five-dollar coffee a block later. I feel alienated, I wrote again, stating the obvious but not caring, because it was my own personal list and not something I planned on publishing. (Sip of Canada Dry, bite of shawarma.)

Conclusion: it's lose-lose. I'd like to quit, but where would I go? I scrawled. The things I want to be free of are everywhere. I underlined the word "everywhere." And then I felt anxiety swoosh up in my stomach like an elevator when I thought of the career I still didn't have, of my bank account, which never had more than seven hundred dollars in it, of my single film studies class that had cost more money than I would make this summer (I still wasn't an official resident of Quebec), and from which I'd gained nothing except the certainty that I was the least audiovisually talented person in the world and that I would never have another good idea again (I'd had my last good idea when I was fifteen). I thought of my savings account once more, which I'd dipped into regularly over the past year and which now had only two hundred dollars in it, of my three unpaid internships for various cultural organizations that hadn't led anywhere, of my friends, who were disappearing one by one under mountains of stress, work, trials, and relationships, of Jess, whom I could probably never sponsor according to Citizenship and Immigration Canada's criteria, of the money I owed my friends, of the money I owed the City of Montreal, of the money I owed the library, of the money I owed my father, of the cavities in two of my teeth that I hadn't yet had filled, of the ideas for my book that would go with me to the grave, and which would rot along with me, never developed. Around me, the clamour, whiffs of coffee, ice cream, fish, Mexican pulled pork sandwiches, children crying, the admiring *ooh*s and *aah*s that kept me from eating my shawarma and writing my list in peace. Some buskers were playing "Hallelujah" on an electric keyboard and improvising on the flute. Children were asking, "Can I have this?" Adults were exchanging dirty twenty-dollar bills for smelly small change. Carbon copies of me pulled on aprons and invited customers to taste the plums and tomatoes. Trucks backed up, car trunks opened, cart wheels squeaked against the concrete and the gravel. Couples with their arms around each other's waists exclaimed, "Oh, I just want to stop by

Première Moisson," and parents commanded, "You have to stay with Mommy and Daddy." Nothing ever happened that didn't fit with the idea of the Jean Talon Market. I was imprisoned in an ad for the market, an ad that had already been running for several weeks. Was this endless carousel of customers real? Maybe it was just a hologram projected by the market management in the hope of attracting real customers. I lowered my eyes to avoid the gaze of these virtual customers to whom I would soon be selling fruit. I was hot, I was trembling with nervous tension, and my lunch break was coming to an end.

SPRING GAVE WAY TO SUMMER. I still hadn't gone camping, I still hadn't learned how to identify any local plants, I still hadn't done a single push-up. I hadn't managed to get past page fifty of Foucault's *Discipline and Punish*. I often wore the same T-shirt for three days in a row, since I never had time to do laundry. I'd get back home at seven and start drinking. I cooked and listened to music for an hour, I ate too quickly, I took long showers, and then I put on my T-shirt and boxers. Sometimes Céline called and asked me to go out, but I said no, I was always overwhelmed with fatigue. I would watch an episode of *Breaking Bad* and regret it, and then watch a few episodes of *Buffy the Vampire Slayer* to get over it. Before I went to sleep, I'd drink a few beers in bed and start reading a page of *War and Peace*, only to realize at the end of the second paragraph that I'd been on the same page for three days. I fell asleep to recordings of different versions of *Starmania* that I found on YouTube. I would write at night, whenever I woke up, drenched in sweat after an alcohol-induced nightmare. I'd turn on my bedside lamp and scribble down descriptions of ghosts, precipices with crumbling walls, rowboats on dark waves; then lose my notebook in the sheets and never again read what I'd written.

"It takes me back to my childhood!" a customer said one day as she tasted the currants that Gélinas Fruits sold at that time of the year.

The customer's skin was wrinkled and very tanned. She had blue eyes and hair the red-wine colour that some women in their sixties think it's a good idea to add yellow-orange highlights to. Behind her, to her left and right, three other customers who looked dangerously like her were also shopping. Since I didn't want to be rude and let them see I couldn't tell them apart, I'd developed a system based on their clothes. Basket of blackberries and half a crate of strawberries from the Île d'Orléans: peach camisole. Three baskets of raspberries and a small container of *gadelles* just to taste: long blue dress. It was working for the time being.

"Are these little bitty ones good? Aren't they bird food?" asked the man accompanying the woman with burgundy hair and the blue dress (bald head, big clean hands, Swiss Army watch, red striped polo shirt, fat stomach, beige shorts with a visible wallet bulge in the pocket, piercing, mocking blue eyes: definitely a retired police officer, I decided).

"You've never eaten *gadelles*? Well, in *that* case!"

I realized she was about to change her order.

"We'll take a medium *gadelles*," she said mischievously.

I gave her a complicit smile. I lifted up a basket of *gadelles*, which I put down on the work counter, not without having first pulled two off the bunch to stuff into my mouth. I delighted in the bitter spikes that splurted out of the red balls. I rubbed my fingers together on either side of a plastic bag to separate the sides, I pulled it off the roll of bags hanging from the cupboards, I put the basket at the bottom of the bag, and I knotted the bag handles underneath the basket's handle.

"There you go," I said, in the tone a mother might use with her baby as she latched it onto her breast.

"Thanks, hon," the customer said, without giving me a tip. After all, the joy of working with *gadelles* all day should surely be enough.

Gadelles are shiny little red fruit that taste deliciously bitter and grow in bunches on bushes. People often get them mixed up with redcurrants, "which taste similar but are bigger and less juicy." Mrs Gélinas had to explain that to me, because I'd never actually heard of *gadelles* before I entered the world of fruit selling. Now I was the one who explained the difference to confused customers. Redcurrants? No, *gadelles*! They're slightly bitter. Every time I sold some and the customer said, "Redcurrants?" it reminded me of my grandmother's voice, tuneful, high-pitched, and nasal, when she used to sing the nursery rhyme "Five Currant Buns in a Baker's Shop" to me.

The customers were transported back into their memories by the display of fruit in general, but especially by that specific fruit. Anyone over forty, in particular, got excited when they recognized the *gadelles:* "My grandmother had a bush of these in her yard! All right, then, we'll take a small container!" And then they recited a few phrases and made a series of gestures (going into raptures, getting out the wallet, paying, leaving happy) as if it was a comedy sketch they'd learned off by heart. Pretty much all our white Québécois customers of a certain age had had a grandmother with a *gadelle* bush in her yard. I would have liked to know whatever happened to all these customers' grandmothers' yards with their *gadelle* bushes. Maybe they'd been sold and demolished. Sold to the suppliers of Gélinas Fruits? I laughed at my own joke as I counted out the change and said, "Can I help the next person please?" and saying, "Here you go!" "Here you go!" "Here you go!" I didn't know much of Quebec outside Montreal and Gatineau, but once I'd gone to a friend's cottage in the Laurentians and I'd noticed several properties for sale. If I ever had a piece of land with a *gadelle* bush on it, I'd never sell it, I promised myself, all the while knowing that I would probably never have to keep this promise. I wanted to know: Who could really justify having left a place where this delicious red fruit grew in the yard?

SOMETIMES, WHEN THE WEATHER WASN'T as good, there was more downtime, so the people who worked at our stall had to find things to say to each other.

One day Ahmed told me that when he wasn't working at the market, he also taught history, math, and science in a high school and that he had once been a university math prof. He was one of the most senior people at Gélinas Fruits.

"The subject doesn't matter. I'm interested in everything. But what I'm really passionate about is teaching. It's having students who say, 'I hate math,' and making them love it. I ask them, 'Why don't you like math? Did a teacher once tell you you were bad at math?' It's almost always what happened. A student got intimidated by an impatient teacher. I tell them, 'Listen, we're going to look at this a different way. Math can be enjoyable, just take it one step at a time.' That's what I like. And that's how you get the student to trust you."

There was also Melanie, a woman in her forties who dressed like a teenager. One day she told me she had a fifteen-year-old son.

"He really likes rap. I don't know much about it, but he's introduced me to some pretty good stuff! Ken West? Kanye West, that's the one. It's pretty good. Martin's a good kid, right. I just want him to finish high school. He's smart. Really smart. But he doesn't love school. That's fine. I told him, there's no need to go to Cégep. You just have to find something you love, stay on the right track, and stay out of trouble."

Loan was twenty or twenty-one, and one day she told me she'd broken up with the guy she'd been dating for several weeks.

"There were signs. The other day, right, we went to mini-golf. And he was always wanting to get past the other teams, even the kids. I was all like, relax, it's just mini-golf. But he wanted to win. The worst part was that I won. And then he sulked, like seriously, super bad loser. The other thing is, he always drives way over the speed limit. And when I tell him to stop, guess what? He doesn't stop."

And in this way, thanks to language and the short minutes when we weren't machines packing up *gadelles* or counting money, but people speaking to each other, I got attached to them. I found them interesting, I wanted to be sure everything was going to work out for Martin, I wanted to go to one of Ahmed's classes, I wanted to invite Loan out on a girls' night. I talked to them too. I told them I was from Ottawa originally ("Right, that explains the accent," they said kindly), that I had a boyfriend in California. I wasn't ashamed to say I worked full-time at the market, nor that I was a full-time waitress before that, nor that I would probably be on welfare after this. After all, they were all there too, on their own journeys.

The days went by more quickly when it rained. But soon, the sun came out of hiding and with it a new procession of customers who'd recharged their batteries and were readier than ever to buy, buy, buy. My colleagues and I stood up straight. I lost sight of them. I heard them saying, "Would you like anything else with that?" their voices an echo of mine, my movements a reflection of theirs, my existence the shadow of their existence.

I OFTEN THOUGHT ABOUT RIOTS. I'd dream about overturned stalls being used as barricades, barbecues on fire, cash registers gaping open. I'd dream about vegetable oil spreading on the ground, broken eggs, crushed strawberries, smashed glass falling from the shelves, forming a jagged, viscous waterfall that spread out among the rows and made all the clients slip and fall, cutting their faces. I told myself: I will never clean up the day after a riot. But deep down, I didn't really know. How can we know where life will take us? How could I know what I was made of, if I could withstand prolonged intimidation, interrogations, and torture? I got lost in the dark fantasies of uncertain post-apocalyptic futures, revolutionary times, military regimes, robotic autocracies, I imagined myself as the heroine, as a prisoner, as a happy old woman. And then Mrs Gélinas would come over and I would rush to fill in the empty gaps on the counter with baskets of raspberries. For now, that was all fiction. For now, I had accepted I'd be standing up for the whole day at a stall selling strawberries and blueberries, because I didn't know what else to do to make money and because I didn't know what else to make except money.

"THESE ARE WILD BLUEBERRIES FROM Lac Saint-Jean!" I had to repeat like a broken record when Gélinas Fruits' most profitable season began, the season of the fruit the French always confused with *myrtilles*. Our white customers from Quebec liked to joke about it. "Look out, Louise, these blueberries are wild, they might attack us!"

No, I'm going to attack you, you bunch of settlers, I screamed silently.

I DIDN'T WORK ON TUESDAYS. I put my face on, put sunscreen on my shoulders, and rejoiced in being beautiful. I sunbathed in my sundress at Jarry Park, exchanging loaded glances with hot cyclists riding on the Rue Boyer path. At least I'm beautiful, I said to myself. But on Wednesdays I went back to work and remembered that beautiful is exhausting and ridiculous. It's just another thing to give the customers a positive market experience. I could sense the guys trying to catch a whiff of my scent as they bent over to breathe in the strawberries, no doubt comparing my cleavage to the curve of a juicy peach. They cast me covert looks, asked me how old I was, told me to smile, said I looked just like Jennifer Somebody-or-Other, or teased me: "Don't eat all the strawberries, you little rascal!" Rebelling where I could, I didn't bother cleaning my teeth or washing my face. I let my eyes go misty, get crusty, and I looked daggers at people. And then I remembered my two unfilled cavities, and got scared, and started brushing my teeth three times a day again.

AROUND SEVEN ONE SATURDAY MORNING, I was leaning on the counter doing a few stretches.

"Tough day, huh?" said François, one of the other employees, with mockery in his voice.

"Yes, my body hurts," I said, in a tone I hoped was smug.

"That's what happens when you do silly things at your age," François said.

"Silly things—" I began, wanting to explain that it wasn't my night out the night before but the work itself that was making me sore (although admittedly I'd overdone it the night before anyway).

But François interrupted me. "No, no, no, don't tell me, I don't want to know!"

I didn't understand these kinds of games among the employees, this obsession with teasing. But it was so common, and so spontaneous, that I ended up giving in to it myself. One rainy August day I saw François arriving at work soaked through and I burst out laughing and pointed at him. Who the hell am I turning into? I wondered.

CUSTOMERS OFTEN PRETENDED TO BE jealous of my job. "Don't you have it good, out in the sunshine all day long!" "Pretty sweet summer job, hey, getting to eat strawberries all day!" I would smile modestly. "Yes, I'm pretty lucky." They probably assumed I was getting ready to go back to school in September to finish my environmental sciences degree, like most of my colleagues whom I resembled (pretty and agreeable young women). But the reality was more alarming: my summer job wouldn't lead to anything more than a period on welfare, followed by a winter job, then a spring job, and so on. I already felt old, I felt as though I'd missed the boat and that underneath my appearance of freshness and health I was actually rotting away. One day when I was wearing overalls, a mother said to her little girl, "Look, Mathilde! That's the lady who grew these strawberries in her garden!" The boss winked at me to encourage me to go along with this customer's fantasy. I smiled, said nothing, and felt soiled. But I wondered, for the first time that summer, who actually had picked these raspberries, strawberries, blackberries, *gadelles,* ground cherries, and wild blueberries?

"WE MUSTN'T COMPLAIN, SABRINA, RIGHT?" Mrs Gélinas would often say. "We have our health, we're alive, so we should try to be happy! We are happy, we mustn't complain." I added a layer of strawberries to the basket I was preparing. Mrs Gélinas, who must have been around seventy-five, put down her knife to go and welcome a bunch of customers with more energy than I would ever have. "Smile, it makes the time pass!" she said to me over her shoulder with a meaningful look.

FROM THE FIRST OF SEPTEMBER, the tropical fruit suppliers were replaced by the fall produce suppliers: squashes of every colour, apples and apple products, edible and decorative pumpkins.

"A pumpkin without a stalk is like a drag queen," remarked Réjean, the grower from the stall next to Gélinas Fruits, one day.

Réjean had already told me, in the same exuberant tone, that he was afraid of nothing except death.

"No, Réjean, it's the other way around," I said.

Réjean squinted at me as if he thought I was a bit sleazy (or maybe impressive) for being so knowledgeable on the subject. Then he smiled at me. I smiled back.

AT THE END OF THE first week of September, Quebec had an unseasonable cold snap. The wild blueberries shrivelled up and the customers moved on to hot cider, soups, and cappuccinos. Mrs Gélinas thanked me for my service. François, Ahmed, and some of the others had more seniority. "It's just how it goes, but you did well, Sabrina!"

I carried on working for two weeks and then I found myself on welfare. I started to sleep late in the mornings. I went through the chaos of my bedroom with a fine-tooth comb into the smallest drawers looking for a life plan. I got soppy over letters from Jess, pictures of Jess, memories of Jess. I counted the days: two more months to go. We'd split the cost of my plane ticket, I would go see him in California. I spent my days putting ads on Kijiji to sublet my room and asking my friends if I could leave my stuff at their places. My hips were tight, knotted. I didn't touch anyone and nobody touched me. My heart, fibrous and contaminated, floated in an endless stream of Boréale and Grolsch. Several times I left messages on Jess's voice mail. Jess called me back three days later. *"Je t'aime! Je m'excuse!* I'm super busy these days!" Which reminded me that I had nothing to do. In the pocket of a pair of clean jeans, I found the receipt paper where I'd written my lists.

The washing machine had erased most of the words. Anyway, I didn't want to remember everything I'd thought myself capable of accomplishing if only I'd had more free time back when I didn't have any free time.

I'd seen it all coming while I dawdled behind the counter in a big wool sweater, my fingers frozen and sticky with blackberry juice, a few days before my last shift.

Ahmed was reading *The Unbearable Lightness of Being* as he leaned on the counter, his back to the non-existent customers. He blew into his fists to warm them up every time he turned a page.

"Is it a good book?" I asked absent-mindedly.

"You know, Kundera is kind of misogynistic," Ahmed said after a moment of hesitation. I frowned, admiring my male colleague's insight. Everything was more relaxed when Mrs Gélinas wasn't at the stall, but we still had to stand there the whole day.

The first chance I got, I went off to smoke a cigarette and buy a coffee. It didn't comfort me to know that I didn't have much longer to go, quite the opposite. I gazed scornfully at the customers who were still impressed enough with the Jean Talon Market to take photos of apples. I saw two white guys in their twenties with dreads and patched overalls, carrying boxes overflowing with vegetables they'd obviously taken out of the garbage. I hadn't dared do that a single time this summer, afraid of Mrs Gélinas catching me. I sat down on an upturned milk crate to smoke. Then I got out my notebook and turned the pages until I got to the list (which was practically a beat poem) on the pros and cons of living in Montreal. Even if I did move to the country, it wouldn't be this year, I admitted. I don't even have my beginner driver's permit. I thought about my bank account, in which I had about the same on September 15 as I had had in April, when I was on welfare. I read the list again, drew an X underneath, wrote the date, and tried to justify my life choices in writing. "I meet tons of people here and make contacts." Even as I wrote it, I knew it wasn't true. My only contact was a job at Jean Talon Market next year. Maybe.

THE MASSAGE

MY TEN-YEAR-OLD BROTHER HAD JUST burped with his mouth wide open for the second time. The first time, I'd burst out in a big, coarse laugh. This time, I reached my arm out over the plates and offered him my open palm to high-five.

"Stop encouraging him," my father said, putting down his chopsticks to pour himself some more wine.

"Why?" I said affectedly. "Are we offending your bourgeois morals?"

"Bourgeois morals, what are you even talking about?" said my mother.

A discreet waiter came to fill our water glasses, and then moved off toward another table, where a woman dressed like Ms Frizzle from *The Magic School Bus* and a man with grey, curly hair and little round glasses had some questions about the least spicy dishes on the menu. I turned back to my parents, who were innocently sipping their glasses of red wine.

"What am I talking about?" I said, holding back my anger. "We're in a bougie restaurant and you're a bunch of petits bourgeois."

I swept my arm around the room to prove what I was saying. Ms Frizzle was singing the praises of Pepto-Bismol while the man tasted the wine the waiter had brought. In one corner, a civil servant in a rumpled suit was eating alone reading a Stephen King book. My parents chuckled.

"Well, that would make you the daughter of bougies," my mother said, while my father, who found me so funny that his French had all but disappeared, said, in English, "Well, excuuuuse me, Little Miss Working Class!"

I squirmed, my lips pressed together, my eyebrows raised.

"If you're not comfortable here, you can pay for your pad Thai and take the bus home," my father said, wiping away a tear.

I stood up, making my pleather chair squeal. The waiter was at the counter talking on the phone. As I passed him, I took a lychee candy and he gave me a thumbs-up to encourage me to take another, which I did. I walked out without looking back at my family, and without paying. I set off at random on one of Old Hull's main streets. It was a beautiful spring Friday evening.

Ruined. The evening was ruined. I'd promised myself to stay calm and mature, and just have some nice family time for once. I shouldn't have gone for dinner with them and given them a reason to say whatever they were saying about me now that I wasn't there. I'd been at war with my parents for about a year. I kept pledging I'd do my part to improve our relationship, but everything they did seemed so insipid to me and all their rebukes stung badly. I had just a few months left before I finished high school. As soon as I graduated, I'd be out of there, I promised myself.

Lost in my thoughts, I didn't see the man with the unlit cigarette coming up to me.

"Excuse me," he said, almost plowing right into me, "do you have a light?"

He had enormous, bulging blue eyes, brown hair that was starting to thin, and was just a tad on the plump side. He was wearing a black duffle coat, as did most male students in their early thirties who, at the beginning of the 2000s, used to hang out at Le Troquet, a restaurant in Old Hull that often held poetry nights and where we, the young, sparkling girls from Ottawa high schools, could get in without being carded.

I didn't have a light, but I was flattered that he'd thought of asking me.

"No, but do you maybe have a cigarette?"

"What's the point, if we don't have a light?" He was amused.

"Let me do it," I said, without knowing exactly what I was going to do.

I took the Gitanes he offered me and headed off onto Promenade du Portage. Government buildings stood alongside bike shops, travel agencies, and nightclubs with their pink-and-green neon signs (COMEDY TUESDAYS, NO CAPS, TOQUES OR HEADBANDS ALLOWED). Girls in minidresses and high heels chatted and smoked on the sidewalk beside guys with big muscular arms and skinny legs wearing chains, rings, perfume, huge watches, light-coloured jeans, and Ed Hardy T-shirts—but these people repelled me and actually kind of frightened me, and I didn't want to talk to them, not even to ask for a light. Farther on were dive bars, a Subway, the Pizza Italia, and a National Bank. A grey-haired man came out of a bar. In my cutest voice, I asked him for a light. He gave me one, kindly and lecherous at the same time. I ran off to catch up with the student in the duffle coat, who looked at me as if I'd just robbed a bank for him.

"You're amazing! Listen, you are seriously smart. Wow! Well, thanks..."

He lit up by puffing on his cigarette as I held mine against it. After a good long pull, he held his hand out to me.

"Philippe. Pleased to meet you."

"Céline," I said, forcing myself to look him right in the eyes and suck confidently on my cigarette.

Philippe didn't give me any details about where he was going or what he'd been doing before he met me. We set off at a gentle stroll toward the river and started exchanging all kinds of fascinating remarks about the philosophy dissertation he was writing. He talked to me about Nietzsche and Spinoza as if I were the same age and moved in the same circles as him. Since I'd often seen those names on the spines of my father's books, I didn't mind pretending I knew them well. I certainly wasn't going to admit to him that I was reading *Peter Pan* by J.M. Barrie and loving it. In the pauses when he wasn't speaking, I nodded my head and even interjected the occasional "Um..." as if I knew enough about it to disagree with him (or with Nietzsche). I hope Mom and Dad are worrying right now, I thought.

"Hey," Philippe shouted suddenly. He was pretty energetic for a pudgy old guy. "Look at this building. There's a ladder at the back to get onto the roof. I do it all the time with my buddies. Wouldn't it be a blast to go up there together?"

"Yeah, sure!"

He must have thought I was at least twenty-two.

The ladder was stable, but I got dizzy. Something inside me wanted to stop me from climbing up. Maybe my super-ego or my animus. I always got those two mixed up in my grade eleven psychology class. Eventually my inner Tinker-bell won out, she who is so small she only has space for one feeling at a time. You're in the middle of living through something intense, she said. It's the beginning of a long life full of adventures. Go on, get up there!

I followed Philippe up to the roof. In the distance you had a good view of the Museum of Civilization, the Ottawa River, and the Houses of Parliament lit up on the other side.

"Look at that!" Philippe crowed, waving his arms around the city lights. "It's not Europe, but it's still pretty damn good!"

I agreed. It was good to see Ottawa from a distance. It helped me imagine my not too distant future when I would leave for good. I didn't plan to live in Ottawa or Hull or even Montreal. I wouldn't be going to university. I would read Nietzsche alone as I went along. I'd go off on a sailboat, first as an apprentice and then on my own.

I turned a few pirouettes and did some cartwheels. Philippe clapped. I put my jute bag down on the ground and sat on it. Philippe slipped out of his duffle coat and sat down next to me. Then, as if he'd just had this totally crazy idea, but also totally appropriate given the unusual context, he said, "Hey, can I give you a massage?"

A massage? It's not something I'd have suggested myself, but sure, why not? It would fit with the atmosphere.

"Go ahead."

Philippe got up on his knees behind me and started massaging my shoulders. I was wearing several layers of jackets, sweaters, and hoodies.

"Can you take something off? It'll be better if you do."

I took off one jacket and one sweater, and held my shoulders out to him again, hoping that this massage wouldn't take too long.

Philippe moved from my shoulders to my neck. Then he got up to change position. For a moment, his body completely blocked my view of the city. He started massaging my arms. Then he kneaded my breasts for a good long while. "It would have been weird to leave them out," he said to justify it.

He carried on talking about philosophy and I carried on trying to keep up, but I thought my voice sounded cracked. After a minute I stopped nodding in agreement, and I even stopped listening. It suddenly seemed really obvious to me that he knew I was an imposter, that I was seventeen years old and didn't know anything about anything. A passage from *Peter Pan* went through my head: "I'm grown up, dearest. When people grow up they forget how to fly." I put my sweater and then my jacket back on.

Once we were back in the street, Philippe told me he was meeting some friends at Petit Chicago. That bar wasn't like Le Troquet. Unfortunately, he couldn't invite me to join them. "Maybe in a few years." I walked to the entrance with him. He asked the doorman for a box of matches. On the box he wrote his name and phone number. "It was really, really, really nice meeting you," he said. I thought I saw a flash of disgust in the doorman's eyes. Philippe turned on his heels and I noticed that he had actually already started losing his hair on top.

I walked back to my parents' house, without my super-ego or my animus. Someone somewhere had said they didn't believe in fairies, and mine had dropped down dead. My heart was so big that there was plenty of room in it to accumulate shame, anger, fear, disappointment, envy, regret, embarrassment, and contempt.

THE STARS

ZOE GETS UP FROM THE table to make coffee. She steps over the laptop cable and the overflowing recycling bin, goes over to the stove, gets out the bag of coffee and a spoon. She washes the machine, puts water and coffee in. When she puts it on the element, she is more aware than ever that this machine, an Italian percolator that Céline bought on Kijiji for fifteen dollars, is made of aluminum, and whatever Céline says, aluminum gives you Alzheimer's. Zoe wanted to buy a better one, but Céline mocked her paranoia so much that she changed her mind. When I move in with Laurent, I'll buy a good one, she promises herself.

The coffee takes about seven minutes to make. While she waits, Zoe sits back down at the end of the table, between Céline and Laurent.

"It really helps me to put things in perspective if I tell myself that we're nothing more than grains of sand in the universe," Laurent says. He keeps touching his hair, and he's constantly crossing and uncrossing his arms, rubbing his knees, and tapping his fingers on the table.

"What things? What are you 'putting into perspective'?" asks Céline, making air quotes with her fingers.

"Well, our love-life dramas, money issues, family stuff … When you realize that the earth is basically just one rock among hundreds of millions of rocks in the sky … you take yourself a bit less seriously."

Laurent taps the table three times with his finger, then shrugs his shoulders as if to say, "I don't care what you think, that's what I think." Céline laughs and nods her head slowly, to suggest that Laurent is talking without considering his words, that she's not personally offended but feels obliged to stand up for all those people whom Laurent, not even realizing how stupid he is, has insulted with his empty words.

"Well yeah, who cares about war, who cares about rape, we're just a bunch of grains of sand killing each other." Laurent wants to reply, but Céline raises her voice. "So if I'm getting this straight, you compare yourself to a rock every time you feel sad or guilty, and that *works* for you? Are you sure you're not a sociopath?"

Zoe sighs. Is this coffee ready or what? Not yet. She decides to water the plants. She drags a chair noisily over to the fridge, stands on it, and grabs the watering can. She fills the can at the kitchen sink. When the noise from the jet of water stops, Laurent says, "Don't put words in my mouth."

Céline chuckles. She doesn't like Laurent, she's never liked him. She often boasts about having good instincts, a gift for *reading people,* knowing in advance if they're worth the bother. Her first impression is never wrong. And she could see straight away that Laurent was neurotic. But she's a good sport, so she still gives everyone a chance, just in case she was mistaken. A year and a half earlier, she'd invited him to her mid-term party. If she hadn't, he'd have been the only sociology master's student left out. That night Laurent and Zoe had met each other and talked for hours. Two weeks later, Céline discovered that they'd stayed in touch, that they'd already met up four times, and that Laurent was "really interesting." And then...

"I'm in love with him," Zoe had said to Céline, the day after an idyllic night during which she and Laurent had made love, talked about their childhoods, eaten Rolo ice cream, made love again, then talked about their respective sexual experiences, confessing their fantasies, their pasts, complexes they weren't used to talking about, then turned on the lights and thrown off all the covers and fucked almost without inhibition, then talked about the weirdest dreams they'd ever had, and then spooned as they slept.

"You're in love with him," Céline had repeated.

"I know you don't believe in love," Zoe had said, already regretting having said anything about it to her. "No need to give me the whole speech."

"I really should have listened to myself."

Zoe has always really liked living with Céline. But these days, the prospect of eating dinner with her when she gets home from work doesn't appeal to her at all. Every time Zoe talks about Laurent, Céline nearly chokes on her scornful, sarcastic laughter. In the hope of making her shut up about it, Zoe sometimes—okay, often—invites Laurent to join them. But that doesn't work: when Laurent isn't there, Céline talks about him behind his back; when he is there, she insults him.

"So, does he … live here?" Céline had asked a few weeks after the "I'm in love with him" incident.

Laurent now had his own toothbrush in their bathroom.

"He doesn't live here. He has his own apartment. He spends time here. This is my home and I want to spend time with my boyfriend in my own home."

Céline didn't say anything, just looked annoyed.

Zoe raised her voice a little and said, "Laurent lives on the blue line, so it's just easier for him to get to Berri-UQAM from here. It makes sense."

Céline had sighed patronizingly, as if talking to someone who was really drunk. "It's just that he's here all the time. Maybe we could ask him to pitch in some cash."

"Is that really the problem?"

"He's just here so much."

Zoe had wanted to tell Céline that she and Laurent wanted to move in together, but she held back. It wasn't the right time. They'd decided they wouldn't talk about it before they'd found a place, especially because Céline would try to convince her to change her mind if she thought it wasn't already set in stone.

"Can't you just be happy for me?" Zoe had asked.

Apparently not.

Céline and Zoe have known each other since their first year of university. They became activists together, they once spent two nights in prison in Toronto together, and they are now together watching the student strike spread across the province, without totally believing it's happening. They even slept together one time, long ago, but they never talk about that. Zoe knows Céline's history. Céline knows Zoe's history. Céline should know that it's a major deal for Zoe to say, "I love a man." She didn't choose him at random. Zoe distrusts men, she's known men who've done her serious harm, who've made her want to die. Céline knows this, but as much as she wants what's best for her friend, she also has difficulty listening when her friend tells her, "I'm doing fine."

A few months before the party, Zoe had signed her name on the rental contract that Céline was renewing for the second time. She'd fallen under the spell of Céline's enormous Hochelaga apartment, and the rent was beyond cheap. The two of them had plenty of space to invite guests and each had their own office. The rent came to less than four hundred dollars each. Céline's former roommate loved the apartment too, but she'd fallen in love with some guy who lived on an island in British Columbia and she'd decided to move out there and start a family. "In ten years there won't be any apartments like this left in Montreal," Céline had said, her eyes shining, as she, Zoe, and the landlady signed the lease.

By comparison, Laurent's apartment was shabby and the rent was astronomical. Zoe knew the two of them would never be able to find such a gem. But she was in love, she wanted to move in with her boyfriend, and she needed to put some distance between Céline and herself. All the apartment's perks were not worth her peace of mind.

At the end of February, the lease renewal notice arrived in the mail and Céline stuck it on the fridge. Zoe knew that Céline would keep the apartment whatever happened. They hadn't officially discussed what she and Laurent wanted to do in July. But Céline had never once mentioned including Laurent in the lease. That told Zoe all she needed to know.

And then one morning Laurent had left really early to go and work in the quiet at La Grande Bibliothèque. Céline had found some of his beard hairs in the sink. Zoe had heard her shouting from the kitchen. A second later, Céline was standing in front of her, her face all red.

"I can't live like this anymore. I just can't take seeing his damn rusty razor every time I go into my bathroom or wiping his piss off the toilet seat. I can't take getting up in the morning and seeing his boxers on my table. And do you really have to make out right in my face at breakfast?"

Céline had exploded so suddenly that Zoe hadn't managed to formulate a response, nor even get mad herself. She listened without moving, without putting her fork down, her eyes open wide. Céline had launched into an endless tirade, drunk on the sound of her own voice.

"That guy is a time bomb. He knows you're worth so much more than him. If you ever question his masculinity too much, one day he's gonna lose it."

Here we go, thought Zoe. She's lost touch with reality. She felt as though Céline was describing a total stranger.

"He'll shut himself up in his parents' cottage and drink all day long, cut some wood, and then start writing a dystopian novel set in a matriarchy in 2072. Or he'll get really into conspiracy theories or become a prepper..."

Where is she getting all this stuff from? Zoe wondered, torn between the desire to shake her, to make her shut up, and curiosity at what she might come up with next.

"Or he'll dump you to go fruit picking in BC and come back with a nineteen-year-old girlfriend. And who's going to suffer the most? You, Zoe. You. And it makes me so sick to be able to see all this coming and not be able to do anything about it."

Zoe forced herself to laugh and put her fork down on her plate. She said, with difficulty, "You're delusional, sister."

They never again spoke about her relationship with Laurent. Céline never apologized. The lease renewal notice stayed uselessly stuck to the fridge with its Red-Square magnet.

NOW IT'S MARCH. ZOE WATERS the many plants in the living room and goes to empty the recycling into the bin on the back porch and then comes back to the kitchen. Laurent points his chin toward Zoe, half-authoritarian, half-anxious.

"So, do you think comparing your problems to the cosmos to put them in perspective is stupid?"

"I don't know," Zoe says with a sigh. "I don't really care. If it helps you, then do it."

She turns toward Céline with eyes that say, "Please drop it." And her mouth says, "And if *you* think it's stupid, then don't think it."

"Yeah, but we're chatting, it's an interesting philosophical question," says Laurent.

Laurent often reproaches Zoe for not taking more of an interest in current affairs and for not having enough cultural knowledge. It irritates Zoe ("Come on, Zo! Hamas! Ahmed Yassin! 1987! First Intifada! No?"), but she sees it the same way she sees her father's crazy love for televised boxing. Well, no, she doesn't know all the fascinating details of Mad

Dog Vachon's career, any more than she could explain why the demonization of al Qaeda or Iran by the United States is "deeply hypocritical" (Laurent's phrase). She actually finds it quite cute that they're so obsessed. Everyone needs a hobby, Zoe thinks. Laurent reads the news. She's interested in plants, beekeeping, fermenting. Every summer she works on two gardens, one plot in a community garden and one plot at a neighbour's house, to whom she gives preserves and jam in return. She has a biology degree and works for an environmental organization. She loves Laurent because he's Laurent, but she doesn't feel the need to be like him. She knows that, deep down, Laurent feels the same way about her. She also knows, because he's always telling her when they're alone together, that he feels powerless and guilty for not being more politically engaged, and that compulsively consuming the news helps him ease his conscience.

But Céline can't understand the subtleties of their relationship. When she hears him exclaim, "Come on—Hamas!" she's quick to tell him to take a hike and stop treating women like children. Zoe finds Céline's way of defending her just as patronizing as Laurent's attempts to educate her. "But I just don't care if I don't understand everything about the Middle East. That's not me. I understand other stuff."

Céline's intolerance for Laurent isn't really justifiable, Zoe thinks, given that in her various political projects she regularly associates with anarchists who aren't feminists, Indigenous people who aren't anarchists, feminists who come down on either side of the prickly sex-work question. "Against dogma!" is what Céline moos when it's her business, as long as she's the one with the power to say who makes the grade and who gets thrown in the trash. "Deeply hypocritical," Laurent would say.

So, for some time, Zoe hasn't asked her any questions. She makes do with half listening—while she cooks, or answers her emails, or gets ready for work—to these conversations that often last from breakfast to lunch and even late into the afternoon. Zoe misses the time when Laurent and Céline had classes to go to and work to hand in. Since they've been writing up their dissertations, they both spend around an hour a day hitting the books and the rest of the time lounging around. It's been even worse since the strike: they're totally overexcited, endlessly analyzing every statement Premier Jean Charest or the Minister of Education, Line Beauchamp, makes, every attempt the journalist André Pratte makes to justify police violence and the use of tear gas, or to equate students with consumers; they debate the real or imagined sexism of the various student unions and the charisma of their spokespeople. Céline has made new undergrad activist friends. Once a week she goes with them to classes to throw out the students and profs who crossed the picket line, and then she spends the rest of the day with the strikers. In the evenings she makes banners and plans flash actions in anticipation of the demonstration on March 15. As for Laurent, he isn't going to brag about it, but he prefers to carry on writing his dissertation so that he can hand it in as soon as everything is all over. Céline says she's afraid of getting her heart broken when the inevitable moment arrives and the movement is crushed by police batons and special laws, but she can't just leave the young people to do all the work. Zoe leaves home on her bike around eight every morning and gets back around five, sometimes finding Céline and Laurent still in their pyjamas surrounded by piles of dirty dishes, still arguing or winding each other up.

"He's bluffing!" Laurent shouts. "The rector will never cancel the semester, even if the strike goes on for six weeks!"

"I hate the way everyone's fawning all over Gabriel Nadeau-Dubois. The student groups seem to have decided he's Jesus!" yells Céline. "We should abandon the discourse of legitimate members of society, we should seize the moment to take the revolution further. I don't want free education, I want this to go on forever, for us to keep organizing among ourselves, I want to burn the university along with the capitalist world to the ground!"

On weekends, when Zoe would like to wander around the city or go out for brunch, the same scenario plays out again.

Today it's Saturday. Zoe looks up movie times on her laptop. Laurent and Céline are in the middle of criticizing the movies currently playing, even though they haven't seen them. Zoe tells herself that if this carries on, she'll leave the house without saying anything to them and go and watch *Hunger Games* by herself. It might even be better that way. Then she could go to the StarCité theatre on Pierre-de-Coubertin and watch the movie dubbed into French, without worrying about Céline, who thinks it's ridiculous not to watch movies in their original language, or Laurent, who would no doubt prefer to go see *Melancholia*.

"Does anyone want a coffee?" Zoe asks when the machine starts to gurgle.

"I'm good, I'm all coffeed out," Laurent says.

"I'd like one, but my period's starting soon," says Céline.

"What's that got to do with it?" Laurent asks.

Zoe pours herself a coffee and sits down at the table in front of the computer. She can't believe Céline could be so manipulative, but she wonders whether Laurent has just fallen for a piece of bait delicately dangled by her roommate. She grits her teeth, and nervously opens her emails, Facebook, Radio-Canada, and three or four other tabs, drinking her coffee too fast and burning her tongue.

"It's the acidity," Céline says acidly.

Laurent widens his eyes, turns his palms to the ceiling, and purses his lips, as if to say, "Go on."

"Lots of women get cramps when they're menstruating," Céline says, as if she's talking to a child, not mockingly, but as if she is literally talking to an eight-year-old child who has demonstrated enough maturity to be given honest information about the menstrual cycle. "The acidity of coffee makes the stomach pains I already have even worse. Now you know."

Laurent says nothing.

"You're already starting?" Zoe says, half believing her. "I thought we were in sync."

"I don't know, my cycle is really short," Céline says. "Sometimes it's only twenty-four or -five days, or even less. Wouldn't it be awesome for my cycle to be longer than normal? I'd like a cycle of, like, thirty-five days or something."

"Why thirty-five days?" Laurent asks. "I mean, if you could choose anything, why not forty, or eighty, or ..."

"Because I like having my period," Céline says gently, as if she's been waiting all along for Laurent to make this exact comment. "And I like it for several reasons. It's nice

54

to have something cyclical in my life. And there's the whole emotional aspect. Sometimes, just before, I get anxious and depressed, I think I'm going to lose it. And then I start to bleed and I'm so relieved. While I'm on, I don't want to drink beer, I don't want to go out, I just want to be with myself, to find myself. I write a lot and have a lot of baths. It's like a ritual."

Zoe knows that Céline never takes baths. And she's often seen her drinking beer to relieve her cramps. But she says nothing.

"Yeah, I can see that," Laurent says.

"I doubt that very much," says Céline, cutting him off with a snort. "I mean, have you ever menstruated? No? Well, there we are, then. Nothing against you, Laurent."

A silence follows. Céline seems to enjoy it.

"I mean, it's not like it's that pleasant," she can't help continuing after a moment. "It's really not. Sometimes my cramps in the first few days are so intense they make me throw up. But I still have to work, so I grab some ibuprofen and just deal with it. I think if men had such intense cramps once a month, they'd get paid leave for it."

Zoe can't stand hearing Céline, the scholarship student and rich kid, talking about work and money. But she says nothing.

"When you're on your period," Céline continues, "you get really aware of how your body works. Your body just knows it's time to empty your uterus. You know me, I have no time for astrology or fate or Gaia, none of that stuff, but all the same, there's something about the menstrual cycle that makes me feel close to nature. It's almost spiritual. We don't have that many sacred things in our modern society, but menstruation does feel like something sacred. Don't you think so, Zoe?"

"No, not really. I'd get on just fine without it."

Céline throws her a furious look. Then she gathers herself and makes disappointed eyes. "Fine. Anyway, that's not what you said last time, when we were comparing our cycles to the cycle of the moon and then we talked about the tides and said how magical it was that we got in sync when we moved in together."

"Well, sorry to have to remind you, but we had just smoked a big spliff."

Céline puts on a wounded expression, frowns, and reveals her teeth in a pout.

Laurent jumps in: "I wonder what your queer friends would say if they could hear you now, Céline. Sacred uterus, lunar cycles, what is all this essentialist crap? Is that your definition of femininity?"

"Who the fuck do you think you are? You think you know what my queer friends would say? You think queer people aren't interested in lunar cycles?"

Laurent starts wriggling in his seat. "You're putting words into my mouth."

"You *said*—"

"Come on, admit this isn't really you, talking about nature and how wonderful it is to be a woman and have a uterus that bleeds every month because it makes you feel closer to 'nature' and your 'sisters.' You were ready to strangle me the other day when I said—"

"You said"—and now Céline is shouting and looking back and forth from Laurent to Zoe—"you *said* that rape is a natural thing we will never eradicate because humans are animals and many male animals rape the females. *That's what you said!*"

"Yes, I did say that," Laurent yells. "But that doesn't mean I was defending rape, for fuck's sake, why are you always attacking me?"

Zoe brings her palm down loudly on the table. "Stop! Fuck!"

The other two slump back on their chairs.

Zoe makes a little *pfff* of disbelief, looking from one to the other. Then she smiles bitterly. "Wow," she says, snorting through her nose, disgusted.

At this point in the story, the three characters are starting to feel infinitely alone and infinitely sad.

Zoe says to herself: "I'm the excuse they use for spending all their time together. They both claim to love me, but actually, neither of them loves anybody but themselves. If they want to spend so much time together, it's because they're mirror images of each other. When they can feel more intelligent or less crazy than each other, they feel better about who they are. I pity them. What the fuck are they doing with their lives? Why isn't Laurent out in the streets demonstrating, if he's so sure he has the answers to all the world's problems? And Céline! She's gonna wake up in a few years and realize that she still thinks like a teenager. But I'm not going to wait around for that. I'm ready to live in the real world, I want to have children, I want a house with a yard, I want a real coffee machine. That's what I was expecting when things got serious with Laurent. I was thinking of our life all coupled up, about everything we'd build together. I fell in love with him, I could see him changing diapers, getting a good job, being strong when I was vulnerable and sensitive when he needed to be. What am I getting myself into? Is he really the right guy for me? I just don't know anymore."

Laurent is thinking: "I always screw everything up. I can never express exactly what I'm feeling. I get caught on the defensive and just react to other people. Every day, when I wake up, Zoe's already getting dressed for work. When I wake up before her, I pretend I'm still sleeping because I'm ashamed of not having anywhere to go, because I know my master's dissertation isn't worth shit. When I'm alone, I get up thinking about her, I take a shower, and I get straight to work: maybe I'm not totally stupid. But then barely three paragraphs later I get discouraged. I don't want to go to the protests. I hate crowds and I'm afraid of getting beaten up by the police. There's no shame in wanting to avoid suffering, everyone knows how it's going to end. I'm just going around in circles. Sooner or later I end up on Facebook, or with Céline, which is basically the same thing. I get sucked into the hoax of the scrolling screen, or the sound of her voice putting me in fake dilemmas: 'Is this right or is that right?' I fall into her trap and get all fired up even as I'm saying to myself: if only I could focus on the philosophical issues of the moment, if only I could just dismantle her phony arguments, I would at least have accomplished *something* today. I always regret our quarrels. I always feel even worse than I did before when I go on Facebook. The protests are pointless. Basically, all I want is to know whether Zoe sees me for who I am. Does she love me because she's seen deep inside me? Or has she actually fallen in love with something I've already lost, or something I'll lose soon? Have I tricked her, has she fallen in love with the character I was playing at the beginning but can no longer keep up because I can't stop myself from telling and showing her everything?"

Céline is thinking: "Why am I still in my pyjamas? I'm always inventing these dramas. But am I inventing them? Or do I just think I'm inventing them because everything tells me I'm inventing them? Is heterosexism contributing to this situation we're in? Ever since Zoe's been with Laurent, she talks less to me, we do less stuff together. She's abandoning the struggle, soon she'll just be like everyone else. She's choosing romantic love and abandoning her friends, she's giving up on her beliefs, she's dreaming about forming a nuclear family, which is so gross, we've been friends for years and now she's replaced me with this jerk just because they're sleeping together! I have every right to be mad! Every right!"

Satisfied with her mental pirouettes, Céline gets up and goes into her bedroom, gets dressed, goes to the bathroom, brushes her teeth, ties her hair back, gathers up her stuff, and disappears into the city.

Zoe and Laurent look into one another's eyes. Laurent gives a deep sigh.

"I'm sorry," he says, frowning and waving his arm around the room as if he has no idea what got into him, what just happened.

After a silence, Zoe laughs. "You boxed her into a corner. That doesn't happen very often. You should be proud."

Laurent laughs too, relieved. They tidy up the kitchen and then go back to bed.

"I think it's a sign," Laurent murmurs in Zoe's ear after they've made love. "I think it's time."

"Yes," says Zoe as she hooks one naked leg around Laurent's waist. And then she says softly, "There's a really cute one on Rue de Bellechasse."

"What are you doing today?" Laurent says, all lovey-dovey now. He walks his fingers across Zoe's stomach. "Maybe we could ... go see it?"

Zoe giggles. "I don't have any plans," she says.

CRIMINAL

HE WAS CÉLINE'S COUSIN. THE one who still lived with his mother at the age of twenty-six, not paying any rent, spending his days playing video games. The one who sold bad pot but smoked White Widow. The one who had massive temper tantrums. The one who always claimed he'd read everything. The one who ate all the food in the fridge and never got groceries. The one who knew a ton of sleazy guys and called them "my contacts" or "my boys." The one who played bass in a ska band.

Everything I knew about him was through Céline, who did not like him (she called him "the parasite").

"He'll try and flirt with you," she warned me. "Be on your guard. The only cool thing about him is that he sometimes has magic mushrooms."

"Let's ask him," I said, already intrigued.

I knew her warning had two meanings: she didn't approve of my own habit of testing out my powers of seduction on every man and boy I met. Actually, it made her really mad. I didn't get why.

Céline and I were sixteen. That night, I was having dinner at her place with her parents, cultured people who worked in theatre. The cousin was there because they'd all just been to a Mother's Day brunch with aunts, grandmothers, and all the rest. The cousin had come by himself. His mother couldn't make it to the brunch because she was working. During the afternoon, I spied on him by going to the bathroom more often than I needed to. The bathroom was right next to the living room, where he was slumped in front of a documentary about Tupac Shakur and then *Ocean's Eleven*.

"Dinnertime!" Céline's mother called out around 8 p.m. (they liked to do things the European way), interrupting our rhetorical conversation about the guy in our group of friends I was obsessed with—"Tell me all his good points. I'm sure you won't be able to come up with more than three." "It's not about counting his qualities or grading him out of ten, it's just about how you feel. I like him." We abandoned our cigarettes and the notebooks where we'd been copying out Jacques Prévert poems and interrupted Jeff Buckley, who just had time to murmur, "Don't be like the one who made me so old," before Céline pressed Pause on the CD player and we raced upstairs to the dining room.

I took my place between Céline and her little brother. The cousin sat down sulkily opposite me. On the table there was a spread of bread, cheese, wine, salad, and dishes that I could never remember which order to eat them in, so I waited for someone to offer me something before I started helping myself.

Céline's parents started talking about the play *Incendies*, which the whole family had been to see at the National Arts Centre.

"I've rarely seen the cruelty of capital-H history so brilliantly illustrated by a family story," said Vivianne, Céline's mother.

"Hmmm, I don't know," said Pierre, Céline's father. "Mouawad has real flair, it was a spectacular show. But wasn't it a bit over the top with all those incest plot twists at the end? It wasn't very believable. It was like, I don't know, like he skim-read Freud."

"Who hasn't skim-read Freud?" Vivianne said.

They both laughed.

With one ear, I was staying alert for chances to make adults notice me, to show that I was interested in the arts too. With the other, I was listening to the sarcastic commentary the cousin was muttering about everything: "Wow, you guys know so much about Lebanon now, don't you?" He seemed to have no respect for his uncle and aunt, except when they asked him if he'd like some more wine or cheese. I thought he was quite impressive, with his olive skin, his cruel lips, and his black eyebrows. Céline's parents deliberately ignored him and passed him the wine and cheese brusquely; no doubt they knew even more about him than Céline did.

"So, Sabrina," said Pierre with a sweet smile, looking up at me as he cut up a rare lamb cutlet. "Céline said you'd both read Sartre's *No Exit* at school. Did you like it? What did you think of it?"

Céline's father always gave me the contradictory impression of treating me as an adult while still subjecting me to the exact same tests of knowledge, manners, and charm as some of my teachers, as if trying to catch me out in a lie, to get me to say one thing where I should really have said the exact opposite. I found dinners with the Milans both stressful and exciting: I didn't know when it would be my turn to flaunt my knowledge of culture and speak without letting any anglicisms slip out.

"It was good, it was, uh, frustrating! You really get into the craziness of the characters and uh, and, uh... Sartre really gets us to understand what he means."

"I'll have some more salad, hon," Céline's father said to his wife, visibly disappointed with my answer and no doubt enjoying my failure.

I glanced over at the cousin. He rolled his eyes and winked at me, which gave me butterflies in my stomach. He had an earring and was wearing a hoodie under a denim jacket with the sleeves cut off: so cool.

Around 10 p.m., the parents went up to bed. "Night, kids," they said, as if Céline, her nine-year-old brother, her twenty-six-year-old cousin, and I could all be grouped into the same age category. For the next hour we played Cranium. The cousin brought out all the possible sexual innuendo in the game's questions and snorted when the brother didn't get what he was alluding to. I think Céline thought we were all a bit of a drag: the cousin and his jokes, her brother, who kept saying it *wasn't* time to go to bed, her parents who had gone to bed without taking care of the brother, and me, flirting with the cousin. Eventually she stood up, cleared away the game, and said kindly and firmly: "Up we go. You can sleep in my bed tonight." Her brother followed her, happy to have all her attention. I looked at Céline, hoping for an approving smile, but she ignored me.

As soon as the other two had gone, the cousin's tone changed.

"About time," he said, touching my arm as if we'd just made it through a particularly annoying traffic jam. "I couldn't wait to be alone with you."

He asked me questions about my life and I gave him honest answers. Every time I said a word like "school" or "homework," he laughed out loud, raised his eyes to the ceiling, and shook his head as if I was twisting his arm and he really liked it.

"Sartre, eh? They still make you read that in high school?"

"Yeah, it's pretty stupid," I said, even though Céline and I had stolen her parents' copy of *Nausea* and had underlined pretty much every sentence.

"If you wanna read something really sick, you should try William Burroughs."

I went out into the hall where I'd left my backpack. I rummaged around in it to get out my notebook and then remembered I'd left it in Céline's bedroom. I picked up a marker and said, "William who?" as I headed back to the kitchen. He spelled out the name and I wrote it on my arm. He told me the story of Joan Vollmer (without naming her), of the gun, the apple, the death. I laughed at it because he was laughing at it. A few months later I tried to read *Naked Lunch* and hated it.

We emptied the bottle of wine and then went looking for another (a vintage Beaune du Château) in the secret cupboards whose location we both knew. "You're immoral," he said. We downed the bottle, then went back to the cupboards and took another one, which we drank as we talked about the whole Mother's Day thing and our respective mothers, whom we didn't find the slightest bit impressive. ("She's just ... mediocre," I said. "*Mediocre!* Mine too," he said. "That's the exact right word.")

Totally drunk, we stomped upstairs like elephants, probably waking up my friend, her brother, and her parents. In the hallway, I caught Céline's eye in a black-and-white photo taken by a photographer friend of the family. We were giggling as though we were about to break and enter some super-fancy place we had absolutely no right to go into. "Here," the cousin said. We got into Céline's brother's bed, under his Spiderman sheets, and took off our clothes.

This wasn't my first sexual experience, and the present scenario contained several familiar reference points: drunkenness, an inappropriate and uncomfortable place, other people close by. The big difference between now and the other times was the age gap. He kept going on about it—at first, I thought it was because it made him uncomfortable. "You don't have the right to do this to me," he said, kissing me and pinching my breasts. Do what to him? I was barely doing anything. He was the one climbing on top of me, licking me all over. "I adore your little ass," he said. I stifled a laugh. The other guys I'd slept with hadn't said anything like that to me. I kissed him back, my eyes open, looking out the window at the blue light from the above-ground pool in the yard. He gave one buttock a ringing slap. I widened my eyes in the darkness. Over his heavy breathing I could hear the pool's water heater and the little brother's computer. "Do you think they can hear us?" he said, panting even harder. A cramp in my stomach was distracting me. I decided I wouldn't answer, and I tried to enjoy what he was doing to me, but events had overtaken me. He was touching me so fast, in such a complicated rhythmic way, that I felt as though I was on the set of a porn movie. "I adore your little pussy," he said. There were glow stars stuck to the ceiling. "Stop it, you're crazy, you don't have the right to do this to me." A clock on the bedside table showed 2:07. He put a finger inside my ass. I coughed to suppress a cry of pain and moved away from him.

He pressured me into sucking him off. "You don't know how, eh? I knew it, I adore you, you have no idea, you're so cute. Come here, look at my cock."

He spat in his hand and, looking me straight in the eyes, with his mouth open, he started jerking off, totally unembarrassed. "Your turn now. Here, try it." Stunned and ashamed, I started in. He laughed. "I'd give you six out of ten." I suggested we could do something else. "Slut," he said. He flipped me over onto my stomach, spat on my ass, and then forced his way in without any warning. I couldn't feel anything except serious dizziness, almost fear, and the premonition that I would never be able to talk to anyone about this night, least of all Céline—but this dizziness, even though it was having zero effect on my erogenous zones, was enough to make me pant almost as much as he was, in a way that made me panic, and made me feel disgusted with myself. "This is criminal," he said, pumping away faster and faster, and suddenly I knew. I had my head pressed into the pillow where Spiderman was climbing New York skyscrapers, and even through my drunkenness I knew I would never forget the words he'd just said. I understood that this idea—especially now he'd put it into words—he was putting into action right under the noses of his hated uncle and aunt, in a child's bed, laying all the responsibility on me, far from disturbing him, was getting him closer and closer to climax.

I DIDN'T HAVE TO TELL Céline what had happened. The next night, she called me to ask if I was all right. She hadn't slept that night. Luckily, her brother had. I'll never know about her parents. I went back home once the cousin had gone to sleep, and the Milans weren't weird with me next time I saw them.

On Monday, I arrived at school with my legs still rubbery and my neck stiff. When I got off the bus, I saw Céline and Julie smoking on the sidewalk on the other side of the road. Céline was explaining something and gesticulating, and Julie was laughing like a hyena with her head thrown back. Céline was wearing a hoodie with thumb holes over a plaid shirt, and the hems of her jeans were tucked into her soccer socks. Julie had paired her turquoise vest with a pleated net skirt. I was happy to see them but not sure I wanted them to see me. Too late, the other students were crossing, I was caught up in the general movement. My friends saw me and said, "Yo, yo!" in their shrill voices.

I mumbled an almost inaudible "Hello." Julie took my arm and leaned over to whisper in my ear. She was super-excited.

"We're gonna steal underwear at La Senza after school. Wanna come?"

"No thanks, I have a ton of underwear." I didn't share their addiction to shoplifting.

Julie got out her Discman and played me "Une année sans lumière" by a group called Arcade Fire. It had just come out. I felt my eyes pricking. Céline passed me her cigarette. She mouthed, "Are you okay?" just as Win Butler was singing, "Hey, your old man should know / If you see a shadow / There's something there." I smoked and nodded, but my eyes were filled with tears. Julie took my hands and made me dance from left to right. At the end of the song I agreed with her that it was amazing and we arranged to meet up at my place after their trip to the mall so we could listen to the whole album. I gave her her Discman back and she went off with the cigarette, blowing us a kiss.

"Did you tell her?"

"No."

"Good."

I didn't know why, but it seemed really important to say nothing about it to Julie. Céline got out her packet of cigarettes and we both took one.

"I hate him," she said.

"No, it was … no, it was funny," I said, as if I found her a bit old-fashioned.

She sat down on the edge of the sidewalk with her feet in the street. I copied her. "I still hate him."

A group of pot smokers were playing Hacky Sack not far from us. One of them came up to ask if we'd be at the bush party on Friday, in Vincent Massey Park. I wanted him to disappear.

"Fo sho!" Céline said.

The guy pointed at me. "You too, Sab?"

"I dunno," I said, too serious, as if he'd asked me to tell him the meaning of life.

"Come on, you have to come, and Julie has to come too. I love that little pyromaniac."

Whenever we had a fire, Julie spent the whole night by it, not drinking any alcohol, just throwing pine branches and insecticide on the flames.

"Well, she's not interested in you," I said to the pothead.

He gave me the finger and went back to his friends. In the distance, the bell rang. I threw my cigarette away and put my backpack on, but Céline put her hand on my arm. "Wait a second. I have to ask you something."

I sighed. I wanted to say again, "It was funny, I swear." The echo of my lie was coming back to bite me, liquid, and forming a protective layer. I didn't want to cry anymore. I just wanted Céline to leave me be.

"Did he wear a condom?"

I reacted like a child. I burst out laughing and hid my face in my hands.

"Sab, I'm serious."

I didn't look at Céline. I let the question's meaning penetrate my mind. And then I went back over my memory of the night before last and I found the answer, which surprised me.

"Yes, he did."

I could see his hand reaching into the back pocket of his jeans, and I could smell the latex again.

"Okay, good," said Céline. "At least that's something."

She admitted that, before asking me, she'd asked her cousin. She'd followed him outside before he left their place to yell at him.

"What did he say?"

She hesitated. "That he was really high and didn't remember anything."

I opened my eyes wide. "Right. What do you think? Do you believe him?"

Céline looked at me and flicked her butt into the street. "No. But what does that change?"

And she was right, it didn't change anything.

REUNITED

AND THEN, WHENEVER SHE DOES have time off, she spends a good chunk of her free days getting angry, being cold and then hot, being alone in the big city, ignoring and being ignored. Several times she pays for things she'd have preferred not to buy, and that she wouldn't have had to buy if she'd been less disorganized. Several times she gives in to the temptations of candy, carousels, to her desire to be surrounded by bodies, even if those bodies mean nothing to her. She racks her brains in vain, she doesn't know where to stop. She's in movement, in waiting. She keeps an eye out for chances to start "real" life, but they don't come. "Maybe the day will surprise me," she says. "I'm going to ride a bit more."

She pedals to the Baldwin pool, which she likes because it's the one where Pascale Bussières breaks in and goes for a night swim in the movie *Eldorado*. She goes through the changing rooms without having a shower or getting undressed. On the other side, a crowd of families splashes around and single guys, gay and straight, moisturize their skin, which they have muscled, waxed, and squeezed into flattering swimsuits. She feels superfluous. She takes off her dress and boots and leaves them in a pile next to her backpack. For a swimsuit she wears an old sports bra and worn-out cycling shorts. She jumps into the pool and stays under the water for a few seconds with her eyes open. Sexy male legs in conspicuous shorts. A little girl in a lime-green bikini and diving goggles pinching the belly of a little boy in blue shorts. Her own hands, dirty. Her own body, hairy, covered in bruises and cellulite. She comes back up to the surface, breathes, wipes her eyes, and gets out of the water. She picks her things up and goes back to the changing room. She dumps her bag out on the bench and finds her underwear and bra. She takes off the wet cycling shorts and sports bra, pulls on her dry underwear, and puts her dress and boots back on. Her hair makes her dress wet. She shivers and digs through her things. Shit. No plastic bag to take her swimsuit home. She gets back on her bike and heads north, with her wet suit gripped between her hand and the handlebar.

She stays in Parc Laurier for an hour, changing benches every ten minutes, trying to catch the eye of people passing, to show off the title of her book in case someone finds it interesting (*Memories, Dreams, Reflections* by Carl Jung). At every stop she takes care to spread out the swimsuit in the hope that it will dry, but it's futile. She sits in the sun, the shade, on the edge of the fountain. She tries to be like Jung with dreams, to find meaning in everything that surrounds her: This half-eaten apple in the grass with a dozen ants milling around. The mouths leaning over the fountains to drink. The ice cream melting between the fingers of the child whose eyes are wide with worry. The big muscular guy and the woman in a black dress, both wearing straw hats, trying unsuccessfully to light a little charcoal barbecue, about to start arguing. The group of guys who look as though they don't get out much (pale skin, glasses, stringy hair), with the most talkative one explaining in full detail to the others how he managed to win a Magic: The Gathering tournament. The giddy Black and Latina teenaged girls leaning on each other, gossiping and teasing, almost gambolling across the park, the little white spheres of their earbuds bouncing against their necks. The young woman in running clothes sitting on a bench, her arm resting on a stroller, looking exhausted, wiggling a stuffed elephant in front of the baby's face without looking at it. The old homeless man bawling out some person who's invisible to everyone else. The white francophones in their thirties, with their pétanque balls, gang of kids, salmon, rosé wine, slaps on the back, expensive but dull clothes, glasses with thick frames, probably Ubisoft employees, gripping their children's shoulders to steer them away from the homeless guy. The dogs, the squirrels. The hot topless men heading to the other side of the park to train on the adult play equipment. The two old ladies with nice calm smiles, sitting side by side on a bench. Herself, alone. She wonders if she hasn't made a mistake, coming to spend the day reading at the park, if she wouldn't have been better buying herself some hard liquor and staying at home to watch eight episodes of *Girls* in a row.

She leaves the park, takes the cycle path to Rue Boyer, and climbs up to her neighbourhood, Villeray. She turns left on Jarry, parks her bike, and goes into Café Riviera. The guy behind the counter, Karim, tells her he likes her dress. "Thanks," she says without looking at him. His compliment does her good. "I like what you're wearing too," she says, and she thinks it: Karim is always well-dressed, he has nice eyes behind his stylish glasses, and she's noticed that he always speaks politely to the customers, without judgment, whether it's her, yelling teenagers, or a hunched-over old man. "Thanks, Karim!" she says again, to show him that she remembers his name. Karim takes her money and hands her a filter coffee with two creamers on the saucer. She goes to sit down. She hangs her swimsuit over the chair opposite, shorts over the bra. Good, now I'm going to read, write, and have a nice day.

She drinks some coffee and the coffee opens the dike that's been holding back her anxiety. The anxiety climbs up to her lungs, her forehead, her teeth, and even her fingers, which she grips, twists, gnaws, and passes over and over her face. "I'm wasting my time," something inside her screams. "I am not the person I could be."

She escapes the Riviera and realizes her stomach's empty. That's why I feel so bad, it's not that hard to figure out, she thinks. She eats poutine at Corvette Express, sitting all alone in a banquette in this Italian-Greek-Québécois restaurant. The employees seem as glum as she is when she works, and she's annoyed with herself for giving them more work. Why have I just eaten poutine, she wonders, as if someone else, just twenty minutes earlier, had made this irrational choice. She leaves a huge tip, exits the restaurant, and walks home counting her money, after she's stuffed the still-soaking swimsuit in the front pocket of her bag, praying that her books and notebook will be spared. Then she realizes she left her bike outside the Riviera. She turns back (it's no big deal, I'm not working, there's no need to get mad, calm down, calm down). By the time she's opened her lock, she no longer wants to be alone at her place, or see her roommates. She gets on her bike and rides along the bike path to Beaubien. She is almost crying, convinced she's stupid and not knowing where to go or how to live.

She gives her last thirteen dollars to a young man wearing a shirt with a dainty hummingbird motif buttoned up to the neck in exchange for a movie ticket and she goes to sit in the theatre more than fifteen minutes before the movie starts.

She's alone in the red chair, alone in front of the screen.

She keeps her eyes open, her body stays seated, but she leaves the place. There's nothing but buzzing and big red-and-grey pixels. Her heart is shared between her chest, her head, her vagina, and her legs, and it is beating slowly but strongly. She feels a stinging sensation on her eyeballs, as though she's almost falling asleep and is ready to close her book. It's the same feeling of detachment, of leaving: whatever was hurting is no longer hurting, because you know that everything is over. Whatever was serious becomes picturesque, fluid, liquid, like a sunset. "We've been running around like headless chickens and now it's time to collapse." Her eyes sting and she moves above anger, above analysis and her constant inner monologue, above stress, raised fists. She lets herself slide.

But she wakes up with a jump: she's not in bed, she's not alone, her day isn't over. She thinks: the day hasn't finished yet, but it's already finished me off.

She remembers: I'm sitting in a movie theatre that can accommodate more than a hundred people. And there are already at least fifteen who've come in and sat down, like me, in the red armchairs. We're getting ready to watch *De rouille et d'os*, not all together, but together anyway. Gathered together. It's not enough, but it's better than being home alone. Isn't it?

I can't manage to feel any tenderness.

I hope that by continuing to read, work, do what I do when I'm not asleep, do my best, I will feel tenderness again, enough tenderness to attract people to me to whom I would like to give my tenderness. You always have to search through the crowd to find human beings.

She writes this, more or less in these words, in a notebook that she keeps in the same pocket as her wallet. The theatre is starting to fill up. She tries not to listen to the conversation of her neighbours, who are talking about their participation in Canada World Youth. Then she tries to be interested, to be open-minded. The lights dim. The show is about to start. She hasn't seen this movie yet. Give yourself a chance. Anything could happen. You don't know what the future has in store for you. She tries to stay awake. She tries to like people and carry on living. At the same time, she wants nothing more than to close her eyes and imagine a red setting sun, as hot and sweet as opium.

MAX, BOB, JOHN, BRUCE, DOM, AND ME

I GET INTO THE SHOWER, but I won't get my hair wet. Max is waiting for me in the living room and then we're gonna get out of here. The air in the apartment is heavy. We watched a movie earlier and it ended badly. The characters were American and implausible, which is usually the case in the kinds of movies we love. But Max and I always find a way of putting ourselves in their shoes. That's where our problems start, because we rarely identify with the same character. When our characters annoy each other, we annoy each other. When they fuck, we fuck on the couch. When they're yelling and killing each other, we yell, we kill each other.

Since Max and I are both intelligent, we know it's ridiculous to behave like this. But we smoke a lot of pot, we watch a lot of movies, and sometimes the notion of reality gets away from us.

I wave my hand under the stream of water. It's hot. I turn it up so it's even hotter. I have half an episode of *Family Guy* to leave the world and plunge into the deaf and absolute state of well-being that having a shower always gives me. The bathroom is shitty and grimy, but my world is enormous and all-consuming.

I don't need any soap or shampoo. I'm honestly not dirty. My hair is still wet from my last shower. But the water cleans more than just my body.

The thoughts I don't need go away. I stop thinking about the TV shows (particularly cartoons for adults) that play on a loop at our place. I forget them. The tiresome credits aren't in my head anymore, I'm not automatically analyzing the characters anymore, I'm not taking sides, I'm not trying to guess the ending. I'm at peace.

I forget the money I owe and the money owed to me. I forget the name of our street, the name of our town, the name of our landlord, and even my own name. But I don't forget everything. I remain aware of Max's presence. I count his swallows of beer.

Then, without thinking about it, I sit down in the shower. I hold myself in my arms the way a uterus holds a baby. I've disobeyed my orders and not kept my promise. The water floods my head with warmth, my hair is soaked, and the time passes. I forget, or I pretend to forget, that the water relieves me but doesn't fix anything, and the feeling of having stepped out of time will disappear the moment the water disappears from the shower head.

I'm just comparing the meaning of the words "fix" and "relieve" when Max bursts into the bathroom and then into the shower. It's like he managed to open the door and the curtain at the same time.

My instinct is to pretend to be asleep, but then I remember that I'm in the shower, and the strategy is applicable to a comparable situation but not this exact one. I take a second to create a fantasy in which I find myself in a group of strong, gentle women, all of whom have known Max or someone like Max and to whom I would say, as I took a handful of chips and adjusted a comfy cushion behind me: "My instinct was to pretend to be asleep, am I crazy?" And the women would say warmly, "No, Katherine, you're not crazy, I've done the same thing myself."

Yes, why not? I could pretend to have fallen asleep in the water. I smoked a joint before I got in the shower. I dozed off: it happens.

But no. No: my eyes are open, and Max is looking at me.

His fist makes contact with me at the moment when I see he's seen my eyes. I saw, I saw everything, don't try to lie to me, his fist seems to say, his eyes green with anger seem to say, his dick that I know will be hard right now seems to say. You wanted to make me think you were asleep? Then go to sleep.

VIOLENT NEON LIGHT. WHITE NOISE of the fan. Creaks of the fan, which is stuffed up with quivering dirt. Cold ceramic on my cheek. The sides of the bath covered in a thick layer of grime. Cracks between the bathtub and the wall filled with a brown paste mixed with hair and pubes. Dried piss and dust cover the base of the toilet. The garbage can is overflowing with toilet paper rolls, tissues, cigarettes. The water is still falling on me. I'm naked. I don't dare touch my nose. Max isn't there anymore. Right now, I'm bleeding and I have a good reason for staying in the shower.

AS WITH "FIX" AND "RELIEVE," there's a subtle but crucial difference between the words "shame" and "guilt." Shame implies that you have a solid background of an identity you are proud of, which softens the blow of a mistake you've made without it defining you. Guilt is both deeper and more superficial. More definitive, more pointless. I'm not ashamed because I don't really know who I am and I haven't done anything bad. But I feel guilty. I don't know why.

Am I feverish?

Will Max be out of my life one day? I hate myself for asking the question in such a passive way. The question a good warrior would ask is: Will I have the chance one day of getting rid of this brute for good? But even saying it like that, I feel cowardly. It's like I'm breathing faster. Yes, I'm breathing... but barely. It would take so little for my breath to leave me. My lungs aren't strong enough, my heart isn't beating fast enough to follow my head, which is screaming.

I get out of the shower. I get out of the bathroom.

The living room is ugly. The living room is overflowing with memories. The shelves are full of DVDs, the scenarios Max and I spend our lives acting out. The glass coffee table is covered with cannabis stems and crumbs, blown glass pipes, rolling papers, cigarette packets whose closing tabs have been ripped off to make filters, dirty dishes, dead batteries, empty pens, rusty nail clippers, dirty bills, old unread flyers. The walls are covered with posters of peaceful scenes and peace symbols that make me think of violence. There's Bob Marley and John Lennon, in colour, in black and white, in yellow, red, and green. Bob and John have never helped me fight Max. They just stay stuck to the wall like cowards, joints in their hands. There is nothing nice about this living room. The carpet is still full of the hair of Scruffy, the cat who died more than six months ago. The ceiling is low, the light is darkroom red because of the sarong covering the naked bulb. The smell of cigarettes will never come out of the couch, which is a shame, because it's a good couch. There are no windows, no door. There are holes the size of Max's fist in the walls, but I don't know how to make them bigger to escape. And I, who love being outside in the sunshine, the snow, the grass, can never go outside again. I am in a dark, damp room and there is no door. There isn't even a crack, and nobody knows where to find me. I think about my cellphone, stuffed in a jean pocket somewhere. Is it a real phone? Maybe I carry around a toy phone without even knowing it.

Calm down. Why get worked up? I know how things go. The worst is over. He'll come back around eight with a friend, maybe Dom the dealer, maybe Bruce, the guy in his sixties who only ever hangs out with people in their twenties, or maybe both of them, and he'll heat up some chicken nuggets in the microwave. Maybe he'll even have bought a pizza. Between now and then I'll have cleaned the glass table and wiped up the blood in the bathroom. He'll tell himself that cleaning must have acted on me like some memory-loss balm. Max, Bruce, and Dom will smoke pot. Max will be nice to me in front of his friends. I'll smoke too, and we'll watch *Futurama, South Park, The Simpsons,* maybe a movie, maybe *The Godfather* or *The Matrix*. I'll fall asleep. And that will help my head to slow down, my lungs to work. I will sleep tonight. At least I can count on that.

THE CHILD

ON THE BUS, A CHILD leans on me to pull itself up (without looking at me or apologizing) and I feel totally absolved by its little hand that touches me without invading, that trusts me without knowing me.

PART 2

PART 2

Born for love and nothing more
Given away 'cause we was poor
Will you wait, will you wait for me?
My hair was black and my eyes was bright
Never gave pleasure to my parents' sight
Will you wait, will you wait for me?

I'll be waiting by the river my love
I'll be waiting by the trees
Will you wait, will you wait for me?

My face was brown and my hair was long
Cut my hair, hushed my song
Will you wait, will you wait for me?
All my life I've been forced to roam
Never had a place to call my own
Will you wait, will you wait for me?

I'll be waiting by the river my love
I'll be waiting by the trees
Will you wait, will you wait for me?

—ROBBIE BASHO, *"Orphan's Lament"*

THE MEETING

ONE DAY, YOU COME INTO the world. Someone comes into your life and you no longer know what you knew yesterday. You are no longer who you were yesterday. Someone has come to seek something in you that was going to die and will save its life. You are amazed at not having had the idea yourself of saving that something's life. You are amazed that you were one of those people who lets things die. You love being alive so much. You love loving so much. Someone has come to look for you and you are no longer in your head. You are in the world. Alive. And then time goes by. The person comes around less. The person moves on to something else. You make a bed on the couch and you forget to come into the world. You only come to yourself. You turn in on yourself, you rub one hand over the other again and again, from one side of yourself to the other. You wait for someone to come and look for you. You forget that every time someone found you, it was because you, too, had gone out looking.

MAYO THORN

AS SOON AS I WOKE up, I wanted to carry on with the conversation Jess and I had started during the night, and which I'd interrupted by falling asleep.

"I slept well," I lied. "You? I'm sorry I shouted, I'm sorry I fell asleep. I had too much to drink. Carry on with what you were saying. Tell me how you feel about me." I propped myself up on the pillows. "We can take it chronologically. What's changed? When? Can you put your finger on it? Did something happen in July? In November? What was it? I just want to know. Let's talk."

But Jess didn't want to talk anymore. We'd talked enough. "I've said everything I have to say."

I tried to remember what we had said in the night, but in vain.

"What do you want from me?" Jess buried his head in a pillow. "You want me to explain again why I don't love you exactly the way you want me to love you? There's nothing else to say, Sab."

So that was that. He didn't love me. Why was he here, then? Why did he get on the plane if he wasn't crazily in love with me? I looked at him. He made a face at me, in a desperate effort to lighten the mood. I hated seeing him feign casualness, but I also needed to relieve the tension. I asked him to lick my breast. He did it. It was the first day of 2013. We'd slept in a bedroom at Céline's parents' country house, where we'd celebrated the new year. Around three in the morning, while the others were trying to allocate the beds, I went upstairs with Jess. "Come, I want to talk to you." I dragged him far away from the party, where he was having a good time. I locked the door. The house was full of people. I knew some people would end up without anywhere to sleep. I didn't care. I had to pour out my terror of feeling him slipping away from me, confirm my doubts. Maybe I'd accused him of spending the whole night chatting with Kat instead of sitting by the fire with me. Maybe he'd reproached me for drinking too much, for falling into one of my famous beer spirals, doing imitations of famous and made-up people, drinking Jack Daniel's, and singing call-and-response songs. Maybe he'd said something like, "I'm just a bit homesick." And then I'd fallen asleep, dead drunk, in the middle of a lamentation.

We both came and it was almost noon. We needed to stir ourselves and go and join the others. Here's a fact, I said to myself. He licks my breasts. He puts his fingers in my vagina. I'm the one he does that to. Take that, Kat. I extricated myself from the quilt to pick up my clothes.

Yesterday's alcohol rushed to my head and I felt heavy, unbalanced. Jess sat on the edge of the bed with his back to me. I wanted to run my hand down his spine, engrave on my memory all his vertebrae and all his discs, but he got up and pulled on his T-shirt, black jeans, and wool sweater.

We went down to the kitchen, where my friends were busy little bees making breakfast. Almost everyone had left. There was just our group of close friends left. The morning seemed nice and pleasant for the people who hadn't drunk too much. Estella was doing fifteen things at once, as usual. She hadn't drunk a thing. She was panting a bit, I thought, as a way of showing everyone how devoted she was to other people's happiness. She greeted me with a quick peck on the cheek, which I tried to wipe away with the back of my hand. Out of the corner of my eye I saw Jess venturing into the living room. Vivianne and Pierre, wearing linen pyjamas, were sitting at the kitchen island having coffee. It wasn't the first time they'd seen me the morning after the night before. As a teenager I'd spent countless nights and weekends in their basement listening to music, smoking joints, drinking wine, and having intense discussions with Céline and Julie Grive, a blond with sad, intelligent eyes, with whom Céline and I were both vaguely in love and with whom we'd lost touch after high school. Since they'd retired, the Milans had pursued their passion for voluntary simplicity, far away from the society of book launches, cocktail parties, and private viewings that their careers had obliged them to attend more often than they would have liked. Their retirement was like our most desperate fantasies: buy a plot of land, build a house with your own hands, grow garlic and herbs, and spend your days between the garden and the living room, where there was a bookcase full to bursting with literature, poetry, practical books, cookbooks, gardening books, and political works—a mixture of their student reading (Marx, Lévi-Strauss, Derrida, Lacan, Deleuze, Malcolm X, Beauvoir, Greer, Friedan, Barthes, Artaud) and Céline's suggestions (*Tiqqun,* Giorgio Agamben, *Letters of Insurgents,* Alfredo Bonanno, *Baedan: Journal of Queer Nihilism,* Andrea Smith, Donna Haraway, *Caliban and the Witch*). Céline got on really well with her parents. A few years ago she'd even stopped calling them bourgeois. Around once a month she went out to Mayo, Quebec, to visit them and get drunk on a great vintage Saint-Émilion.

"Hi, Sabrina," Vivianne said to me.

I stretched my lips without looking at her. I'd noticed the benevolence mixed with pity in her voice. My legs were weak, I felt frail and slow. My friends were drinking coffee in the dining room, which was flooded with light, chatting around a great wooden table that Céline's father had made himself. Jess reappeared and I sank into the chair he'd found for me. He sat down on the piano bench next to Kat.

"What wood is it made from?" Tahar asked, caressing the table.

(Like he would know anything about it, I thought evilly.)

"It's actually wood from a hundred-year-old barn that I bought by the square foot," Pierre said. He'd been sporting a beard since living full-time in Mayo.

(Barn boards! What decadence, I thought, but thinking was exhausting, so I stopped doing it.)

"You have an incredible house," Tahar said, his eyes dreamy, as if he was trying to figure out the life plan that would get him from this moment to the day when he would be able to acquire such a place for himself.

"Thanks," said Céline's mother. "*House Beautiful* wanted to do a piece on us for their 'dream house' section, but we said no. It's not really our sort of thing."

(How noble, I spat, silently.)

Vincent had also drunk too much the night before, but he was fine, he actually seemed quite comfortable with his hangover. Settled in his chair, a guilty smile on his lips and a sparkle in his eyes, he was telling the others about his night, and they were laughing heartily.

"It's your fault," he said to Céline in his hoarse voice. "What were you thinking, bringing out that bottle of tequila at one in the morning?"

"I was inspired!"

Céline was wearing a silk dressing gown over a *No Olympics on Stolen Native Land* T-shirt.

She smiled at Estella, who was pouring her a coffee.

Estella smiled back, then rushed back to the stainless steel gas stove, where she was in the middle of making a mountain of French toast. Why didn't someone get up and help her? They annoyed me. Estella annoyed me too.

"There's no better place than the woods to get drunk," Céline said philosophically.

"What happens in Mayo stays in Mayo," said Kat.

Everybody laughed at this ready-made idea, which wasn't even that appropriate, even the parents (who lifted up their terracotta mugs to say "Cheers" so they could emphasize that they were cooler than the vast majority of parents), even Jess, who'd got the general thrust of the conversation thanks to Kat's sentence in English and the word "tequila." I bit my lips. I had the feeling that their laughter was somehow directed at me.

"I'm going to throw up French toast later on," Vincent declared cheerfully, biting into the egg-soaked bread that Estella had just put in front of him.

I saw Vincent following Estella with his eyes. They must have slept together the night before, and that must be why Vincent was in such good form this morning, poor guy. Vincent had always had a soft spot for her, and I thought she led him around by the nose. He uncomplainingly accepted Estella's lack of communication and her vague talk of polyamory and "erotic friendship." But at the same time, I could understand why he was attracted to her. I'd been living with Estella since moving to Montreal three years earlier. She was seductive, somehow magnetic despite having an angular and unusual face. The night before, she'd arrived at the party wearing a long bottle-green velvet dress decorated with lace, with a tiara on her head and wearing furry mauve boots. She was both open and mysterious, as if she belonged to a dozen worlds at the same time. Not a weekend went by when she didn't go out dancing. She'd picked up a few minor roles in Quebec feature films, without ever explaining to us how she'd managed to find her way into this closed world. She always had weird, precarious jobs she would only vaguely tell us about. She also had several other groups of friends we didn't hang out with. Behind her extravagant airs, she was a reserved person. Estella liked encouraging others, complimenting them to give them confidence. ("Don't let them walk all over you! You're the best!") She treated the children she knew as equals. She didn't play with them to entertain them, or to give their parents a bit of a break, but because she actually wanted to, and because she had as much imagination and energy as they did. I suspected that she believed in fairies and elves. Vincent also had a childish side. I remembered seeing them, last night, a little way away from the fire, making snow angels and renaming the constellations Big Vajayjay, Little Vajayjay, and Anal Corona, and laughing like maniacs.

But you would never have caught Vincent being optimistic. He was the kind of person who was never surprised by other people's pain, someone for whom pain was always present, by turns strident and quiet, but always there, impossible to forget, like an old back injury. Sometimes he was at peace with it, and then he was a good person to confide in or to drink endless beers with, sitting on a balcony complaining and watching the cars pass. Other times he shut himself up in his apartment and called me up at two in the morning to tell me things that frightened me ("I dream all the time that I'm drowning and I'm finally free"), a fear that I chased out of my mind by calling him a drama queen, rolling my eyes at the other end of the line. Vincent was, generally speaking, too much. He talked too much, he laughed too much, he drank too much, he took stupid risks, he was all roller coasters and cliff edges. And then, from time to time, he would stop to look at a starry sky or an expanse of lichen and he seemed, just for a moment, to achieve an interior peace to which I couldn't even aspire. He had wolf-dog eyes, muscular forearms from his landscaping job, his skin constantly scratched by raspberry bushes or concrete blocks, and brown hair down to his shoulders. He had neither had the money nor the grades nor the interest nor the concentration to go to university. Sometimes he said he regretted it. It gnawed at him, the question of doing something with his life. "I have to make a move," he would say during a crisis, pretty much every three months. He didn't love answering "landscaper" to the question to which Céline and Tahar answered "Master's" and "PhD." I was in more or less the same situation as him, having worked as a receptionist at Jule's film studio for the last year. I'd dropped out of university after one term, too panicked at the prospect of owing money to the student assistance program or to my father. I missed the time when we used to answer that ridiculous question, without a trace of embarrassment, with, "We're revolutionaries." That time had passed. We'd moved into the next epoch of our lives, a nameless epoch. We hadn't sold out, but we weren't as ideologically committed as we had been back in 2009. We were awaiting trial, we had seen spurts of enthusiastic revolt explode and spread into the streets like trails of powder before fizzling out a few months later, we all owed money to half a dozen people, we'd lost some friends for personal reasons and others for political reasons. Céline and Tahar had seen it coming, Vincent and I told ourselves bitterly, siphoning off beer by the gallon. Those fuckers had a plan B. Vincent sometimes talked about writing a science fiction novel.

"Stop talking about it and just do it," Tahar interrupted. I thought his tone was abrupt, but he probably wasn't wrong.

"How was your night, Jess, did you have a good time?" Kat asked in English, putting her hand on my lover's arm.

(Take your hand off him, I thought, despite myself.)

"Yeah," Jess said, in that particular tone of his that was polite, aggressive, and engaging all at the same time. "I loved all the Québécois singalongs."

Kat laughed and they looked at each other, no doubt remembering the great complicity that had drawn them together the night before as they watched us with anthropological detachment while we were singing those old songs. Kat was Céline's new roommate. It was only the second or third time that Céline had invited her to one of our get-togethers. She was from Toronto and had moved to Montreal a year earlier with Ruby, her three-year-old daughter. Céline had met her at some feminist symposium and had formed a one-person welcoming committee to her new life. They were now very close, as if some major events had taken place since they'd met. Kat was also a student. She was a beautiful woman, calm and obviously very intelligent, and I didn't especially like her.

"Don't say that, you'll start them off again," Estella said, sitting down at last.

Estella and Céline tended to get fed up after half an hour of the call-and-response songs that Vincent, Tahar, and I particularly liked, and that we carried on belting out even when someone else took possession of the guitar and tried to pick out a Gillian Welch song.

(A little flash from the night before suddenly came into my mind: I remembered shouting, "You're so out of tune!" at Céline, who was trying to bury us by singing "Winter's Come and Gone.")

"Girl, girl, woman, and a boot-root-toot rigodee aday!" Vincent whispered, batting his eyelashes in Estella's direction.

"Noooooooo!" said Estella, staring at the ceiling as if Godzilla's foot was about to crush us.

"That's not the words," said Tahar obsessively. "It's 'Girl, girl, girl-woman, and a boot-root-toot rigoday diday'."

"Who cares!" Vincent said, throwing a piece of French toast at him.

Tahar ate the piece of bread and gave Vincent a kiss and a wink. He was his best friend, they'd been inseparable since kindergarten, which they'd both attended in Longueuil. Today Tahar had bags under his eyes and whisky breath, but I knew perfectly well that his hangover, probably similar to mine, would not prevent him from going home soon and plowing through a hundred and fifty pages of a Mishima novel for his thesis (*Modernity, homosexual literature, something and politics in something-something*). He was like that, he never stopped working. Even right now he looked busy. I watched him cutting up his French toast. He picked up the can of maple syrup, poured out just enough, and then straightened it back up without spilling a drop and passed it to Estella, almost as if it was the plan of a model they were making together. Then he did something he often did: abruptly change the subject, or start a conversation of his choice, so he could monopolize the discussion by starting his sentences with, "No, but..." This time he wanted to talk about the protests against the new constitution in Egypt.

"No, but seriously, Morsi is finished, he'll be out before the end of the year. It's inspiring, what's going on over there, but I think the army will soon be wading in. It's gonna get ugly."

Pierre weighed in on the situation in Egypt. I stopped listening after three words. Jess was cutting his food up meticulously into small mouthfuls. His well-defined jaw moved under his stubble as he chewed. The intense winter light made his eyes shine. His hair standing up on his head, his big hands, his protruding collarbones between his wide shoulders, and his narrow chest made me want to start crying. I mentally reviewed all of Jess's tattoos, starting with the Buddhist mantra around his wrist, which was the only one visible now. Nobody but me knew the one on his shoulder, the one on his left pec, the one on his thigh, the one on his right shoulder blade. I couldn't stop myself: I put my hand over his.

"I'm trying to eat, Sab," he said in my ear.

His smell made me want to go and shut myself up in the office with him, his words made me want to break down. Tahar skilfully contradicted Céline's father, dismantling his arguments and politely calling him a bourgeois liberal. Pierre cleared his throat and reminded us of the firewood stacking that awaited us shortly. "It was part of the agreement, remember," he said drily.

"We haven't forgotten, we haven't forgotten," Céline said, holding her hands out in front of her chest to show she wasn't armed.

Jess asked Vincent and Tahar how they knew so many songs. Céline pointed a finger at Jess, opening her eyes wide to show that it was an excellent question, and thanking him for having changed the subject. Vincent looked up at the ceiling and shrugged his shoulders.

"I don't know," he said. "Sab?"

"Huh?" I said, as if he'd just sprayed me with water.

"How do we know so many songs?"

"It's because of the music game," I said in a whisper.

"The what?" Jess and Kat said in unison.

"Nothing."

I didn't have the strength to explain and, weirdly, the music game was the one thing I'd never wanted to share with Jess. It was our thing, my friends' and mine. I mumbled: "It's our oral tradition."

"Check out the little Queb, all proud of her roots," Céline teased, cutting me to the quick. "Please pass the local maple syrup."

"Here," said Vincent, handing it to her. "In memory of the fur traders."

"My word," Céline said, "this syrup is as sweet and smooth as a fille du roi."

"Have mercy," said Kat, who, I was just realizing, understood French. "You're killing me."

"I don't get it," Jess said, leaning toward Kat.

Why didn't he lean toward *me?* I thought, on the verge of tears.

"They're emphasizing their shared colonial heritage," said Tahar, deadpan.

"What's with the 'Queb,' Céline?" Vivianne said. "Sab's Franco-Ontarian like us."

"I know, we just use it as an insult."

"Ah, okay."

Vincent held his finger in the air. "Count yourself lucky we didn't get into the Richard Desjardins. That's Sab's specialty, and once it starts, it never ends. And don't forget I love old Rick too. *J'ai autant d'amis que mille Mexico-oooo!*"

He tried to catch my eye. I ignored him.

"This is really good, by the way," Céline said. "Thanks, Estella."

"Thanks, Estella," said everyone else except me.

"My pleasure," Estella said in a singsong voice. "Aren't you eating?" she added in a low voice to me.

"Yes, I am eating," I said, determined and on the defensive.

I forbade myself from going any further in my contemptuous thoughts, ordering myself to keep quiet and eat, to focus on my dehydrated brain and my poison-saturated soul instead of listing out the tiniest faults of my friends and the Milans. I could be so hypocritical. Céline's parents had always been kind to me. They had money, so what? Their projects were a lot more respectable than my father's annual new car, Rolex watches, and endless tide of Heineken, and he was drowning in debt. My father! Why was I thinking about him when I already felt like throwing up? He'd always mocked Céline's parents. He called them "crunchy granola." Was I like him? Was I destined to become a bitter, alcoholic old spinster?

I brought my attention back to my friends, who, after a few mouthfuls' pause ("You know it's good when nobody's talking," Vivianne said brightly, provoking polite laughter from her guests), had started analyzing the effects of the 2010 Toronto G20 summit on "the movement." I told myself I should join the conversation as a way of improving my mood, but I got caught up in a long series of acrid burps and changed my mind, listening to them in silence and telling myself that they were just blabbering on and they really just liked hearing the sound of their own voices.

"Basically," said Tahar, "it was after the G20 that we realized that counter-summits are pointless."

He'd finished his French toast, pushed away his plate, and folded his hands—with their clean nails—on the table. As for me, I was drinking little sips of water and still hadn't touched my breakfast.

"There are a lot of young people who'd never been on the wrong end of a baton before who got radicalized during the G20," he continued. "But with all the arrests and the injuries, as many people ended up traumatized, some of whom are still out of the game today, and it's from that—"

Céline interrupted him. "I'm not sure I agree with that. People were already talking about that before and during the Olympics. We started criticizing people who just showed up at the counter-summit at the last minute for a bit of fun. I was in Vancouver during the Olympics," she reminded a tableful of people who already knew.

Jess screwed up his eyes in concentration. Over the last six years he'd learned to speak French pretty well, but he would lose the thread when people spoke too quickly. I loved him, I couldn't get over the fact that he existed, I wanted to brush off my friends like crumbs from a table and say to him, "Okay, seriously, nothing you saw me doing last night or over the last few months is really me. You'll see, I'm going to show you what I'm capable of, and together we're going to build something really solid."

I heard him murmur, "*Contre-sommet*... Oh, I get it, summit hopping."

"Yes," Tahar said. "But it was after the G20 that people were really, like, beaten down."

"True," said Céline with her mouth full. "I think the criticism of counter-summits had already started before 2010, but the whole G20 experience kind of confirmed that we had to move on to something else."

I crossed my arms over my chest in the hope of containing the malaise that was starting to spread from my brain to my whole face, my chest, and even my arms and legs. It was just so typical of Céline and Tahar to badmouth the G20 today, two and a half years later, after talking my ear off for months with their stories and their subtextual reproaches, as if I ought to have understood back in June 2010 that my job at Jean Talon Market was pointless compared with the historic moment they were taking part in, and that one day I would regret my lack of recklessness and dedication if I didn't quit so I could go with them to Toronto for the weekend.

"The G20 wasn't that ridiculous," Vincent intervened. "We gave them a ton of trouble, and new links were formed between several groups ..." He was floundering for words.

Estella nodded encouragingly. Tahar had put his elbow on the table and was holding his chin, looking at Vincent over it, channelling a cross between Michel Foucault and Stokely Carmichael *circa* his time as honorary prime minister of the Black Panther Party.

Vincent spoke more quickly. "Okay, so nobody predicted there would be so many arrests, but at the same time, we can't really say it failed. I don't really see the problem. As long as it gets people engaged. Seriously, what's the difference between the G20 and the riots that start whenever the cops kill someone, or what happened here in 2012?"

Estella had been nodding her head the whole time. Vincent tucked his hair behind his ears and looked nervously at Céline and Tahar. I was embarrassed for him. It wasn't that what he was saying was stupid, it was the tone he was using, like a kindergartener trying to stand up to an older kid in the schoolyard, knowing he's already lost, by saying, "I know you are, but what am I?"

"There's a big difference," Tahar said. "When the cops murder someone, anything can happen. They don't have time to see us coming. Same thing with the strike. There was a moment. There was potential, in an organic way. If the students had refused to negotiate, and if the unions weren't such sellouts, it could have become something really effective."

I sighed as best I could and made a superhuman effort to swallow a sip of water. The water tasted of metal and rotten eggs. I wished that someone better informed, wiser, and more experienced would suddenly show up at the Milans' house and put Tahar in his place. But it didn't happen, and he carried on yammering.

"But what did the G20 do? We blocked Toronto for a weekend? It mostly just helped the police state. They got to try out their new toys, they got loads of people on file, and in the end their fucking meeting just went ahead anyway."

"Yeah," Vincent said, "but it wouldn't have been better to just do nothing. The G20 was inspiring. I came back inspired, even if I did end up in a cell and now I have a criminal record. When I came back, in my head it was as if everything was starting, everything was possible."

"Exactly. In your head," Tahar said.

I agreed with Vincent and hated Tahar's arrogance. I slowly opened my mouth to say something, but Céline beat me to it.

"Whatever," she said decisively. "Everyone agrees that there was a before and after with the G20."

Vincent threw his head backwards to get his hair out of the way without using his syrup-sticky fingers. He raised his eyes skywards and shrugged his shoulders, but he was obviously hurt. I wanted to give Jess a headset with simultaneous interpretation so he could understand all the subtleties of this demonstration of power masquerading as an interesting conversation.

"And that's why Occupy was so shit in Canadian cities!" Tahar said, croaking out a laugh.

They really didn't get it. They really thought they were the avant-garde. They were such Leninists.

"Don't forget the infiltrations," Estella said. "I even know someone who discovered later that she'd slept with a rat."

"Melissa?" Céline asked, a bit too loudly.

Estella gestured to show that it wasn't important.

"Of course it was Melissa," Tahar said. "It's important to talk about it. The rat called herself Judith. White lesbian woman in her mid-thirties, grey hair. She testified against Melissa and other people afterward. We should share this kind of information."

Another couple of words and he'd have been wagging his finger at Estella. But Estella wasn't intimidated. She called on her secret strength to carry on, graciously and almost poetically. "It's true what you're saying, Céline. For people our age especially, the G20 was absolutely like a line in the sand. After the G20, half my friends were radicalized, and the other half withdrew from the struggle."

"They got into self-care or anti-oppression politics, or they moved to the country," Tahar spat.

At the words "moved to the country," Pierre looked up from his crossword. Vivianne put her hand on his arm. I saw her roll her eyes and smile. Now I had a hole in my head and my liquefied brain was leaking out through it. I felt as though someone had thrown a basketball at my nose, caught it again, and kept throwing it at my nose over and over.

"There is some good to those things," Céline said, signalling with her hand for Tahar to calm down, her spread fingers patting an invisible dog's head. "If people had 'got into' it before, we might actually have come out of the G20 in better shape."

Céline had picked up the habit of doing air quotes with her fingers and was doing them almost every sentence.

Kat was following the conversation attentively without speaking. Tahar hadn't said anything for at least a minute. Then he took the floor again. "No, but it's like ... I don't know. Jess, you live in Oakland, the people there, are they as cowardly as they are here? When they feel they've been pushed around too much, do they just become herbalists and yoga teachers?"

"Oh yeah, for sure," Jess said, nodding and raising his eyebrows to indicate "more than you can even imagine."

"Here, too. They abandon the struggle, start families, write books, and never do anything again."

"Ladies and gentlemen, here's the regular teeny-tiny generalization we've come to expect whenever Tahar Merad takes the mic," Vincent announced.

It was a poor comeback, but at least he tried.

Jess started explaining the situation in Oakland. Several anarchists had moved there in the wake of Occupy in 2011, and then they stayed to start squats, join some subculture, or to "spread anarchy" (I managed to grind my teeth to support Estella, who snorted scornfully). Others fled to Oregon after they had their bikes stolen.

Everyone laughed this time, even me. Jess was funny, everyone thought he was funny, everyone loved him. Jess shrugged his shoulders.

"Occupy really divided people. Not much is happening now. We have the same problems as you, the same false debate about violence and everything, the hijacking of the movement by the political class, and then so much of the media plays on the racial divides to demonize either young Black people or anarchists."

My head was too heavy, my neck couldn't hold it up anymore. I put my elbows on the table, rested my chin in my hands, and looked out through my half-closed eyelids, soothed by Jess's voice. I could see bare trees. I could see the barn. I could see Tahar's 1997 Camry and the Zipcar Estella had rented.

"It's complicated," Jess said. "There's a lot of history there. As you know, that's where the Black Panthers started, and pretty much everyone from there understands that the police are not on our side."

As long as Jess is talking, it'll be okay, I won't die, I said to myself. I wonder how many words I've heard him say in total since we've been together. I wonder what words I've never heard him say. I wonder the exact date of the last time we'll be together. I wonder if it's possible to survive my soul being integrated into someone else's; if, when he leaves me, I'll become some kind of zombie, a half person, a shapeless sack filled with phantom limbs.

"It's a city with a lot of poverty, and it's been gentrifying into a commuter town for San Francisco for the last fifteen years, and you can't help wondering if the anarchists who move there after studying at UC Santa Cruz are actually doing more harm than good."

"But at least during Occupy you blocked the port," Tahar said, one hand stretched out and his fingers pointing at Jess.

"Yes, once."

Jess scratched his neck, both alert and calm at the same time, listening carefully. He always looked comfortable in his skin, even though he often wasn't. I wanted so much for him to feel good with me, feel he could tell me anything, that I was his partner in crime.

Tahar continued, "That's what we should be moving toward. Blocking things. Not symbolic gatherings where we smash a couple of windows at Starbucks. Block the movement of goods, organize unpredictable interruptions in communication systems, that sort of thing."

"You'd be a good party leader, Tahar," said Céline's father, looking up from the books section of *Le Devoir*.

Céline's mother got up to go into the living room, from which she returned with her Christmas present, an electronic tablet. "Okay, dear, help me out," she said, pressing herself against her husband, who seemed to be getting more and more annoyed. "How do I play Scrabble on this?"

"I think so too," Kat said, although it wasn't clear whether she was agreeing with Tahar's proposal or Pierre's.

"Obviously, we all think so," Vincent said. "But to go from that to saying that counter-summits—"

"And maybe this way of thinking is more widespread in the US," Kat continued. "I don't know, but in Canada, there aren't many people who are ready to take real risks."

Vincent puffed out his cheeks and blew out slowly,

probably disgusted at being interrupted, but interested, as we all were, by Kat's grand entrance onto the ice.

"Actually, the only ones taking risks are Indigenous people."

"And yet," said Tahar, "they are sadly easy to buy off."

"You keep making generalizations," said Kat, who was now monopolizing the respectful attention of all the guests. "We don't hear everything that's going on. There are often blockades in communities that nobody in Montreal knows about. And sorry, but letting an election kill the strike and going back to school to get the piece of paper that leads straight to your career as a prof is selling out too, just as much as accepting revenues from mining."

I looked at Jess, who, to my great horror, was gazing at Kat as if he was impressed, inspired.

"The only resistance right now is against the pipelines, and that's happening at Unist'ot'en."

Everyone nodded their heads thoughtfully.

Yeah, yeah, I said to myself, rolling my eyes.

I took a bite of French toast, just a single bite, and knew I was going to throw up. "Emergency!" I said, getting up.

My chair fell over. Vivianne frantically pointed to the bathroom, saying, "Quick! Quick!"

I thanked her with a thumbs-up with one hand and hid my mouth with the other. Vincent and Céline started laughing. "It's not funny!" I wanted to scream, but my mouth was already busy regurgitating my single mouthful of French toast. I heard Tahar saying, "Poor old thing." I'm not a poor old thing!

Someone followed me into the bathroom and closed the door.

"Oh, Sab."

It was Jess's voice. I wasn't even embarrassed about him seeing me like this. He'd seen worse. I was just relieved he'd followed me. I heard Vincent's big voice saying, "Tequila, Heineken, no time to fuck around." Shut up, I thought, but when I heard the others laughing, I almost wanted to smile myself.

Jess rubbed my back while I threw up water and air. My closed eyes fluttered to the drum of my pulse. Just a hand on my shoulder made me dizzy. I wanted to die.

"We love you, Sab!" they shouted as I threw up again.

Did they really love me? Yes, probably. They probably loved me more (and Céline had also loved me longer) than Jess did. But I didn't want anyone else's hand, I wouldn't have accepted the damp face cloth if anyone else had held it out to me. My friends knew me and loved me—but they didn't know me with my head thrown back, tears blooming, arms lowered. They didn't know what I looked like when I opened my mouth to kiss, lick, suck. They didn't know me when I had the flu, and I rolled up into a ball like a kitten and demanded to be brought tea in bed. They'd never met my eyes in Arrivals at an airport, had never heard me say, "You're here," with as much relief as despair in my voice. Only Jess knew me like that. And what do you do when you know someone that well? You love, no? You can only love when you know someone that well, when you've taken such care of another person, when the other person has made you tremble so much.

That's what I was thinking, vaguely, as I flushed the toilet. I felt better.

ESTELLA WAS WAITING FOR ME in the hall with a big glass of water. She handed it to me when we came out of the bathroom.

"Maybe we should go out and get some air," she suggested.

"Yes, let's go right now."

Jess, Estella, and I put on our coats and boots. Estella's coat was silvery pink, with a black fake fur collar. I was really proud seeing Jess wearing his grey Sorels passed down by my father, even if I hated my father—Jess was practically a member of my family! Vincent had gone to lie down on a couch in the living room. Ruby, Kat's daughter, who'd slept later than everyone even though she hadn't had a drop to drink, was sitting on top of him and calling him Horsey. She was trying to convince him to give her a horse ride on all fours, but Vincent was saying no. "I'm a very sick horsey, you'll have to give me some magic hay to make me better."

Ruby got right to it happily, giving him cushions and books to eat. "Here's your hay, Horsey!" Kat was sitting on the floor and laughing as she watched them.

In the kitchen, Tahar and Céline's mother were clearing away the dirty dishes. Céline had joined her father at the island and they were talking about Paulo Freire as they drank another coffee. I heard Céline saying, "Don't worry, Dad, we're not that hungover, we'll get the firewood corded."

Tahar was explaining to Céline's mother that he'd started reading a book about post-punk and was methodically listening to all the music it discussed. He couldn't get over discovering all this at the age of twenty-nine. Céline's mother seemed to find him interesting, and she was encouraging him to plug his iPod into the music system.

"Let us discover it too!" she said.

Nobody knew what had happened, I realized. All they knew was that I was drunk and we'd slept on the futon in the office and locked the door. Even Kat didn't know how much I'd suffered seeing her move away from the fire with Jess to "go and explore the barn." After I saw their silhouettes disappear behind a beam then reappear at the top of a ladder among the shadows of the hay bales, prettily framed by skylights, I had to down a whole beer to sing "Mon Joe" without fainting. Nobody knew that I was sure of nothing, that my notebooks were full of complaints and theories about Jess's real intentions. Nobody knew how I interrogated him, that he answered with, "I've told you everything," and that I insisted because I didn't believe it. They didn't know it, and they didn't think about it. They'd had a memorable time, or upsetting, or pleasant, they too would remember this New Year's at Mayo, but for different reasons.

I heard the first notes of Tahar's choice, New Order's "Age of Consent," just as we went outside and Estella shut the door behind us.

The snow was so bright it hurt my eyes. The trees were quilted with snow. The sun was high in the piercingly blue sky, there was so much light I knew I'd be temporarily blind when I went back inside. Nature was alive and dead at the same time. And I felt the same way as soon as we started walking, relieved and awakened and so sad. I no longer understood who I was, why I always had such a toxic taste in my mouth, why I hated my friends so much, why I couldn't make Jess love me. Whenever we stopped to look at something, the dizziness came back. I needed to walk. The winter silence was soothing. I needed to walk. I thought maybe I, like winter, could stop talking.

Jess made a snowball. He gathered it, shaped it, perfected it. I wanted him to throw it at me and hit me on the neck, but he just kept it. He didn't look at me. Estella skipped from one wonder to another, and then galloped over to me to help me stay on my feet. "It's fine, you don't need to wait for me," I said. She kissed my hand. I lost them from sight. It wasn't a problem, our tracks in the snow were obvious enough, I could have retraced our steps and gone back to the house.

I cut into the woods and went forward with my arms lowered, with my eyes closed, the way a camp counsellor had shown me once. If you hold your arms out in front of you to move the branches apart, they'll whip you in the face when you let them go. In the snow, there were bits of down a bird had shed. I could hear chickadees, and the noise of the wind sounded like a river.

I love them, I thought, thinking about my friends—of course I loved them. But it wasn't enough. Or rather, it was too much. I wanted their friendship to be like weather so ideal one doesn't notice it, rather than being like lifebelts or old wives' cures, these bottles of hard liquor held out, the sad smiles that reminded me that when Jess wouldn't want me anymore, they would be there to pick up the pieces.

I found a bush of wizened red fruit and sharp thorns. I didn't touch the fruit. I pulled off a thorn and put it in my coat pocket. To stick into my throat the next time I wanted to talk too much.

EMPLOI-QUÉBEC

I WALKED INTO THE EMPLOI-QUÉBEC office. The floor was covered in slush. The receptionists were sitting behind glass with defensive, sarcastic expressions on their faces. Every window had two slits, one for talking and the other for sliding documents through. A few weary faces turned toward me then went back to staring at their crossed hands, their forms, their babies, or their cellphones. I pulled off my snow-encrusted toque and mitts. I immediately started shivering. I'd just walked forty minutes through the snowstorm. I wondered where I could put my toque and mitts to dry. The other people in the waiting room seemed wet. Some had kept their coats on, others had taken them off.

Standing in front of one of the windows, a man was wringing his hands and talking to the receptionist in a quavering voice. "Are you going to help me?"

"Okay, sir," the receptionist said. "Take your time to

read everything before asking questions. It's all written down there. Your case has been closed."

You could hear in her voice a mixture of restrained exasperation, scorn, and gratuitous toughness.

"So how am I going to pay my rent? If I could just talk to someone..."

"You have to fill in a form, that's our procedure."

"Listen, you can't just close my case like that, it's not fair. It's not fair."

The man's voice climbed an octave with every word he spoke. Everyone could tell he was going to cry. The receptionist sighed, as if to say, "You think you're the first person this has happened to, but I see tears like yours day in, day out."

"Go and read the documents. There are people waiting."

The receptionist went back to her papers. The man she'd just humiliated was at least forty-five. I was still standing, looking for two empty chairs where I could sit down and lay out my clothes to dry. When I saw the man turn around and head in my direction, I quickly folded my toque down over my eyes so I wouldn't have to look at him, but there was really no point, there were about thirty people in the room, we'd seen everything.

"Heartless jerks," said an old tattooed man.

The man pushed the door open without looking at anyone. I watched him as he walked, with his head down, to the café a few steps away from the Villeray–Saint-Michel–Parc-Extension Emploi-Québec office. I went to sit down, and I tried to disappear into the blue plastic chair. As there were people sitting on either side of me, I kept my coat on and put my bag, hat, and mitts on the floor underneath my chair.

"Where's your form? I'm asking for your form. *Your.*
Form!"

At another window I noticed Dan, the man who had
"lost everything" and who was "no longer conventional,"
the man who'd come to my place two months earlier to see
a room for rent. He was wearing an alpaca hat and sunglasses on his messy salt-and-pepper head. He rummaged in his
hiker's backpack, revealing a Thermos, two apples, several
books, and a rolled-up yoga mat. He pulled out a nest of
crumpled papers that he placed in front of the receptionist.
She sniffed in his face and said, "I can see you take good care
of your things."

I sank down into my coat so he wouldn't see me. The last
time I'd seen him, I'd told him I'd let him know, and then we
never called him back because we thought it was a bit weird
that a guy like him would want to live with two girls like us.
I was an idiot.

A group of new social security claimants headed toward a
meeting room for an orientation session, led by a red-haired
woman only a few years my senior. How I pitied them. I
remembered my own session, two years earlier, during which
the man leading the orientation had explained to us that if
we thought six hundred dollars a month wasn't enough to
live well on, we were right. "It's not enough to live well
on because we don't want you to be dependent on benefits
forever. Benefits are a last resort. We're here to get you on
the path to the world of work." Then he'd tried to frighten
us, clearly taking a virtuous pleasure in it. Who were these
people who worked in job centres? How could they live with
themselves, how could they not collapse under the shame?

117

The man had told us that the Ministry had eyes everywhere, and it would know, he would make sure it knew, even if it took him years, if we tried to defraud it or leave the province. In my mind, I rolled my eyes, convinced that it wasn't true, but the people around me seemed to be afraid. And then a few months later I discovered that perhaps I should actually have taken the threats seriously: Vincent hadn't declared his savings account and after three years on welfare he'd been sent a letter from the Ministry demanding repayment of five thousand dollars for "false declarations" or "illegitimate deposits" or something. Vincent never did end up paying back that debt.

Dan had gone to sit at the other end of the room and had taken out his book. I recognized the cover, *The Power of Now* by Eckhart Tolle. Poor Dan. I looked around me. Over by the window was a row of computers "intended for use for Ministry-approved purposes." In the middle of the room stood the table where people could fill in the forms the receptionists gave them. They all had hunched shoulders, as if an executioner was breathing down their necks.

"Fill in your social insurance number," commanded the all too familiar forms.

It was my turn. The receptionist pronounced my name as if it were a funny joke.

"Mmmmkay, 'Sabrina' 'Cormoran'!"

I felt a wave of nervous heat. Even after two years, visiting Emploi-Québec was like the worst first day of school ever, or the time my mother caught me playing doctor with Mathieu, a little boy who lived in our co-op. It's not like you went there thinking that they were going to treat you with great care, that the employees would be discreet, compassionate, or polite. No. We know when we walk in there that we're about to be infantilized and ridiculed, we know the experience will be a bad one. But knowing this isn't enough to soften the blow. The receptionist's contempt is like a slap, you feel ashamed. I was ashamed as I walked toward her, even as I thought that she should be ashamed of herself for treating people like rats that were hard to kill. Fuck shame, I thought. Let's just be practical.

I threw my documents down on the counter and gave them a little flick so they'd go through the slit.

"Everything's all present and correct," I said.

"You've forgotten to sign here," the receptionist said.

I signed the line she was tapping with her blood-red nail.

"There," I said, my voice pitched a little too high for my taste.

"You can go and sit down again, someone will call you," said the receptionist unblinkingly.

I gave her a crude wink and went back to sit down. I started singing "Jonquière" by Plume Latraverse. The old tattooed guy sitting opposite me grinned and one-upped me with the lyrics from another Plume song.

The receptionist ignored us. She was rubbing moisturizer into her hands and staring into space over the heads of the crowd. At least it's funny, I thought. I looked at the translucent scrap of paper I was holding in my hand, and then the electronic board that dominated the room. I was number 14. Thank you for waiting.

AFTER TWENTY-FIVE MINUTES, MY AGENT came to get me. He was wearing a T-shirt with the Quebec Carnival snowman on it. His name was Rémi Dubé.

119

"Hi Sabrina, how's it going? Ready to get back to the job hunt?"

"I guess."

I picked up my soaked hat and mitts and followed him along a yellow-painted, neon-lit corridor. We went into his office. He took out some papers.

"So I see you finished our volunteer program in … September, was it?"

"Yeah, September."

"And judging from Luce and Patricia's reports, it looks like it went well, your project was successful."

"Yes, it went really well. It was a great experience."

He was talking about the "documentary film" project financed by Emploi-Québec that I, Vincent, and five other friends who weren't studying had "directed." In actual fact, we spent the summer drinking beer and filming "slices of life" in Hochelaga—Vincent's neighbours, their children, ourselves telling stories and jokes, improvising hateful monologues about the Montreal police, smoking cigarettes, playing with water pistols, and introducing our pets. Admittedly, I had learned how to edit and how to use a camera. It had been fun, inspiring even. But I couldn't really see myself carrying on down that road. I was satisfied with the final product, but the movie would no doubt be forgotten forever after a few showings in Hochelaga alleyways; I wasn't going to lick the boots of some producer at the Hot Docs Festival. Dubé and his colleagues were proud of us: in their eyes, we had reached our maximum potential with this documentary. And they were probably right.

I stared at Dubé's nose so that he would think I was looking him in the eyes. Behind his head was a poster with a stormy sky and some mountains, with a quotation from Lao-Tzu, "A journey of a thousand miles begins with a single step." One of the HB pencils on his desk was capped with a pink-haired troll. Rémi Dubé was a bald man who used to have red hair. He sweated a lot, was rather red in the face, and was a lot nicer than my last agent, Frédéric Lapierre, about whom I'd never heard any news since my case had been referred to Dubé.

With Lapierre, my visits to the job centre felt practically like an attempt to cross the American border. Our meetings took the form of interrogations, where each of my answers gave him a reason to suspect me of having lied earlier. If I told him I'd lost my phone, he came right back with, "Did you really lose it, or are you just saying that to make me believe you really did try to get in touch with your last employer?"

"No, I really tried, I showed up at the restaurant three times and then I talked to his girlfriend, he won't give me my T4."

"And when did you go to the restaurant? When was the last time? Friday? Didn't you have an interview at a bakery on Friday?"

At least Dubé made the effort to ask me how I was when he saw me. Right now he was squinting encouragingly at me.

"So, Sabrina, the thing I don't get is, why, if it really went so well, and you made contacts and you got experience, if you really put in the groundwork to launch yourself into the world of documentary cinema"—he listed all the stages I'd valiantly conquered, counting them on his fingers and banging his fist on the desk in between each one—"why am I getting a request to renew your benefits? Huh? Explain it to me."

"Well, because I don't have any money."

"You took an editing course. You made contacts in the field. Have you applied for jobs? Have you signed up with agencies in the industry?"

"Well, no."

I wasn't going to explain to him that I'd just come back to Quebec after three months in the States and that Estella had signed and returned my monthly declarations.

"Okay. We'll do that today, yes? I know you can do it, Sabrina, get your CV out there and get into the world of work."

Could I really do it? Sometimes I thought yes, of course I could. I made do with shitty jobs out of choice, because I didn't want to get bored to death by a job or studies that took up all my time; I was a waitress, fruit seller, and benefits claimant on principle, because I had projects to work on, because I was involved in a great love story that took a lot of energy. But other times I felt as though I'd caught myself lying. What exactly was my plan? What "projects" was I talking about? And what was this tale of all-consuming love that took up so much space I didn't even have time to get anything better than a minimum-wage job?

"You finished your own project, you should be proud of that. But now it's time to work. Okay?"

"Okay."

I saw myself through his eyes. "It's not what you think, Dubé," I wanted to say. I had ambition, I understood the value of hard work, I wanted to accomplish things, deepen my knowledge. Just because I was a prisoner of capitalism didn't mean I couldn't at least try to play my cards right. Why did I need this bureaucrat to remind me? He was right, I was a slacker.

"Good," he said with a thumbs-up.

Why had I thought that Rémi Dubé underestimated me? I was the one who was lowering the bar.

We went to the computer lab. Dubé opened a few windows on the jobs website. "Read that and I'll come back and see you. By the time I get back, I want you to have applied for at least three jobs, okay?"

"Okay."

I started reading, but I was distracted and depressed. I wanted to talk to the men and women around me, but I didn't want to interrupt their job searches, and I suspected that Rémi Dubé was hiding in a crack in the wall to spy on me and make sure I really was doing what he'd told me to do. I clicked on a few links at random, read through a few job descriptions with dead eyes. I regretted all my bad choices, all my days wasted wandering all over and lounging around that had brought me here, to the job centre, forced to present proof of my poverty and to "try to lift myself out of it," forced to admit that I was getting older without becoming anything, forced to take off the rose-coloured glasses that had allowed me to interpret my meanderings as life-enriching experiences, forced to see these meanderings for what they were, detours off the right path, excuses for not simply putting one foot in front of the other and getting ahead in life, idiotic self-sabotage.

IN THE INDUSTRY

IT WAS JULIE'S STEPFATHER. THE guy who was both obese and muscular at the same time. The one who, two months earlier, at his stepdaughter's birthday party, to which he'd mostly invited his own friends, bikers, self-employed plumbers, electricians and contractors, wrestling fans, gamblers, fishermen, hockey fans, had stuffed me with mouthfuls of rare meat sprinkled with precious pink salts and said, "Céline, now that's a girl who can appreciate good food." The one who'd played Guns N' Roses, AC/DC, and Van Halen full blast all day while Julie hung around the stereo system with her Jolie Holland CD. "Give me that old-fashioned morphine," I heard her humming, sitting a little distance away from her stepfather's friends, toasting a marshmallow on the campfire. The one who'd only taken his eyes off the barbecue to pat Julie's mother's butt as she came through the patio door with her arms full of bags of chips.

"That's my wife!" The one who, in the state of drunkenness that comes right before amnesia, and with the support of two other giants, had explained to me that I would never get to a high enough level in martial arts to beat any normal man and who, in order to prove it to me, had insisted that we arm-wrestle.

"See, Céline, I beat you," he concluded as he swayed.

"Be careful, you guys, you'll fall in the firepit!" shouted one of the giants' girlfriends.

Basically, the man you'd get if you put all the big white Canadians into a hat and pulled one out at random.

Julie and I were nineteen. I didn't talk to my parents anymore and had refused to register for university that year. I'd got myself a sublet in an apartment near the War Museum that I shared with four guys, all musicians, and a job at Home Hardware to pay the rent. I was saving money to hitchhike to California with Sabrina in July, when the fifth musician got back from travelling. Sab and I had recently become obsessed with direct action and the deconstruction of everything we'd learned at school. I was sleeping with one of the musicians, the one who'd been on the cover of *Voir Outaouais* and who was supposed to be the next big thing in Franco-Ontarian *chanson*.

Julie still lived with her mother and stepfather in Kanata. That day, I'd taken the 96 Terry Fox bus to her place, something I'd done only once before (for her birthday party) since she'd moved there two years earlier. To be honest, Sab and I had kind of dropped her a bit since we'd met our new best bud, revolution—which still had the abstract shape of a big ideological jigsaw puzzle that we were putting together by reading and discovering that we knew nothing, that the truth was somewhere else and that we absolutely had to go and find it. I'd phoned Julie a few days earlier to ask if she'd give me a tattoo. She'd recently bought a professional machine, which she'd paid for by waitressing at the Royal Oak near her house. It would probably be the last time we'd see each other before I left. Her own plan was to leave the family nest the following year, quit the Royal Oak, and earn a living as a tattoo artist.

"This is amazing," I said to her, looking through the catalogue she'd assembled in a Daffy Duck binder. "If you become a tattoo artist, you can travel, you can go anywhere in the world."

"I'd like that, I'd really like that."

Julie got me settled in the basement, in a chair that looked like a dentist's chair, with a little table nearby where she'd placed clean towels, soap, antiseptic solution, bandages, all the sterilizing equipment, her needles, and her ink. On another table, there was a yellow biohazard container like you might find in a public washroom, with a vaguely tribal-looking logo and the label "biomedical waste." Before starting, she pulled her turquoise hair back into a ponytail and pulled on a pair of gloves. I talked non-stop while she pricked my skin with the machine. It helped me block out the pain, which was like a persistent headache, both sharp and deep. I felt sick and really wanted to move around. As I sat there, I talked to her about my volunteering in a resource and support centre for sex workers. I talked to her about a trip to Toronto I'd taken with my new colleagues to go to a benefit night for Terri-Jean Bedford and the other sex workers who were preparing for the trial where they would take on the Province of Ontario regarding all the laws surrounding their profession.

"Did you know that in Canada it's legal to pay for sex but illegal to live off the profits of prostitution, to publicly communicate your aim of working as a prostitute, or to be in a house of ill repute with the aim of becoming a prostitute?"

I'd repeated the text from the Ministry of Justice website, which I was reciting to everyone I knew that year.

The case would go all the way to the Supreme Court, and the Bedford judgment, favourable to the women, would forever change Canadian prostitution law. I was so passionate about this story that I could talk about it as precisely and in as much detail as if I'd written a book on the subject. I reeled off to Julie everything going through my head about feminism.

"Wow," she kept saying, without taking her eyes off her work. "Wow." Julie had never expressed any jealousy about Sabrina and I getting closer and planning a trip together, without her—but still. I was ashamed, which was why I was babbling on so much.

All afternoon, her stepfather kept coming around inconspicuously, jogging down to the basement several times to count his Canadian Tire money, get his sausages out of the freezer, or pretend to be looking for the remote control, stopping each time to comment on the tattoo.

"Why a snake? That's not very uplifting, Céline! Why not a rainbow or a peace sign?"

"It means something to me."

We took breaks to go to the washroom and stretch our

legs, but I really wanted the tattoo to be finished in a single sitting because my departure date was approaching fast and I wouldn't have time to come back to Kanata again. When she had finished, around four thirty, Julie slathered my arm in healing cream and then handed me a mirror, which still had a few Spice Girls stickers on it, the kind you used to get in the packages of merchandising bubble gum. I remembered putting makeup on in front of that mirror with Julie when we were between elementary school and high school, before going to a dance in Overbrook or spending the afternoon at the Genest pool, without ever actually swimming because it would wreck our makeup. I gazed at the snake now winding its way around my arm.

"It's perfect."

I wasn't surprised. She'd always been so good at art.

"I'm glad you like it, but I can do better."

She turned and bent down to look at the snake from every angle.

"Next time," I replied. "I think it's true, what they say: once you start, you can't stop."

She pulled up her shorts to show me her thighs, decorated with flowers, mermaids, stars, and colourful geometric shapes.

"Hey! I didn't know you had all this!"

"I get out my needles when I'm bored."

She laughed her sharp, jerky laugh, so particular to her.

Now that it was all done, I realized I was shaking. My fists had been clenched the entire time. My arm was tingling. Julie unwrapped a transparent Tegaderm bandage and stuck it on my snake. She rubbed my arm so that the bandage would stick well. She pulled off the plastic backing and smiled at me. "You okay?"

"Yeah. It's crazy, isn't it? I'm going to have it forever."

"Um, ya," she said, as if I'd finally figured out the magic of what she'd initiated me into. "Do you want to stay for dinner?"

"No, I have to work in the morning. Another time."

"Okay. I'll tidy up and meet you upstairs."

"Thanks again."

"Really, it's my pleasure."

I'd stopped trembling.

When I went back upstairs, I passed an open door and saw a bed with a body moving around under the sheets. There was a dim light on, and on the bedside table I saw multiple pill bottles lined up perfectly next to a big glass of water. I hurried to shut myself in the bathroom to look at my tattoo again. I loved it so much I had butterflies in my stomach.

When I came out of the bathroom, I came face to face with the stepfather, almost crashing into him. He told me to look where I was going, and then asked me to show him the final product. "Let's see, let's see!"

I showed him. Julie came up from the basement carrying the mirror. He let out a little whistle of admiration and ruffled Julie's hair as he pulled her to him proudly. I looked in the mirror, thinking, I hope she doesn't drop it.

"You're the best, Julie," he said, pronouncing her name *Jew-lee*, the English way.

"*Touche pas mes cheveux,* Barrie!" Julie said, turning red. "Don't go yet, Céline, I want to give you some extra bandages."

"Okay, and I have to pay you, too," I said.

She went back to the basement to look for the bandages, then we sat down together in the living room. The stepfather followed us, turned on the TV, and said, "I just wanna check the score." He flicked through the channels until he got to TSN. Then he turned off the TV and stayed standing in the door frame. I took a hundred and sixty dollars out of my wallet. Julie counted the money. She kept a hundred and stuffed sixty into the neck of my T-shirt.

"Hey! What are you doing?"

"You're gonna need it on the road."

I put the money back into my wallet and thanked her for the discount. She gave me a little packet of Tegaderm.

"Okay, now you're all ready. And don't forget the soothing cream. You can buy it at the pharmacy."

The stepfather offered to drive me home. I accepted. He put on a pair of flip-flops and a Senators cap. We got into his black Jeep, this year's model. He started the engine.

"I love Julie," he said immediately. "She's an absolute diamond. She's not like other people, you know. She's younger. She's younger than you, even though you're the same age."

He merged onto the 417 and turned the radio on (Matchbox Twenty, Shania Twain, Patrick Bruel), then turned it back off. Silence. The windows were closed, the AC was on full blast. He asked me if I liked the car. I said yes, even though in my mind I was calling him a polluting, over-consuming, dirty capitalist. He cleared his throat and said:

"So, you were talking about prostitution back there?"

It took me a moment to reply. It was strange to hear him say the word "prostitution," this guy who normally spoke in monosyllables or in set phrases like "Fair enough!" or "What a goof!" or "Get 'er done!" I thought he was playing the doting father, and that he was going to tell me to stop influencing his stepdaughter with all this stuff, or maybe that he wanted to know what today's young people were interested in but didn't know how to start. I talked to him about Terri-Jean. But he interrupted me. He was well aware of all that, he told me, because he too was "in the industry." I asked him to be more specific. He refused. Then he carried on talking, putting out feelers to see if I was disgusted. I acted like I wasn't. I still don't really know why, because to this day I wish I hadn't heard what came next: "There are things you don't know about, I'm sure of that," he said, a veiled threat in his voice. I let him flounder around with a few similar lines without giving him a reply. Eventually he decided to stop beating around the bush and explained that he worked as the final interviewer for the escort agency that some of his friends ran. I asked him if sexual favours were part of the hiring process.

"Of course! You think I'd do it if I wasn't getting some nookie?"

I wanted to throw up. I was afraid of him. I didn't understand why he was telling me all this nor why I'd asked him questions.

We were coming up to Parkdale Avenue. He tried to make me promise that I wouldn't tell his stepdaughter. "It would be better if you kept this to yourself. It could hurt people if you talked about it. Family is everything to me. You'll understand one day."

My legs were covered in goosebumps from the AC. I focused on the strip of skin I was peeling off my thumb.

"You think you know everything, but you don't know anything really." This time his tone was laughing, tender, paternal. He was relaxed now that the cat was out of the bag. "It feels good to talk about it," he said.

At the top of Sir John A. Macdonald Parkway, I told him to make a right and go down Wellington. When we passed the Parliament Buildings, he let go of the steering wheel to point at the Centre Block and gloated, "Excellent customers."

It was starting to get dark. My hands twitched on my chilled thighs and I kept my head turned to the window. Tourists from all over. Groups of overexcited, red young men wearing shorts and boat shoes. People buying and selling drugs in front of the McDonald's in the Rideau Centre. A trio of Inuit walking slowly along the sidewalk with their heavy backpacks. At the corner of Rideau and Cumberland, I told the stepfather that I lived on campus and gave him instructions for dropping me off "at the door." I pretended that this had been an interesting conversation and wished him good night. "Thanks for the ride!" As I watched the Jeep drive away, I started walking toward the Rideau Centre on Besserer, stumbling a few times and breathing quickly. On the way I passed a group of tourists getting ready to take part in the Haunted Ottawa Walk, led by a teenaged girl in a black hooded cape. She was holding a lantern. The bluish-white light danced in the shadows, making her face look deformed. Shivering a bit, I walked through the Rideau Centre, which was as chilly as the stepfather's car. I went past the iron shutters lowered over Club Monaco, American Eagle Outfitters, and Mrs Tiggy Winkle's, I held my breath instinctively going past Moneysworth & Best Quality Shoe Care—the shop was closed, so it wasn't emitting its usual toxic scents—then I left by the third-floor doors and waited at Mackenzie King station for the 97 bus to turn up, which I took to LeBreton station. Then I walked along Preston to the street where I lived.

When I arrived, I saw my musician lover sitting on the steps in front of the house. He was singing a Grateful Dead song and accompanying himself on the mandolin. It seemed strange to see him; and his relaxed expression, his leather jacket open over his naked chest, his red bandana in his messy hair, and his big toes visible through his woollen socks all seemed somehow inappropriate. I sat down on the other side of the steps, with my arms and legs crossed, and listened to him without speaking. He looked at me out of the corner of his eye, happy to have an audience. "I set out running, but I'll take my time, a friend of the Devil is a friend of mine." At the end of his song, he turned to me with such a sincere, hopeful smile that I clapped. Then we went inside together and I slept in his bed without telling him anything about my evening after the tattoo. He said the snake made me look badass. I accepted the compliment, but I looked at him differently. He seemed young and naive, this guy who was three years older than me and who'd been on the cover of *Voir Outaouais*.

A FEW WEEKS LATER, I received a CC'd email that the step-father had sent to a woman he knew who managed a Keg restaurant on York Street. He described my numerous qualities as a potential employee and asked her if she could give me a job as a hostess. "Thanks, Sally, I owe ya one! ;)." "Sally" never called me. I never wrote to either one of them to explain that I already had a job at Home Hardware.

I saw Julie just once more after that, a few weeks after my ride in her stepfather's Jeep. It was a cool, pleasant day in June. We met at the Second Cup on Laurier. I had a black coffee and she had a sparkling Italian soda. I talked about my travel preparations, and the places Sab and I wanted to go.

"When are you leaving?"

"In two weeks."

"Lucky you."

"Yeah."

We went to feed the ducks in Strathcona Park and laughed when we discovered, on a picnic table, a message we'd carved together in the not so distant past when we'd gone there after school just about every day to smoke joints and sing our favourite songs, trying to harmonize. The message, in two different handwritings, said, "One day I am gonna grow wings, a chemical reaction, hysterical and useless." The letters she'd engraved were well-formed and stylized, while my own were barely legible and too big.

"That was a long time ago," Julie said. "It feels like a long time ago."

"Not that long," I said, shrugging my shoulders. "I still listen to Radiohead."

"Me too, and I still smoke pot."

We laughed some more.

"I still smoke pot at Strathcona," I said.

"I still buy pot at Major's Hill Park," she said, taking a spliff out of her bag and waving it in front of my face.

This time we laughed long and hard, more and more, until we were holding our sides, we had tears in our eyes, we thumped each other on the back, and we only calmed down to look each other in the eyes and roar even more. Then we smoked the joint, went back up the hill as far as Laurier, turned onto Nelson, and wandered toward the ByWard Market just as we'd done so many times with Sabrina. We went to Nepean Point to watch the sun set. I gave her a lecture on the colonial horrors Samuel de Champlain was responsible for. She replied that she'd really like to learn how to use an astrolabe. Then we went to wait for our respective buses at the Rideau Centre and went our separate ways.

I hadn't told her anything.

She'd started an unpaid internship at a tattoo studio and was feeling discouraged. They'd told her they'd only start paying her once she'd proven her worth. When she'd tried to find out how long that might take, the other tattooers had laughed. At the Royal Oak, the boss had scolded her when he saw her refusing a beer from a customer. And her tips were smaller than they used to be. "Ever since I dyed my hair blue, basically!"

She said she was thinking of moving to Toronto or Vancouver or Montreal and going to university. I felt sick about it, but I didn't say anything.

"Yeah, you should go," I said. "There's something rotten in Ottawa."

FEBRUARY

A WHITE WOMAN GOES INTO a convenience store. She has big glassy eyes, a hat hiding her forehead, a flash of blond hair at her neck, and a runny nose. She buys two beers, a can of Molson Ex and a bottle of Canadian. She doesn't have cash, so she pays with debit. The man behind the counter is patient.

The woman starts entering her pin and then stops to say, "Are you cousins?" to the cashier and another man, sitting on a stool in front of a small television. They don't look like each other, but both are Asian.

"No, we're not cousins," they say.

"But you look alike," the woman insists. She seems to have forgotten that she's in the middle of paying.

Vincent is also at the convenience store. He's left his apartment for the first time in a week. He's "going through a phase," as his mother puts it. No matter how diligently he leafs through his (happy) childhood photo albums again and again and scrolls through the long list of contacts in his phone (dozens and dozens of friends he doesn't have the courage to call), he's feeling himself sliding into an abyss of solitude, toward a point of no return. The abyss seems appealing. He's been on welfare for six months, for the third time in five years. People he knows think he's "working on a novel," but he's not actually working. He's looking at photos and phone numbers. No, I can't. I can't do that to them. Take your mind off things. He goes out. He goes to the convenience store to buy a can of beer. He's breathing through his scarf because the convenience store smells of damp.

"So you're brothers, then?"

Not that either. The men exchange a few words, obviously annoyed. The one behind the counter takes Vincent's money over the woman's shoulder.

Two kids come into the convenience store and ask for cigarettes. The man at the cash asks for ID. They show him proudly. The woman still hasn't taken her bottle and her can. She's trying to get her card back into her wallet, but her aim is so bad that after three attempts she just chucks both the card and the wallet straight into her purse. Instead of chucking the beer in too, she says, "I need a bag."

Her voice is thick. She turns to the teenagers, lifting her finger as though she is about to impart words of wisdom. "Usually it's always the other guy at the cash. Today's the first time it's him."

"We're honoured, then," says one of the teenagers.

Vincent notices that people have the nasty habit of pointlessly running their mouths. The man behind the counter puts a plastic bag over the woman's beers and gestures with the back of his hand to say, "Sort it out yourself."

The teenagers have to walk sideways to get around the woman to the till without knocking into the display of gum and candy. They pay cash, stuff the packs of cigarettes into their coat pockets, and head to the door. They whisper to themselves, giggle, and, as they push open the door, shout, "Hey, ma'am, your store is open!"

Despite himself, Vincent's gaze settles on the woman's crotch, where he does, in fact, discover a lowered zipper. The woman barely twitches, too busy making the men behind the counter admit that they're related.

"Oh yes," she says, leaning her arms on the counter, over the scratch cards. "They're good guys. The Chinese are good guys."

"Ma'am."

It's Vincent who spoke. He's about to leave, but he stops. He opens the door for her. "After you."

And he smiles at her. The woman takes her bottle in one hand, and the bag and the can in the other. She goes out. He goes out. It's winter in Montreal. The woman skitters on the ice and disappears into the night.

Vincent slips his tall can of Boréale into his inside coat pocket. He goes back home and drinks the beer without taking his coat off, sitting on the floor in the hallway. He never wants to go back to the convenience store. He doesn't ever want to see snow again. He doesn't want to live in this apartment anymore. He doesn't want to live in Montreal anymore. Nor anywhere else. He can't do it. He just can't make himself want to stay.

VICTORY

OVER THE YEARS, IT ATE away at my soul. I told myself,
I kept telling myself until my head was spinning: I'd like
to spit in his face, I'd like to tell him to fuck off, hurt him,
really hurt him, give him a long-term headache. I'd come
out of it safe and sound and he'd have migraines. A headache that would last for years. Too sick to speak. Too sick
to screw. Too sick to sleep. A balloon that is going to burst,
that is bursting, that is going to burst, that is bursting, endlessly. In his head. You can't go out anymore, so you can't
make friends. You can't listen, you can't learn, you can't
have fun. Especially, especially, especially, you can't fuck
anymore. Never again. You become a wreck.

For years, I've been fantasizing.

And then one day it happens. I do it. One day I plow
into you hard. I see your legs flailing. I see you turn blue,
then confess. You have the nerves of a child. Hot lungs. You

139

don't scare me. Your pains are nothing but little pricks. I turn myself into marble and stay like that. You cry, I overwhelm you. I turn your weight into feathers. And then I leave. I sleep, one hand on my stomach, uncomfortable on the Greyhound seat but at peace.

You will never again pretend to have forgotten.

I have a heart in my stomach, I am absolutely sure of it. I haven't seen a doctor, but I can tell. That's what gave me the courage to leave. It beats with my own heart, it sings, not very fast, not very strong, but it is firmly attached. It says, "Here I am, and I need you to go far away." A little ruby sheltered deep inside me.

One day you shut your mouth. It's a small joy, but so long hoped for that I let it melt in my mouth.

THE SHARED APARTMENT

IT'S MORNING. THE ALARM GOES off at six thirty. Kat hears it but doesn't move. She doesn't hit Snooze. A few seconds later the second alarm, the one she set on her phone, goes off too. Kat does nothing. A minute goes by. She's asleep. She can't do anything. She's asleep.

Ruby's been awake for a half-hour. She's dreaming in bed like she does every morning. She's inventing colours and flowers she never tells anyone about. The alarm going off reminds her of the inevitable: snowsuit, bus, schoolyard, boys, girls, desks grimy with fingerprints, orange splatters, pencil lines, French class, the stinky eraser, markers that smell nice but that she doesn't dare sniff in front of everyone, pencil shavings at the bottom of her backpack, the banana her mother stuffs in her backpack every day that gets covered in pencil shavings, the exercise books that smell of banana because they've been in her backpack, the words "time out," "quiet," "line up," "quiet," "everyone." The gymnasium she would really like if she could just sit there, lie down and sing, and listen to the echo answer her, but which she hates because she has to run around it and avoid the basketballs that move so fast and make you cry the second they hit your nose and the boys who move so fast and never miss the chance to laugh at the girls who don't catch the ball.

Ruby gets up and climbs into bed with her mother. She sits cross-legged, finds the cellphone, and turns off the alarm. Then she bends over the older technology of the alarm clock. Kat stretches out an arm heavy with sleep and touches her daughter's hair. In the darkness, Ruby pokes at buttons, and plastic dials and sides where the racket is coming from. Kat rolls over in bed. She's floating in the most torturous, delicious state there is, a half sleep you're aware of, when you surrender to the pleasure of sleeping. Just five more minutes.

The clock is still screaming. Ruby decides to press all the buttons starting on the left until she finds the right one. On her third attempt she finds silence, which is never really silence but a space where new, quieter noises reverberate. She likes it when a loud noise goes quiet and reveals another one. This morning she can hear the refrigerator's hum. She goes to it, opens the door, and stands there looking at it, the foods she doesn't yet know how to put together to make a meal.

"Get dressed, Ruby!" shouts Kat with a tiger yawn.

Ruby gets out the jug of orange juice, which she needs to carry with two hands. She walks slowly, half a step at a time, her hands firmly gripping the jug, over to the table. She puts the bottle down, which is cold and wet from condensation. It sticks out a bit from the table. She wipes her hands on her pyjamas and pushes the jug on a bit more. Then she drags a chair over to the cupboard where the glasses are, climbs onto the chair and then the counter, opens the cupboard, and takes out a cup. To get down, she sits on the counter then puts one foot at a time on the chair and then the floor, holding the cup to her chest. She turns back to the jug and tries to lift it with one hand. It's too full, too heavy. She puts the cup on the table, goes back to the cupboard to get the chair, kneels on it, and, concentrating hard, lifts the jug with two hands (not too high) and tips it until the orange juice starts gushing out (not too fast). She aims at the cup. It fills up. She pours juice until the cup is full (not too full). She puts the jug down. I did it, she thinks.

Céline, whose bedroom is just off the kitchen, gets up and thuds toward the bathroom. When she gets back, she throws herself into making coffee without even looking at Ruby. Then she gets out the bag of oats and a saucepan.

Ruby says, "Good morning, Céline."

"*Salut, Ruby. Bien dormi?*"

"*Oui.*" She doesn't like answering that question. "Ooooh, oatmeal," she adds.

Ruby gets up and presses herself against the counter right by the oven and raises her head to Céline, who's pouring a portion of oats into the water.

"Can I have some?" Ruby says.

"Sure," Céline says, a little annoyed.

Céline adds water and oats to the saucepan.

Five minutes later, Céline places a steaming bowl in front

143

of Ruby. Ruby races over to the fridge and gets out the maple syrup, which she pours gleefully on her oatmeal.

"*Et beaucoup, beaucoup de sirop d'érable!*" she says triumphantly.

"Do you want some oatmeal with your maple syrup?" Céline says.

Ruby laughs. Céline goes back into her room to get her laptop, which she puts in front of her on the table. She opens Facebook.

I knew that racism had deep roots in Quebec, even among activists, writes Abla Mimouni, one of Céline's Facebook friends. *But I thought I'd at least be safe among feminists. I was wrong.*

"You're reading at the table! How rude!" Ruby says.

Céline carries on reading. *I was invited to a discussion about women and Islamophobia at Café Aquin at* UQAM. *Everything was going well until the questions. One girl puts her hand up: she tells me I'm exaggerating, that Islamophobia isn't the norm in Quebec. I try to answer, but she cuts me off. She cuts me off!*

Céline clicks Like before she finishes reading.

Kat wakes up, puts an elbow on her pillow to help herself get up, and goes back to sleep. Then she wakes up again, but her body is all tangled in the sheets.

She was studying until three in the morning. She's only on her fourth hour of sleep. It's all too much. She has too much to do. University isn't made for single mothers. She depends on the pity the profs might or might not feel for her. She's going to go crazy. She isn't sleeping enough. She's getting paranoid. She feels attacked on all sides. Ruby's teachers accuse her of neglecting her education. The landlord, who lives below them, threatened to take away the dryer that came with the apartment because she put a soaking quilt in it. Céline doesn't take her side in the war against the landlord, which goes further back than the dryer incident. The landlord turned against her after they refused the rent increase a year ago; they refused together, but the landlord turned against Kat alone, she sends her emails that say things like, "I don't need the problems like that with my building, I never have problems with tenants before you, don't bring your problems to here."

"She's a bitch, but it could be worse," Céline says, who doesn't want to lose this great cheap apartment she's been living in for nearly ten years.

One Monday evening when Kat and Céline are having dinner with some girlfriends and their children, the landlord tells Kat off for making too much noise. First she bangs on the ceiling underneath her bedroom, then she sends a text: "SILENCE PLEASE!!!"

"Why does she think it's me and not you?" Kat rants.

Céline shrugs her shoulders. The landlord bangs hard for a long time.

"It's intrusive," Kat says. "Why doesn't she just knock on the door like a normal person?"

She ignores the thumps, which get more and more insistent. The landlord starts yelling in English with her thick Quebec accent; they can hear her clearly through the floor, "Fucking bitch! Fucking bitch! How did I deserved this fucking bitch like tenant!" Kat grits her teeth and serves everyone more wine, saying that the landlord is stark raving mad. The landlord shows up at the door, red with fury. She's losing it. Céline assures her that the guests were just about to leave.

"And where are their fathers, hey?" the landlord says as she goes back down the stairs.

Whenever she sees Céline, the landlord is polite and nice. She gives her meaningful looks and makes pointed comments, looking for complicity. "Your roommate isn't easy, hey? I don't know if it's just a language barrier thing or what, but something's not right in here!" The landlord taps her head three times to indicate that Kat is crazy. Céline doesn't contradict her, she explains to Kat, out of strategy, to keep some room to move.

"She's a racist," Kat says.

"Hmmm ... I don't know if she's a *racist*," Céline says.

"It's not for you to decide," Kat says, trying to stay calm. She thinks: I don't have time for this. "She's a racist. You wouldn't know, you're white."

Céline wants to answer, but Kat puts her headphones back on and makes blinders with her hands so she can concentrate on the thirty-five pages she has to read.

Kat feels the first symptoms of an anxiety attack, but she doesn't have time for an anxiety attack. She has to study, she has to write a fifteen-page essay, she has to pass her four classes, she has to get her degree, she has to find work, she has to pay back her student debt, she has to bring up her daughter.

"Ruby, go and get dressed," Kat says, as she finally tears herself away from the warmth of the sheets.

"I'm eating oatmeal! I'll get dressed after!"

She cuts me off so she can ask what I can possibly know about Islamophobia. I don't wear a burka. I don't even have an accent. Basically, I'm not a real Arab, Céline reads, not paying attention to what is going on around her.

Kat takes shelter in the shower and stays under the hot water for a long time. It's the only thing that helps. It's almost eight. The school bus left a long time ago. If she drives Ruby to school, she won't be back to the house before nine. Her first class is at nine thirty.

I'm so mad at myself for freezing. I should have eaten her alive. Another one who thinks she's special, thinks she gets it all. I don't have the energy for it anymore. They all say the same stupid shit, but the ignorance of people who've never experienced racism will never cease to amaze me, hurt me, and waste my time.

"Right on, well said!" Céline comments under the post, but something stops her from pressing Send.

Ruby remembers she hasn't studied for her French dictation. She feels a ball of playdough inflate in her stomach. For now, I'll just pretend dictation doesn't exist, she decides.

Céline, who's already downed a pot of coffee, takes a second one off the stove just as Kat walks into the kitchen holding a handful of elastics. The shower has done her good. Kat is beautiful. Even when she doesn't get enough sleep.

Kat pulls out a chair, sits behind Ruby, and starts gathering her hair into two bunches. Ruby purrs. Céline pours Kat a coffee. Kat decides to tell Céline her dream. Ruby stays sitting in front of her empty oatmeal bowl. She enjoys every second that she's not at school. Céline is aware of the time passing. So is Kat. But nobody gets up to get dressed.

"And then suddenly we were walking in the desert looking for a spring. We were all made of wood except for the guide. He had skin. After walking for hours, we finally found water. The guide got down on his knees to drink, and we went up to the water to drink with our feet."

While she's talking, her phone starts ringing and vibrating. Messages pop up on the screen. She mutes the sound. Céline looks from Kat to the phone.

"Mom?" Ruby says.

But Kat carries on telling her dream. The more she talks, the more details she remembers. "We saw a parrot pecking at the ground and understood that it was him who had dug a tunnel to let the underground water out. He told us he had to fill his beak with water and take it to a village in the forest to put out a big fire."

The vibration stops and Kat immediately forgets about the phone. She carries on talking, as if there were no longer buses to catch, lunches to make, no more school.

"And then a woman in our group recognized her village, it was her village that was on fire. I tried to console her, but it didn't work. She was crying so hard."

The telephone starts vibrating again. Kat doesn't look at it. The buzzing grates on all her nerve endings. She is so tired. She knows her dream had at least one more scene, but she can't remember it. Ruby turns toward Céline, then to her mother, with questioning looks, but Kat is looking over her head, out the window.

"Dreams are crazy," she murmurs.

The phone vibrates. Its vibration fills the whole room and nobody moves.

A PUPPY'S CRY

I THOUGHT I HEARD THE cry of a puppy whose tail had just been crushed by the boot of a man, who, walking single-mindedly toward the object of his anger, didn't see that the puppy was there (and didn't flinch when he heard it cry).

A NEST, A KNOT

A RIDICULOUS JOB WAS WHAT had brought them together. A sandwich shop. Cassandra got hired in April. Raphaël had been working there for six months. They appreciated one another's twisted humour, tattoos, and music snobbery.

The sandwich shop was called All Dressed. On the restaurant's sign, a woman was eating a big sandwich with one hand and taking off her shirt with the other. "It's a pun!" the boss explained.

"I would hate this place no matter what," Cassandra mutters in Raphaël's ear while the cheese is melting on a Philly cheesesteak she is making for a customer. "But that sign!"

"It's obscene," Raphaël agrees, admiring the pretty curls on Cassandra's neck.

"At least the music is good!" A Bruno Mars song is playing on the radio.

Raphaël laughs out loud and puts one plastic-gloved finger on the tattoo of a skull, Gothic letters, and bleeding roses that covers part of Cassandra's shoulder. "You're kidding me, right?"

"I pay you to make sandwiches, not stand around flirting," the boss grumbles.

"I'm going to kill him," Raphaël says.

"I'll help you," Cassandra says.

They steal bread, sausages, litres of milk, money. He comes by her place to give her some of the booty.

"See you tomorrow," he says.

"No, no work tomorrow. I'm going to set fire to All Dressed tonight."

"Don't tell me that! But know that if someone was going to set fire to it, they'd have my blessing."

He looks her in the eyes for a second too long, then offers her his hand for a high-five. She takes his hand and grips it for a second. He laughs, revealing large white teeth, and shakes his head. He throws her a look that means, "What are you doing? What's happening? Are you feeling what I'm feeling?"

He pulls up the hood of his black hoodie, goes down the spiral staircase, and gets back on his bike, his now half-empty backpack on his shoulder. He disappears.

Cassandra stays rooted to the spot on the balcony and watches him roll away. She feels dizzy. Darsha, her roommate and best friend, comes out.

"Who was that?"

Cassandra jumps. "I didn't hear you!"

Darsha raises an eyebrow.

"That was Raphaël. He's just a guy who works at All Dressed."

Darsha crosses her arms over her chest, which is covered with strings of fake pearls. "Just a guy who works at All Dressed, eh?"

She folds her hands under her chin, lifts her eyes skywards, and sighs amorously. Cassandra gives her a jokey punch and escapes into the apartment.

A few weeks later, spring settles in for good. Cassandra and Raphaël wait for each other at the end of their shifts. They walk around together and tell each other their life stories. They like the same things, they hate the same things. They compliment each other and make confessions.

"I have a monster inside me," Raphaël says.

"Me too," Cassandra says.

"Mine's kinda hard to control."

He comes to meet Cassandra at All Dressed even when he's not working. They see each other every day. They start drinking a lot, make a ruckus from one apartment to the other, one alley to another, together, all night long. Then they start kissing. And fucking. A nest or a knot forms between them. Whole days are spent listening to music in Cassandra's bedroom, near the main door of the big apartment she shares with Darsha. There are nights when they don't notice the time passing, when they hear Darsha get up, make tea, walk across the apartment to her sewing studio, and start up her sewing machine, and when they say, incredulously, "It's morning? And we didn't go to bed?" There are the exquisitely hard shifts at All Dressed. The over-the-top breakfasts with eggs *and* pancakes *and* toast *and* bacon *and* sausages *and* fruit. There are the powerful, indelible words: "I love you." "I've never felt like this before." A revenge against the mediocrity of work. The feeling of being superpowered because of the other person. The beauty of one quadrupled by the beauty of the other. They look good when they go up the Mountain on weekends, with their sunglasses, their sketchbooks, and their cameras. They are good-looking in a scornful or darkly humorous way. They don't want to be winners. They think it's kind of loserish to be a winner. "He's just like you," Darsha says.

It continues. It's summer. Raphaël is romantic. He graffitis on a wall that Cassandra walks past on her way to work, writing *Happy birthday Cassandra!* in huge letters. He takes her to see Godspeed You! Black Emperor. He shows up at her window in the middle of the stifling hot nights and makes love to her like a pro.

"I'm spending too much time here," Raphaël says, licking her belly, her pussy. "Will you forgive me?"

"Mi casa es tu casa," she says, laughing.

Her laughter turns into an orgasm. Raphaël carries on kissing her thighs, her breasts.

"My Cassandra is my Cassandra," he says.

On July 1, Raphaël moves into Cassandra and Darsha's place, leaving behind his artist roommate who adores the beatniks in Saint-Henri. The Roots album *Things Fall Apart* plays on a loop for the whole moving day. Around noon, Darsha comes back from a party where she spent the night. She's holding a bottle of Gatorade.

"What the fuck?" she says, staring at the truck full of boxes.

"It'll make the rent cheaper for everyone," Cassandra says.

Darsha looks at Raphaël, who is going down the spiral stairs wiping his hands on his shorts. "You've got to be kidding me," she says. Raphaël smiles and goes to get more boxes from the truck.

"Anyway, we're never here, we work like dogs."

"I work too," Darsha says. "This isn't a rooming house, you know."

"Darsha! You have the whole third bedroom for your sewing business and I've never said anything."

Darsha doesn't say anything else. She changes the music, puts on Crass's "Do They Owe Us a Living?" and helps them empty the moving truck. Raphaël has a lot of boxes. Darsha makes costumes and goes to raves. She takes a lot of drugs. She decides to roll with the punch and move on.

Raphaël is delighted. He's in love. Life is worth living. He decorates the apartment, puts up shelves, makes dinner, greets the neighbours, charms the landlord. Cassandra sings in the shower, buys clothes, makes love-song mixtapes. They're simmering in precious happiness.

But the honeymoon doesn't last. Barely two months. Routine sets in. Raphaël hates his job, and his job eats up his life. After a long day of work, all he has left is his anger, his backache, and enough money to buy a case of beer. "I need to relax!" he explodes. Cassandra's going through the same thing but finds herself having to comfort him. Raphaël drinks more and more. After September, he doesn't have enough money to pay rent. Cassandra tells herself—tells everyone— that Raphaël is bipolar and that she's supporting him. He's suffering, she tells her friends who are worried about her, and she sees them less and less. Raphaël drinks, smokes pot, spends money, stops showing up for work. He's depressed, having more mood swings, sponging off Cassandra. When she tries to tell him about her day, he sighs loudly. When she flinches at his anger, he says, "You take everything too personally." He says, "Stop manipulating me."

Darsha barely talks to them. Whenever she sees them, she greets them with the friendliest, most neutral tone. She takes Adderall every day, which she orders from websites full of pornographic ads. She sews costumes all night and works on her artistic projects during the day. She makes puppets out of papier-mâché and found objects, kittens and sheep whose throats are often slit and the guts hanging out. Once, just once, she decides to write Cassandra a letter to explain that she thinks Raphaël is dangerous and that he should leave, but she gets disheartened after three sentences and rips the paper up.

Cassandra is talking to her mother on the phone. She's trying to explain her current situation, but she feels like she's lying. What exactly is wrong, after all? She can't figure out how to explain it. She wonders if she's paranoid. She describes some incidents, but she tells them badly. She no longer knows what happened.

"He seems nice," her mother says.

"Yes, he's nice," she says.

In October, Raphaël loses his job. This is what sets off his explicitly violent behaviour. He rages over nothing. He throws things. He breaks things. And then, sometimes, he wakes up in a great mood and becomes the good old Raphaël, romantic, sexy, attentive. Cassandra doesn't talk to her mother on the phone anymore, because she feels responsible for her own unhappiness: she can't work up the will to leave him. She waits in hope for his good days. His things, mixed up with hers, have become part of the apartment. One day she comes back from work and finds him on the balcony cooking a sausage over a fire he's made in the little metal trash can with several of Cassandra's books. She threatens to have the locks changed if he pulls another stunt like that. He gets up. He moves closer to her, puts his hands around her neck, and tightens them. After three seconds he lets her go. She shouts, "Fuck you!" in a hoarse voice. He punches her in the stomach. She runs and shuts herself in the bathroom. He follows her and yells through the door that he'll do it again and harder if she ever tries to leave him again. Cassandra stays in the bathroom for an hour. When she comes out, Raphaël is sitting in their bed watching *Game of Thrones*. She watches the show with him, then they sleep spooning. Cassandra wakes up several times with a jump. Raphaël sleeps deeply.

Days pass. They don't talk about what happened. Raphaël drinks, smokes, invites over tons of noisy males who raid the fridge.

Darsha, overwhelmed by events, goes off to take refuge at a friend's place in the suburbs.

"I'm going to pay my rent for three more months," she says to Cassandra with tears in her eyes before she leaves the apartment. "I'm sorry, sweetie. It's too much for me."

Raphaël's violence makes him confident. He moves his guitars and amps into the old sewing room and tells Cassandra she has to ask for permission if she wants to go in there. He hardly ever acts pathetic anymore, and manages to find a new job. As soon as he starts working again, he begins acting as if Cassandra was the one who'd been sponging off him forever. He's found a job as a cook in a restaurant. He earns more than she does at the sandwich shop. He joins the boys' club of restaurant kitchens. He takes coke, drinks, spends the night with a waitress. He doesn't hide it from Cassandra. He says, "I'm going to stay the night at Vanessa's, she's a good friend of mine. Don't go crazy." Cassandra tells him to fuck off for appearance's sake but actually enjoys these evenings when Raphaël isn't there. She digs a little hole in the black cloud that's invaded her brain and tries to get things in order while he's not there.

"He hit me," she states, amazed.

But he didn't *hit* me hit me. He didn't hit me like "A man hit a woman." It was different. They were winding each other up. Things were getting tense. He hit me, but I could have been the one who hit him. He wouldn't have hit me if he hadn't known that I could have hit him myself. He's not like that.

Sometimes Raphaël wants to spend the evening with Cassandra. She doesn't dare make plans, just in case.

"Will you be here tonight?" she asks him on Halloween as she's leaving the house to go to the sandwich shop.

"Stop asking me questions," he says. "I don't have my schedule off by heart, I don't know what time I'll be home. You'll be around, so if I'm here, you'll see me."

She obeys. She gets back from work around four, puts two bags of groceries down on the counter. Children in costumes ring the doorbell even though she's turned off all the lights and there's no pumpkin on the porch. The door-bell is insistent, as if chanting, "It's time." There's no sign of Raphaël. Cassandra goes back to the grocery store and buys a big box of mini chocolate bars and a cauldron in the shape of a pumpkin. She turns off the television, turns on the lights, wraps a scarf around her head, and puts a ring in her ear. She spends a few hours on the porch saying, "Arrrr, I'm a pirate!" and handing out candy. Then she makes herself something to eat, sets a plate aside for Raphaël, and settles down in front of Netflix.

Raphaël comes back around midnight, drunk, also dressed up as a pirate. He smiles and snuggles up to Cassandra, who's dozing on the couch, the empty cauldron on her thighs.

"You're my soulmate," Raphaël says. "Arrr!"

Cassandra holds him tight. Things aren't always easy between us, but we have to stick together, she says to herself. We have a common enemy: work. It's work that stresses us out. People who don't work don't get it.

"You're welcome at Sharon's place," says a note that Darsha slips in the envelope along with her share of November's rent.

"It's sweet of you, but don't forget I signed a lease," Cassandra replies by email, without bothering to write "Hi Darsha" or to sign her name.

She sleeps badly. She's walking on eggshells all the time. Raphaël spends at least two nights a week with "Vanessa." Cassandra doesn't know if Vanessa's a real person or a code name for "some girl." When he's at home, Raphaël wants to fuck. Cassandra rushes to jerk him off instead to avoid catching something. One day, when she tells him his breath stinks of alcohol, he spits in her mouth. Generally, he's so drunk he doesn't have the strength to straddle her. Sometimes he manages, and she lets him.

"Things aren't okay at all," she says.

"We're a very normal couple," he says.

In mid-November, Cassandra gets to work to discover that her boss is going bankrupt and has to close the sandwich shop. She doesn't tell Raphaël. The next day, she leaves at nine as usual and heads to the unemployment office, where she signs on with Sharon's address in the suburbs. Then she walks to the library, joins, and goes online. She scours Craigslist and Kijiji for a place to live in a different neighbourhood. Everything is expensive. She isn't brave enough to rent a place by herself. She looks under "shared apartments." The ads don't inspire her. Nobody is as special as Raphaël. She hates herself for thinking this. She sends dozens of emails flaunting her qualities as a roommate (clean, responsible, chilled out, 420-friendly). The day after, she starts again. She gets a few answers but can't bring herself to go and see the apartments. Some nights they still sleep spooning. She's annoyed that she likes his warmth. She wants to tell him what she's doing with her days, but she holds back. "It's time," the doorbell sounds again.

After three weeks she picks up her first EI cheque and buys a used car, which she parks three blocks away from her place and fills with her clothes and valuables, one trip at a time, for two days, her heart racing, looking over her shoulder for Raphaël with every step.

But Raphaël doesn't catch her. Very early one morning, she comes back to the apartment after putting the final bags in her car, and stands in the kitchen for several minutes with her winter coat on, a pen in her hand. Don't write him a note, she orders herself. She throws the pen down on the dining table, bursts into tears, and drives to the suburb where Sharon and Darsha live.

It's a small, pretty house. Darsha has moved into the guest bedroom. Her sewing machine stands on a table that is too narrow for it. Her fabrics are piled up against one of the walls. Sharon isn't home. Cassandra spends the morning with Darsha and tells her everything. They cry a lot. Darsha says she's sorry that she couldn't support her better.

"You have your own problems," Cassandra says, shrugging her shoulders.

Darsha stares into space, dazed. "What are you going to do now?" she asks.

Cassandra tries to answer but can't. Her head hurts.

"Forget I asked that," says Darsha. "Just rest."

"If the landlord calls you, don't answer," Cassandra says. "And the same goes for Raphaël, but I don't think he'll call you."

Saying his name gives her a lump in her throat. She cries. Darsha hugs her and then makes her a bed on the couch. Cassandra sleeps the whole afternoon.

When she wakes up, the house is all dark. She hears a noise of keys, and then footsteps both resounding and light. She closes her eyes, blinded by the ceiling light as it's turned on. When she opens them, a little deer is standing in front of her and looking at her. She shakes her head. The deer says: "Hello! Um, who are you?"

It's not a deer, it's a child.

"Cassandra," says Cassandra. "Who are you?"

"Isaac," says the child, and then bursts out laughing.

"What's so funny?" Cassandra asks, but soon she's laughing too.

"Isaac's a giggler," says a woman whom Cassandra sees putting grocery bags down on the kitchen table.

I didn't know Sharon had a child, Cassandra thinks. But why would I have known? I never asked.

Cassandra gets up to introduce herself and help Sharon with the bags. But Isaac blocks her way and says, "You can't catch me!"

And he runs off toward the stairs. Cassandra looks at Sharon.

"He's quick to trust people," Cassandra says.

"He's a happy little boy," Sharon says.

Cassandra explains who she is. Sharon seems to be up to speed already.

"I'd really like to go and play with Isaac," Cassandra says.

"Go ahead, please," says Sharon, smiling.

So Cassandra heads to the stairs, her heart beating, almost crying with relief at the idea that this child is hiding somewhere and waiting for her to come and find him.

THE CEILING

KAT THUMPS ON CÉLINE'S BEDROOM door.

"Come in," says Céline almost immediately.

Kat goes in. Céline is sitting on the bed, her back ramrod straight, her eyes wide. She's biting her finger, pulling off the skin growing around the nail.

"Can you hear them?" Kat says.

"Yeah," Céline says.

Kat comes and sits next to Céline on the bed. They hold hands.

"*I need to relax!*" they hear through the ceiling.

They both blink at the shock of the voice. It contains something like a laugh, indignation, a complaint, a loss of control that opens the door to violence.

Kat's eyes are veiled and her lips are grey. She looks as though she might throw up.

"It never stops," Céline says. "They've been shouting

like this for half an hour." She raises her eyes to the ceiling. "What room would that be for them? The bedroom?"

"No," Kat says. "It's their living room. Their living room is next to the kitchen."

"Get away from me, I don't want to see your face! I'm not drunk, I'm tired!"

There's a muffled noise, and then something heavy falls onto the floor. Then her voice: *"You're crazy! Stop!"*

Kat digs her nails into Céline's palm.

"You okay?"

"Too many memories," Kat says.

Céline lets go of Kat's hand and puts an arm awkwardly around her shoulders. "What should we do?"

Kat feels her ears buzzing. She scans Céline's bedroom. Black-and-white photo of Céline and her little brother, maybe seven and thirteen. Dried roses in a Mason jar. Hibernating computer. Cups of coffee, piles of books and papers. Several copies of a brochure called *Accomplices not Allies,* the title in white capitals written over a face hidden behind a black balaclava, eyes and mouth hostile. Pinned to the wall, a scrap of pink fabric with two narwhals kissing: *Fuck Everything.* A Certain Days calendar, open at the photo of a Mi'kmaq woman kneeling in front of a row of riot police, waving a feather. A red circle on today's date: "Meet Johanne," her thesis supervisor.

"Kat," Céline says.

Kat blinks and shakes herself. Breathing as if she's stayed underwater too long, she says, "Maybe we should go and ring their bell. Lower the tension."

"Yeah, okay," Céline says.

They stay sitting there. The man carries on yelling. *"Oh yes, boohoohoo, always whining! It's my fault, right, everything's always my fault! And you're perfect, aren't you?"*

They hear muffled blows after the shouts, as if the man is pacing in the apartment as he screams.

"Bitch!"

Kat and Céline follow the sound of the shouts with their eyes, their heads raised toward the ceiling.

"Or maybe we should call the police," Céline says.

"The police are totally useless," Kat says. "The police never protected me against Max. All they do is make things worse."

"I know, but..." Céline says, pointing at the ceiling, trying to find a better idea.

She doesn't find one.

"Shall we go and see? Shall we ring the bell?"

Kat hesitates. "Someone has to stay here with Ruby."

Céline manages to rip off another strip of skin and starts chewing it. "Who is this dude anyway? I thought it was two girls living upstairs."

Kat tries to concentrate on the question and calm down. "I met him a couple of times when I was driving Ruby to school. I think he replaced one of the girls in July."

"Which one left?"

"The one with the multicoloured hair extensions."

"Ah, right. The one who didn't want to oppose the rent increase."

"Neither of them wanted to. They were both a bit apathetic. I think the whole lot of them do a lot of drugs."

A glass object breaks and yanks them back to the present.

"Fuck!" Kat says. "Okay, what are we gonna do?"

"I don't know," Céline says. "It's stressing me out. I'm scared. Should we call the police?"

"If she's taking drugs, maybe it's not a good idea to send the police there," Kat says cuttingly. "Aren't you supposed to know all this?" Kat takes her arm out of Céline's and gestures toward the calendar, a poster saying *Solidarity with Ferguson: Arms Up, Shoot Back*, and all the anarchist propaganda covering the bedroom walls. She gives her an ironic smile, just for a second.

Céline lowers her eyes and crosses her arms in front of her chest. The shouting is still going on.

"Fuck!" Kat says again.

She gets up, walks over to Ruby's bedroom, opens the door, and stands there without moving. She hears her daughter's breathing. She tries to calm down, to adjust her own troubled respiration to the regular breath of the sleeping child. Ruby is here. I am here. We are together, far away from him. He doesn't know where to find us. One. Two. Three. Breathe.

She closes the door again and goes back to the kitchen, where her own computer is sitting in the middle of empty cups of tea, highlighters, and photocopied course packs. She sees her cellphone plugged into the computer. She grabs it and goes back to Céline's bedroom. She sits back down on the bed.

"Okay. Sorry. I'm on edge. You know what? I think I have her phone number."

"Good idea," Céline says. "Good idea."

Kat scrolls through her contacts. "What's her name again? Oh yeah, C. Cassandra."

"Cassandra," Céline murmurs.

Kat calls the number.

They don't hear ringing coming from upstairs, but after a few seconds the shouts stop. Cassandra doesn't answer. Céline leans toward Kat. Kat frowns, her fingers gripping the phone. "She's not answering."

The man starts yelling again, but not so loud, as if he's losing steam. Kat and Céline look at each other.

"You've reached Cassandra..." the voice mail says. Kat hangs up. They don't say anything for a few seconds.

"Sleep in my bed tonight," Céline says.

After a brief hesitation, Kat says, "All right."

While Céline is putting her pyjamas on, Kat goes to check that the doors are locked. Then she goes back to Ruby's door again and puts her ear to it. She can't hear anything. Her breathing gets faster, too fast. She goes into Ruby's bedroom. Ruby is lying on her back like a starfish, sleeping with her mouth open. She's getting tall, Kat thinks. She goes and sits at the top of the bed, takes her daughter's hand, and presses it to her cheek. "Ruby," she murmurs.

HIS MEMORIES

HIS MEMORIES CAME BACK TO haunt him, he says to me as he looks for his cigarettes (he doesn't have any). His memories, pictures and smells and sounds whose violence I will never know, appeared in the night, he explains as he's looking for his friends (they've disappeared). This morning, he asks me, "You know that awful feeling when you can't tell if it's a cat or a child crying in the night?" as he pats his pockets looking for cigarettes (they've disappeared). Later he tells me, "I've always loved the sea, but it has never loved me enough to keep me, every time it spits me back out on the beach," patting his heart for the memory of his friends (he no longer has any).

JULY

I WALK LIKE AN INJURED wolf on the thick ice, like a lost wolf confused by the trees being too similar, buffeted by the accusatory wind. I am sure of one thing: I won't drown, haven't come across a drop for weeks and my stomach is more jealous than a heart. My scattered blood doesn't heat anything, doesn't make anything melt. I empty myself. Here is the deep lake where I used to dive; all I can do now is limp across it.

METEOR, AUGUST 13

VINCENT GETS UP AROUND SEVEN and staggers to the bathroom. He lifts the seat up with his foot and pees. He flushes
and goes back to his bedroom to look for his glasses. He
puts his glasses on. He heads to the kitchen, unscrews the
coffee maker, gets ready to throw yesterday's dregs into
the sink, then remembers that it's not true that coffee cleans
the pipes. It's an urban legend that his plumber cousin
debunked last week when he came over—funnily enough,
to fix the blocked sink. Vincent throws the coffee into the
garbage. He rinses the coffee maker then fills the bottom
tank with cold water. He opens the cupboard, gets out the
coffee beans and the grinder. He grinds some coffee, gets a
spoon from the dish rack, and puts coffee in the appropriate
section of the machine. He screws on the top compartment
and puts the contraption on the element, which he turns on.

Waiting for the coffee, he goes to get his computer. The
floor is cold under his bare feet. He puts the computer onto

the kitchen table and goes into his bedroom to get dressed. He chooses jeans, a long-sleeved T-shirt, and a hoodie. It's cold for August 13.

Vincent goes back to the kitchen. He checks his email. He has two messages from Emploi-Québec telling him he owes them money. He moves the two emails to the trash. He has one email from Estella, which just says, "Thinking of you, Vincent." His eyes fill with tears. The coffee boils and gurgles. Vincent goes to turn off the element and pours himself a coffee. He's forgotten to buy milk. It's no big deal, he likes black coffee too.

Vincent turns off the computer and takes it back to the desk in his bedroom. He makes his bed. Then he stays standing for a long time. He opens his closet door, chooses a pair of running shoes, and stands for another long while in the middle of his bedroom. Then he goes back to the closet and gets out the rope he bought the week before at the hardware store. He puts the backpack on and remains standing in the middle of the room. He goes to the desk, picks up a pen and a Post-it, and writes, "Password: furorandmystery321." He sticks the Post-it on the computer.

Vincent wanders around his apartment looking for his keys. He doesn't find them. It's better if he doesn't lock up, he realizes, and goes out. A warm wind slips into the cold air, rising toward his face. His already ratty hair gets even more tangled.

He greets the mailman, who's going up the stairs as he goes down. Then he heads to Rue Ontario and walks to the end of it, and then farther still, to the other side of the railway tracks.

TWENTY-FOUR HOURS

THE SECOND TIME I SAW Vincent, it was in the street. I recognized him right away despite his balaclava and black clothes; it wasn't hard with his ice-blue husky's eyes.

The third time I saw Vincent was at a party, and that was when I discovered we were friends of friends and also that he was a funny, intense person, passionate, someone I wanted to get to know.

I can't remember the fourth, fifth, and sixth times. All I know is the single times turned into a long river, sometimes calm, sometimes raging with nights out, conversations, political arguments, confidences, getting up to no good, secrets, crazy laughter.

It was only today that I remembered my first meeting with Vincent. It had completely gone out of my head. I'd rewritten the chain of events, I'd woven the threads of our lives thinking that the time we met in the street was the first time. Of course, that didn't hold water since, as I've just said, I actually recognized him that time.

The first time I saw Vincent, it was around midnight and he opened the convenience store door for me by pressing a button. That was actually his job; he worked at the twenty-four-hour Couche-Tard on Rachel Est. I said hi, he said hi back. I already more or less knew what I wanted, just a bag of chips to soak up the alcohol I'd absorbed. I looked through the rows of tempting candy, but I didn't have time to browse, I had friends waiting for me in the car. They were all drunk (even the driver: "I can hold my drink really, really well") and were convinced they were really hungry. I chose a bag of country-style peppers-and-cream-flavour chips, and I noted that the snack company, if the bag was telling the truth, had entered the world the year before I had. I headed to the cash.

Vincent was standing behind the counter swaying from one foot to the other, probably too tired even to try to entertain himself. Between the two of us there was a wall of bulletproof plastic. He told me how much the bag of chips was, and I slid the money through the special money slot.

When he passed my change back, a moth crossed from his side to mine and brushed against my hands, my wallet.

"A moth," I said.

"Yeah," he said. "There are tons of them around now."

"I have them too, in my garbage," I said. I couldn't decide if I thought the moth was beautiful, disgusting, or terrifying.

He looked at me. "At least they only live for twenty-four hours."

"Moths only live for twenty-four hours?" I said, horrified. I had never thought about it.

He stayed serious. He didn't offer me a plastic bag to put the chips in. He didn't ask, "Is that everything today?"

I said, "Pretty depressing, being an insect."

Vincent shook his head as if he understood what a moth's life was like and I didn't. "I think there are worse things," he said, with an encouraging half smile.

I wondered for a moment what he meant by this. Then I remembered my friends, the engine idling, our desire for junk food. I took the bag of chips, said, "Thanks, have a good evening," and went out into the night to join the others, not yet aware of all the beauty that Vincent would bring into my life.

GOODBYE

"WE HAVE TO GO," I said, starting a new game of *Tetris*.

Jess said, "Okay," and got up from the bed where she was stretched out with her legs spread. I rotated a turquoise *L*. Jess went over to the sound system and turned up the volume. "Soon we'll be done with the trouble of the world," Mahalia Jackson sang.

I reached my arm out toward the nightstand, picked up a Kleenex, and dabbed my eyes without stopping my game of *Tetris*. Jess walked over to the closet, took off her long dress, hung it on a hanger, and took off a black suit wrapped in plastic. I watched her out of the corner of my eye without stopping fitting all the lines, squares, and other coloured pieces that were falling across my screen. I felt some kind of misplaced haste seeing Jess in her clean shirt and pants.

"Here goes," she said nervously before shutting herself in the bathroom.

It made her nervous, wearing ordinary clothes, especially masculine ones, like other people would be nervous wearing an eccentric outfit.

I had to get dressed too. "After this game," I said to myself. I wanted to beat my record, I'd got to level 13. I'd been doing nothing but playing *Tetris* for the last week. I wasn't ready to think about anything else, or dream about anything else. I forced myself to dream about *Tetris*. Two more levels and I would beat the game. And what then? Then I'd start all over again.

I shut my laptop without turning it off and placed it on the bed. It started overheating noisily. I found my black dress in my pants drawer. It was all crumpled, and too light for the season (it was summer, if you could call it that; it was so cold). I pulled it on over the long johns and *I (burning police car) Montréal* tank I'd been wearing for five days.

I looked at myself in the mirror. I didn't think much of the image it reflected back to me. I put on a faded black wool jacket with fraying cuffs and sat on the end of the bed to braid my hair. When I finished, I had nothing left to do, so I burst into tears. It only lasted ten seconds. I put my dead fish face back on, expressionless, exhausted, empty. Then, since Jess was still dawdling in the bathroom, I started to get nervous. I didn't want to go at all anymore. I'm not going, I told myself. People will understand. And if they don't, I don't care.

Jess came out of the bathroom, looking sexy and unhappy. She was disguised as a man and it was pretty convincing. I could see a few sparkles on her temples, but she'd cleaned off all traces of makeup. I was the one who social norms dictated should disguise myself as a woman, but I didn't have the heart to put makeup on. I couldn't put makeup on, not that day. There wasn't any point, I didn't want to hide my tear-swollen face, I didn't want to make the tears more obvious with running eyeliner and mascara, I just wanted to cry, cry, cry, a river howling all alone through the forest.

I went over to the record player, sat down in front of it, and chose a song perfect for tears. "You can take the road that takes you to the stars now," Nick Drake sang.

"I'm not going," I said.

Jess knelt down behind me and rubbed my back as I stared fixedly at the music.

"Okay, fine," I whined, "I'm going, but I have to take a shower!"

Jess followed me into the bathroom and helped me get undressed and take out my braid. In the shower, I shampooed, soaped, conditioned, and scrubbed as if there were a valuable painting under the tat of my body, in the hope that, once clean, I might be revealed as being of good enough quality that I wouldn't break under the weight of this day.

I got out of the shower and put my underwear on. I wrapped a towel around my shoulders and left my other clothes in a ball on the bathroom floor.

My bedroom door had stayed open. Jess was sitting at my desk chair, her back very straight. I saw her frown when she saw me come out of the bathroom wearing my towel as a cape and wander around the apartment, stopping sometimes to pick up a box of tissues and put it back where it belonged, or move a cushion from one sofa to the other. Jess watched me for a few minutes and then she went to the bathroom to get my clothes. She came out to join me in the living room, where I was crouching on the ground with my back against an armchair. Jess held my clothes out firmly and said, "Come on, Sab. I'll drive."

"Aren't we waiting for Estella?" I said. I couldn't figure out why my roommate wasn't at home.

"She's with Tahar, remember? We're meeting them there."

"Oh yeah."

Jess took me by the shoulders and kissed my head. I put my clothes back on, but now that I'd rubbed myself down with Ivory soap, Fructis shampoo, and St Ives apricot scrub, I could tell they stank of sweat, dirt, and piss. I took the hand Jess was holding out and followed her, grabbing random objects between the living room and the door, my keys, my sunglasses, something I'd written for the ceremony and that I might read, but probably would not.

I locked the door, I went downstairs, I couldn't remember whether I'd locked the door, I went back up, checked, came back down, settled into the passenger seat, and closed my eyes.

Jess started the car. I guessed that the world looked more or less the same as it had the last time I had taken an interest in it, but I couldn't be bothered to check.

I thought of Vincent.

You know what I saw, Vincent, when I closed my eyes and thought of you, you know what I saw when Jess was driving like a responsible adult in a city she barely knows, while we crossed the city from east to west and the radio dared to talk about something that wasn't you, dared to play songs you'd have hated?

I thought about your hands sliding an elastic band from your forearm to your wrist, about your right hand bending, your fingers spread, about your elbows standing up on either side of your head, your hands helping each other, joined together to pull your hair back, I could have braided your hair, Vincent, I know long hair, I could have come over any time, you know I never turn my phone off, you would gather your hair in a ponytail or sometimes a bun. I teased you, I said, "Vincent has a man bun!" You said, "I have to hide my rat's nest! A bun's better than a single massive dread." You didn't comb it out anymore, it would have been too long, I could have, I could have come over to your place with a load of brushes, tried them all, I could have, I could have, I could have.

I opened my eyes. The car was driving murderously along. Jess would only have had to give the steering wheel a little twist to assassinate the old lady, the students on bikes, these two punks with dogs, this jogger talking on the phone, all it would have taken was a clumsy (or skilful) manoeuvre to kill us, to shatter our windshield and smash a store window. But Jess was driving in a straight line down de Maisonneuve, without trembling, McGill Metro Presse Café Eaton's Centre TD Canada Trust Canadian dollar exchange rate abandoned grocery cart The UPS Store National Bank vitamin water ad Hotel St-Martin Spa Diva Presse Café Bank of Montreal Peel Metro Pandora (Vincent liked laughing at Pandora stores) another vitamin water ad iTravel2000 Tim Hortons. I closed my eyes again.

It wouldn't have changed anything, your hoarse voice murmured in my ear.

I jumped. Jess was driving, she didn't make any sudden movement, she didn't kill that mother and her baby in a stroller, nor that woman in high heels, she didn't turn her head toward your voice, she hadn't heard anything. I shed a few tears and a good amount of snot. I felt around in my backpack, found a bandana, and blew my nose with it.

"He's here," I said. "I just heard his voice."

Jess didn't push it, she believed me. She had her own dead people. This was my first.

You're my first death, Vincent.

I'm not your death, he replied immediately. I'm just dead. I am my own death. And you have to love me that way.

Okay, I agreed, but it seemed impossible. I wanted to love you alive, I simply wanted to love you alive.

I SPOTTED YOUR MOTHER RIGHT away when I went into the church, she looked even more devastated than the others. I said, "My condolences," to her and my voice seemed fake, deformed, as if I was trying to express myself in a foreign language that I was pretending to speak well for a role in a movie, but nothing mattered to me. I saw Céline, Kat, Tahar, Estella, and at least a hundred other people I knew. I barely noticed if they were crying, if they were sitting or standing, if they talked to me or touched me. I was aware only of your mother, her face burned my eyes when I looked at her and burned my back when she was behind me. Jess busied herself finding seats, handing me another bandana, holding my hand, leading me to the bathroom when I needed to go. After returning from the washroom, I sat down, taking up very little space on the bench, I locked my hand into Jess's, and I tried to disappear: I didn't move or talk or even cry until the end of the service.

AFTER THE PRIEST, THE AUNT, the former boss of a summer camp where Vincent had worked, and a few friends had done readings or told a moving anecdote, it was Tahar's turn, the only one of us who'd decided to step forward. I didn't know what he'd prepared. Tahar sat down at the piano, where a girl around twenty whom I didn't recognize had earlier played while another stranger of the same age had sung "Con te partirò."

I'd known for a long time that Tahar played piano, but I'd never heard him. There was a piano at the house of his ex, Antoine, and we were always asking Tahar to play something. He refused. "I'm not a circus animal," he would say. We rolled our eyes.

He had no music in front of him. Someone coughed in the room. Tahar was wearing a white shirt, soaked through with sweat. We could see his skin and hair through it. He was the only one of us wearing real dress shoes. He gave off an air of fire and ice, as if he was at the same time the drunkest and the most sober person present (weirdly, I hadn't drunk a single drop of alcohol since Vincent's death—I didn't want to at all). Tahar moved his head as if to say, "I'm ready." Who was he talking to? Himself? Vincent? "I'm starting," he said with his head, and he began playing the piano.

When I recognized the song, I felt a rush of wild pain in my chest, no, not this one, what are you doing? A panic gripped me as though it would suffocate me and at the same time it relieved me, like bloodletting performed on my heart, draining it of its poison and lies by gripping it too hard. It was Robbie Basho's "Orphan's Lament," which somehow Tahar was managing to sing without crying. His voice was clear, true, but softer and soberer than the original. I scanned the room and found Céline and Estella. Their faces looked like mine must: we were looking at Tahar as if he was betraying us and curing us at the same time, appalled, outraged, hypnotized by his voice and his fingers on the piano.

"Born for love and nothing more," Tahar sang.

I looked worriedly at Vincent's mother. Was this song too much? Was it going to do her in?

"Cut my hair and hushed my song," Tahar sang.

I came back from my mental vanishing act and rejoined the others, who were crying without restraint, even the children, even Jess, even the friends of friends and the cousins of cousins whom I could see clearly now and who I knew hadn't really known Vincent very well. We were all crying. Something was happening to us, we who could hear this indescribable song. It was no longer just sad, it was no longer just sad in the way that made people shake their heads and say, "So young," no, it was unbearable and at the same time it was the crux of life, it was inevitable, it was what we all had in common and had had forever.

"All my life, I've been forced to roam," Tahar sang. "Never had a ..."

There was nothing left, barely a few lines, but he couldn't carry on. He let his hands fall on the keys with an ugly noise. He was breathing like a dying dog. We all stayed silent and encouraging. I noticed that Vincent's mother was smiling and nodding. Maybe she didn't understand the words. Or maybe she understood them.

Tahar straightened his shoulders and resumed with the last bit of the song. "All my life, I've been forced to roam. Never had a place to call my own. Will you wait, will you wait for me? I'll be waiting by the river, my love. I'll be waiting there by the trees. Will you wait, will you wait?"

Tahar continued, his face clenched, distorted, until the final bar disappeared. I felt as though every person there wanted the music to never end even as they understood that there was nothing more to say, nothing more to sing, nothing more to play.

We clapped. I didn't wonder why I was there, I no longer needed Jess to find my way, I no longer wanted to run back home and start playing *Tetris* again. I was a human being, and human beings need to say goodbye, to get together, to cry in the same room. I brushed my hands together, crossed my fingers, but I wasn't really clapping, I wasn't making a sound. My hands didn't tap, they twirled, and they were made of paper, of scales, of parchment, my hands were the shape of moth wings.

PART 3

I lived like an angry guest,
like a partly mended thing, an outgrown child.
I remember my mother did her best.
She took me to Boston and had my hair restyled.
Your smile is like your mother's, the artist said.
I didn't seem to care. I had my portrait
done instead.
    —ANNE SEXTON, *To Bedlam and Part Way Back*

HORNY

THIS WAS SABRINA'S FATHER. THE one who lived in a condo tower. The one who gave us Lunchables and Capri Sun juice instead of making us something to eat. The one who drove Sabrina's mother up the wall whenever Sabrina came back from a weekend at his place with a new Barbie, a new Gap hoodie, a new Céline Dion or Mariah Carey CD. The one who smoked inside. The one who took us to the cottage. The one who yelled when we got his leather car seats wet with our asses all damp from the lake. The one who took us out on speedboats, the one who said, "Yes, of course," when he took us tubing and we asked him not to do zigzags, the one who betrayed us the second he touched the steering wheel and zigzagged all over the place—I cried, I screamed, I begged him to slow down, and he sang out, "Julie is a wimp!" The one who wore cologne.

"I'm going out tonight to find myself a woman," he said one afternoon as he came out of the shower.

We were at the cottage. Sabrina and I were squashed into the couch with cheese strings and cans of Fruitopia. I was sunburnt.

"Dad," Sabrina said in a warning voice.

"And I'm gonna choose the one with the biggest jugs," he carried on.

"Dad!" my friend wailed in a voice that I didn't know, a supplication that was both strict and panicked, ashamed, and practically ended in a sob.

"I'm going to choose the horniest one there!" he said, enunciating each word clearly. Then he laughed.

Sabrina and I were eight years old. I knew what "big jugs" meant, but not "horny."

"Da-ad!" my friend shouted, and she threw a cushion at him and got all red, and burst into real tears and ran off to shut herself in the bedroom the two of us were sharing at the cottage, leaving me alone with her father and the Family Channel, which was playing *Bewitched*.

"There's no need to cry," the dad shouted. "Baby! Baby, ba-by!"

I pretended to be totally absorbed in the show: "Endora: He has you under a spell … Oh, these male witches are the worst kind! Samantha: He's not a witch. Endora: What? Samantha: He happens to be, if you'll excuse the expression, a normal, mortal, human being." And then, afraid that *Bewitched* wasn't a safe enough refuge, I opened the Notdog book that had been lying on the living room table and I stared at a paragraph for a long time without taking in a single word about the adventures of Notdog and his friends, pulling the woollen blanket over my knees, fiddling with the piece of mica in my pocket, counting to one hundred in

English and then in French up to five hundred, feeling my new adult teeth with my tongue, and especially, especially, not looking at him at all.

MY FATHER IS HOLDING
A REVOLVER TO MY HEAD

MY FATHER IS HOLDING A revolver to my head. I am holding a revolver to my father's head. He's in a dressing gown, I'm wearing a snowsuit, and it's dripping on the wooden floor. I still have pink cheeks from playing outside for so long. The snow melts quickly in the warm, sunny living room. My father isn't laughing anymore. "I'm not laughing anymore, Julie," he says. He takes the safety off his weapon. I hold back as long as possible, but then I start to cry. "Why do you always tease me in front of your friends?" I ask, with my face full of snot. "Don't be a little bitch now," my father says. My mother appears on the stairs. She's picking up, one step at a time, the papers, books, pets, tax returns, and underwear lying around. "Looks like another great intellectual debate," she says. She's wearing a beach dress and sandals.

"Where are you going, Anne?" my father asks, letting the revolver drop to the floor.

"Nowhere, as usual," she says as she heads to the kitchen. I hear her start the dishwasher.

"Let's call it quits," says my father.

"It's not what Chekhov would have wanted," I say to nobody in particular.

My father sits back down in his leather armchair and chooses a book and a Scotch from the bookshelf.

"You want a book? A Scotch?" he offers.

I accept both. We drink, read, and swap complicit smiles. I go to sit near the heater, I stay there until the snow covering me melts. Underneath, I'm wearing a painting apron. I go to see my father and hold out my hand; he spits on it without taking his eyes off the hockey game on the television. I go over to my mother and hold out the other hand. She spits in it, changes my diaper, and wipes up my tears with a cool cloth. I go and sit in a garden chair with a notebook on my knees and draw with their spit, hoping that someone will notice me and hail me as a genius.

THE BLACK DOG

FOR MUCH OF MY CHILDHOOD, I was afraid of dogs. My mother was afraid of dogs before me. She would tell me, over and over again: "It's my fear, you don't need to be afraid of dogs just because I am," but I was still afraid of dogs. After all, it takes time to understand words, but you can taste fear. Her trembling legs, her breathing that went all crooked, her obvious desire to hide behind me—when, in every other slightly worrying situation, it went without saying that I could hide behind her. Dogs were the exception. I'm sure she was annoyed with herself for so obviously wanting to hide from a dog's sight, but she couldn't do much about it. I understood that when it came to dogs, it was every man for himself.

IN OTTAWA, ON BOLTON STREET, our neighbour had a dog, a golden retriever called Arcane. The neighbour was tall and bald, he wore black clothes, a long black coat that dragged along the ground. We used to see him leave his house at strange times to take Arcane for a walk and smoke a cigarette.

"Those people don't work," my grandmother used to say when she came to our house to play with me and bring my mom casseroles, pressing her nose up to the window to see the neighbour better.

"Mom!" my mother said.

"What? I'm just saying what I think."

"I don't want to transmit those values to Julie."

The neighbour seemed somehow magical and unique to me, and I couldn't understand where my grandmother would have seen other people like him.

Whenever I saw the neighbour and his dog when I was out with my father, we would go over to see them. My father would pet the dog and the neighbour would say, "He's friendly, he's friendly!" while I held my fist out to the dog to let him sniff it, and then I would quickly put my fist back in my coat pocket. I never opened my hand, never scratched Arcane behind the ears. Whenever I saw the neighbour when I was out with my mother, the neighbour would say hi to us, my mother would call out "Hello!" nervously and politely, and when he was out of earshot, she would mutter, "That leash is much too long, it's dangerous, he should have a shorter leash for his dog."

The year I turned five, we moved out to the country, my father, my mother and me. My parents had been looking at houses in the city and in the suburbs for several months. They hadn't found anything and their frustration was growing. In our apartment on Bolton Street, there was no longer enough room for all my toys and all my father's books. At least, that's how my parents explained the situation to me.

"That one will need some renos, but maybe it would be good for the kid, it's right next to the woods," the real estate agent had said, showing us some photos of a house for sale at the edge of a village thirty kilometres northeast of Gatineau.

"It's worth going to check it out," my father had said.

We'd followed the agent's car down the highway. Buckled into my car seat, I stared at the rows of trees. I tried to focus on a single one for as long as possible, and when I lost it from sight, I would start over with another tree.

"The new house is far away," I'd said.

"We don't know if we're going to move there," my father said. "We're just going to have a look."

"It would be a long commute for you," my mother said.

"Well, I wouldn't hate that, doing some driving," my father said.

"But, Jacques, the traffic!" my mother said.

"Traffic doesn't bother me," my father insisted.

The house was big and white with no embellishments. Big, bright rooms, wooden floors, a smell of flour, bedclothes and down, and damp cleanness that floated permanently in the air. There were three bedrooms and a little room with a sloping ceiling that my father called "my office" when we were looking around. The house was surrounded by an enormous porch, well-built. In the yard there was an above-ground pool, a sandbox, a firepit, enough space to run around, and in the distance a stream and the forest. There was no fence.

My parents decided to buy the house. They bought it

quickly, on a whim. Neither of them was very handy; they weren't the kind of people who might have noticed that the plumbing was completely wrecked. The real estate agent "hadn't noticed" anything either.

IT WAS VERY HOT ON moving day. The day before, my mother had been busy labelling all the boxes and piling them up in the middle of each room. Right now, my father was giving instructions to the movers. He was speaking to them and using more slang than he usually did. My mother pointed it out to him. My father ignored her.

"Everything's A-okay," one of the movers said, wiping his forehead with his T-shirt, "except nobody told us there was a piano. I don't have enough guys to move a piano."

The mover looked at my father.

"You didn't tell them there was a piano?" my mother said. Without waiting for my father to reply, she went on, "It's my piano. What are we going to do? Let's call your company and get them to send another guy. We have to be out of here by four."

"Don't get upset," my father said. "We'll figure something out."

"I'm not getting upset," my mother said. "I'm figuring something out."

The mover was sweating. My father and my mother clenched their fists. I wandered around the empty apartment saying, "Oh! Oh!" to test the echo. The adults basically had to scream to hear themselves over my shouts, but nobody seemed to even notice, like I was some construction noise in the distance.

"We're super busy today," the mover said. "It's too last-minute to call other guys."

"Not even later today? Tonight? If we offer a bonus, can't you come back tonight?"

The mover said it was a possibility. My mother called the landlord to see if the new tenants would accept this arrangement. From my "Oh! Oh!"s I moved on to full sentences: I recited a passage from one of my favourite movies, *The Secret Garden,* and helped the echo out by using a sharp voice to repeat each sentence.

"Mary! (Mary! Mary!) Come to me! (Come to me! Come to me!) I'm in the garden! (I'm in the garden! I'm in the garden!) With Colin! (With Colin! With Colin!)"

The mover went to drink water from the bathroom tap. My father noticed me and said, "Okay, Julie, turn it down a bit."

My mother and the mover came after my father.

"It won't work," my mother said. "They don't want to. The apartment has to be empty by four."

My father knew what he had to do. "Fine," he said. "I'll help you."

The mover nodded his head, satisfied but confused, probably not understanding why my giant of a father had not suggested this earlier.

The reason was that the giant had no skill. For more than an hour, the three movers had to follow my father's rhythm as his fingers slipped, his knees forgot to bend, and his eyes did not anticipate the corners of the walls. My father was sweating so much I could see drops falling on the floor, and his face was all red.

"You don't even play your damn piano," he said through gritted teeth, a quarter of the piano's weight in his arms, as he went by my mother.

My mother didn't say anything else the whole day.

When the piano was finally in the truck, she drove me to the grocery store, bought Mr Freezes for everyone, then buckled me back into my car seat, drove back to the house, and sat behind the wheel while the guys finished loading boxes into the truck. She turned on the radio. A woman from Radio-Canada was talking about Kim Campbell, the new prime minister. "What's a pry minister?" I asked. Instead of answering, my mother put a cassette on. She turned up the volume. "A strange feeling suddenly crept over me," Laurence Jalbert was singing. "A rising tide, filling me." Underneath the music, I could hear my mother breathing.

OUR NEW HOUSE WAS AT the end of a dirt road. There were no neighbours.

"I'm going to miss that yellow dog," I said to my mother that night as she tucked me in for the first time in my big white bedroom.

"Are you? Did you like the neighbour's dog?"

"Yes," I said, but I was lying.

I was actually going to miss the strange neighbour with his long black coat.

She kissed my forehead and then both cheeks. "Night night, little one." She turned the light out.

Once the door was closed, instead of the patch of red-and-grey sky, the light of the street lamp, and the regular noise of the cars and trucks driving on King Edward that I had grown used to, I could hear nothing but a few crickets and could see nothing at all in the deep darkness. I couldn't even see my own hands when I waved them in front of my face.

"Mommy!" I yelled.

She appeared a few seconds later, haloed in the light from the hall, dressed in high-waisted jeans and a sailor sweater.

"Mom, can you hold my hand while I go to sleep?"

She knelt down beside me and held my hand for a long time. But I couldn't fall asleep.

"What's that noise? It's like a spider."

"No, Julie, it's nothing."

"Are there any spiders here?"

"Just ones that are smaller than you."

She lay down next to me and sang "My Bonnie Lies Over the Ocean." At the end of the song, thinking I was asleep, she tried to get out of the grip of my hot little hand so she could sneak away. I held on to her: "I'm afraid I'll have a nightmare!"

"Would you like me to leave your door open a bit?"

"Yes. And can I have something of yours?"

This was something she'd come up with to calm me down when I couldn't fall asleep without her: she lent me a scarf, a pillow, or a piece of jewellery that smelled of her.

"Here you are, sweetie," she said, taking off her watch and laying it on my pillow.

I grabbed it and breathed in its scent of perfume-free deodorant, skin, tea tree oil, baby lotion, Down Under Natural's kiwi shampoo, leather.

"Good night, Mom," I said.

"Good night, Julie."

She went out and left the door ajar.

OUR LIFE THERE WAS LIKE a bad dream. My parents didn't get on anymore. They loved the house but didn't know how to live there. My father left around five thirty to get downtown, where he worked as a journalist for a daily newspaper. My mother stayed home with me. She'd developed a kind of obsession with laundry: in a little room off the kitchen there were a brand-new washing machine and dryer with tons of options, modes, precise indicators. They'd belonged to the former owners. According to the real estate agent, they were old people who'd moved to Florida. My mother washed all the towels in the house pretty much every day, starting with the white ones, which she bleached. Then she set off with a load of coloured towels and prowled the house looking for any clothes that might be slightly dirty. She sat down in front of the washing machine with the basket of clothes and read the washing instructions on every item, which she followed to the letter. As the machine spun, she went into the bathroom and handwashed everything delicate. She washed my swimsuits, my woollen coats, the dress I'd worn once two years earlier when I was a flower girl at my aunt's wedding. Once the washing and drying was done, she folded everything meticulously, stacked it up, and went to sit in her bedroom, her hands crossed, or holding in her arms a big fluffy orca she'd bought herself before we left Ottawa, until I came to look for her to remind her to make me something to eat. I would often try to figure out the mystery of the orca, to understand why my mother owned a stuffie I wasn't allowed to touch, but I didn't dare ask her. As I waited for her to make an appearance, I took a horse ride around the house on an orange ball that had a face on it spotted with red freckles and whose ears were the handles I could hold on to while I bounced. She spent hardly any time in any room except her bedroom and the laundry room. She seemed to avoid the living room in particular. Sometimes she slunk along the corridor wall up to the entrance to the living room, put an arm through the doorway, and touched the piano keys without actually setting foot inside the room. Since she could only reach the left side of the piano, she played the left hand of Bach's Prelude in C Minor with her right hand, then went back to the laundry room or her bedroom. She found the rooms too big, she said, that was why she stuck to those two. But the rooms weren't all that big. They were just empty. When my father got home from work, he inevitably went down to the basement to see if the pile of boxes had got any smaller, but it never had. Our frames, photos, posters, vases, and trinkets were still wrapped up and shut away behind the furnace. My father had moved into the little room with the sloping ceiling, setting up his Macintosh Plus, his books, his dictionaries, his sound system.

"Help me out a bit," he said to my mother one night at dinnertime, while she was nibbling in silence, her eyes lowered, sometimes even a few mysterious tears flowing down her cheeks even though nothing sad had happened. She talked less and less. The telephone never rang. I went around the house picking up the receivers of all the phones to check that the line hadn't been cut. It hadn't. I rode circles on my bike in the driveway, alone. "Can I have a little sister?" I asked sometimes. In the evenings we ate as a family, then my father or mother took charge of my evening routine. Skip-Bo, Lite-Brite, Connect Four, Snakes and Ladders, and Uno were still in the boxes, so we went straight from dinner to bedtime. My mother sometimes read me Robert Munsch's *Love You Forever* or one of his other picture books. On weekends, my father tried to watch television, but the channels didn't come in very well. I'd never known so much silence.

Late in the evenings, my father went to his office, closed the door, and listened to music with headphones on so as not to disturb my mother, who went to bed right after me. I figured it out one evening when I'd woken up to go to the bathroom and he came out of his office at the same time, an empty glass in his hand. I asked him why he didn't play music over the speakers anymore—I was used to it in Ottawa and it even helped me fall asleep. My father went to fill up his glass in the kitchen, then he invited me into his office, something that practically never happened. He himself emphasized it by saying that just this once I was welcome. He took me in his arms and sat down in his stuffed office armchair. I felt tiny, snuggled up in his lap. He put the headphones over my head—I had to hold them on so they didn't slip off—and smiled at me as he pressed a button. He put the album sleeve in my hands, and with my eyes lowered I looked at the black-and-white photo of a man with his eyes lowered, framed in black and then framed in white. I heard the first notes of the piano. My father was rubbing my back. I stayed there for four minutes thirty seconds, transfixed, listening to Peter Gabriel. "When the night shows, the signals grow, on radios. All the strange things, they come and go, as early warnings."

WE WENT TO VISIT THE village school. "You're going to start in September. You'll make loads of friends," my mother had said. It suited me. I'd had enough of the empty house and the noise of the washing machine. I missed the things we used to do in the city, swimming lessons, parks where we would always see the same kids with the same moms (or the same nannies). I missed the Children's Museum, where I could lose myself for hours, in the magic of the bus, the undersea room, and the market of plastic vegetables. I even missed the Museum of Nature, where I had so often shivered in horror at seeing snakes, flies, mice, and spiders in their vivariums. In a dark room, they broadcast on a loop clips from movies where these terrifying creatures appeared: *The Fly, Anne of Green Gables,* and others that I can't remember now. That room used to attract me like a trap. At the end of several showings of these movie extracts that made my blood run cold, I wanted to go and find my mother again, but, as if hypnotized, I stayed where I was to have one more viewing of Anne plunging her hand into the sack of flour and discovering a mouse, or to see the man appear whose head had been replaced by a fly's head.

"So, did you play the piano today?" my father would ask my mother during dinner. In his tone there was something both kind and cruel. Something kind that could have been mistaken for something cruel, or something evil that could have been mistaken for something kind. My mother answered him with a list of everything she'd washed. My father pointed out that it wasn't just the clothes that needed attention, that it wouldn't be a bad idea to go once round with the broom. "To switch things up," he said ironically, trying to catch her eye with an expression that said, "Yes? No? Hello?" and not managing to do it.

IN THE CITY I WASN'T allowed to cross the road by myself. In the country it was different. There weren't really any roads, properly speaking. My mother and I had done a test. I'd stayed on the porch while she walked off into the forest, a few dozen metres at a time, and then called out, "Hello Julie, can you hear me?"

"Yes!" I would answer.

She carried on walking and asking if I could hear her until I answered, "Not really!" Then she would move back to the last place where we'd been able to hear each other well. She took out the pink fluorescent tape she'd put in her pocket and tied pieces of it around several trees.

"You can play by yourself," she said, "but don't go past the pink ribbons. Deal?"

"Deal," I agreed.

I started school, but I didn't make many friends. On the third day, the teacher organized a drawing competition. To my great chagrin, I won first prize.

"Stop showing off," spat Danika, a little girl who was really good at soccer and children's power games. "Why did your parents move here?" the other children asked. I didn't know what to say, so I held my tongue. Their expressions and their songs were unfamiliar, I didn't know how to play their games. Several of them lived on farms, rode on ATVs, had uncles, aunts, and cousins. I was an intruder. I had nobody.

"You talk weird," they said.

"So do you," I said back.

Except for one girl called Noémi, who was the only Black girl in my class, and who was rejected by the other kids even more than I was, I couldn't trust anyone. Noémi and I hung out at recess, hiding underneath a concrete staircase, to exchange information. We didn't want to be seen in public together: it would have confirmed our status as the lowest of the low.

"I heard them during phys. ed.," Noémi said to me one day. "They're going to pretend to invite you to Jade's party, and then they're gonna say, 'Haha, just kidding,' when you say yes. If I were you, I'd just say no right away."

"Okay, thanks. I saw them putting something in your locker, maybe a mean drawing."

"It's fine, I'll just throw it out without looking at it."

We left it at that. I never went to her house, she never came to my house. Two factions allied in the war against the empire.

AFTER A FEW MONTHS I'D earned my parents' trust. I played in the woods almost every day without getting lost or hurt, except for a few scratches that I didn't complain about. I was allowed to go past the pink ribbons.

On the day before Halloween, I decided I'd go farther than I'd ever been. My father had gone to Ottawa for a few days to cover the federal election and I was alone at home with my mother, who seemed in a better mood while my father was away but still didn't have much energy. I had abandoned the idea of asking her to sew me a costume or take me shopping, telling myself that I'd make myself up to look like a butterfly before I went to school the next day—so what if the other kids laughed at me.

That afternoon, I didn't tell her what I was planning to do. I put an apple and a McCain's juice box in my school bag and announced, with my heart pounding, "I'm just going to play outside!"

My mother was, as usual, doing laundry. She was walking through the house with her arms full of whites. She nodded and smiled at me. There was something slow about all her movements.

In the summer, it had been easy to figure out where I was because all the trees had different-coloured leaves. But now it was more complicated. Only the conifers stood out from the others, and there were hardly any of them in the forest around our house. "I can do it," I said to myself anyway.

For about twenty minutes, I followed the stream. The water burbled pleasantly under the dead leaves. I went past the pink ribbons and walked on, turning around every thirty steps to look at the fluorescent dots in the distance. Sometimes I had to scramble over big rocks or jump from one little rock to another. Then I reached a place where the stream went under the ground and came back up a few metres farther on. I realized that I had gone farther than I'd ever been before. I turned around and I couldn't see the pink ribbons, but I didn't feel lost. "I know where to go to find my way back," I told myself. I decided to celebrate that by eating my snack. I sat down on a big rock and listened to the murmur of the stream hidden under the moss and roots.

That's when I heard some strange noises. Branches cracking, panting, breathing. I let out a little cry of panic, closed my eyes, and brought my knees up to my chest. Then, half opening my eyes, I saw three big black dogs racing toward me. They slowed their pace and skittered around me for a few moments. At last they stopped.

The three dogs looked incredibly alike and at first I thought it was a mirage. Their teeth, their fur, their saliva, their shining eyes were just a few centimetres away from my face. I mustn't scream, I understood. I have to skip the stage of being afraid.

I stood up. I held out my fist. I lowered my eyes. I opened my hand. The dogs sniffed my palm and licked it. They barked for a few seconds, their lips drawn back, their hot breath up close. I started talking. I'd never talked to a dog before in my life. In a kind of encouraging whisper, I said hello to them a few times.

They calmed down a little. They no longer looked as though they wanted to rip my face off, but they were getting agitated again, they were overexcited, they were jumping and running in circles around me.

"It's okay, I won't hurt you," I cooed.

Then I stood up and tried to retrace my steps along the stream toward the house.

The dogs started yapping, but in a chatty kind of way, not threatening. They ran around me and blocked my way. They gazed at me. Not that way, this way, I understood, without really hearing a voice. I turned around and started walking the way they were indicating. That was when the dogs, as if they were a single entity divided into three bodies, followed on my heels and quickly overtook me. I stopped so they could get a long way in front, but they turned around and invited me to follow them with the ends of their snouts.

I obeyed, and walked behind them, keeping a respectful distance.

The dogs were trotting along and turning around regularly to make sure I was still following. After a hundred metres or so, they turned to the right. I understood they were heading toward the road. The dogs scrambled out of the ditch. I did the same. The ditch was steep. I had to grab onto cut roots that stuck out of the ground. I hauled myself up to the road and lay there on my stomach. The dogs were waiting for me, sitting like three chess pieces in the middle of the road. Then they set off, with me behind them.

We were walking on the road I lived on. I could have turned around and gone back home, but the dogs wanted to go in the opposite direction. I decided to carry on following them. On foot, the road seemed different from what I'd seen from the car. Behind the trees there were houses I'd never noticed.

We came out on the road that led to the village. A few cars passed. The dogs looked both ways before crossing, just like my mother had taught me. The drivers of the cars didn't seem to notice us. We crossed the road and I noticed that our road carried on over the other side of the main street, and there were several houses on that side, some with swings and toys in the yards. I froze as I thought of my own toys in my own yard. I need to go home, I thought. But the dogs turned around as one and forbade me with a look.

We'd reached what seemed to be the end of the road, but I wasn't sure. The dogs stopped.

We were outside a dilapidated country house with a badly kept lawn. A car sat rusting under a shredded tarp. Crates of beer were growing mould on the porch. The dogs were panting at my side, motionless. I couldn't understand everything I was seeing. Dismembered bicycles. Craters of brown water. Piles of soaked newspapers. Abandoned tools. A pumpkin with a terrifying smile balancing on the ramp up to the porch, and white smoke puffing out of the chimney. Right in the middle of the yard, in front of the house, was a metal pole, to which someone had attached a long chain. At the end of the chain was a dog the same size as the three I was following, but much thinner, as if ill or underfed.

Its fur was dirty and knotted. It was whining and wiggling about with the striking strength of the weak. The chain was banging noisily against the post. He'd trampled the ground around the post so much that all the grass was dead. The three other dogs looked at me. Then they stopped looking at me. They lay down around the tied-up dog, on the dried ground, cracked in places. They said to me: It's fine, you've seen. You can go.

IT TOOK FOREVER TO REACH the house by following the road. I was expecting my mother to scold me. I had a knot of worry in my stomach, and tears of apprehension formed in my eyes as I walked.

"Hello?" I called out when I went in.

I heard my mother swear. Her voice was coming from the basement.

"Mommy?"

I ran down the basement stairs, which normally scared me badly.

"Stay there," my mother said. "Fuck!"

She was standing in three feet of water, her arms reaching out to the shelves where all our boxes of memories and decorations were stored. She managed to reach one.

"Here, take this," she shouted. "Take it upstairs, quick!"

The water was still rising.

I raced up to the main floor looking for somewhere to put the box and noticed that the kitchen was flooded too, as well as the laundry room, which, I realized, was the source of the leak that had spread all over the house. My running shoes had become sticky and muddy, because of the earth brought in from outside. I headed toward the living room with a bad feeling in my stomach. I saw that the water was even higher than it was in the kitchen. There was a hole in the ceiling, and a great jet of water was pouring straight onto the piano. I didn't understand. The water was coming from the laundry room. How could there be a hole in the living room ceiling? And why was it right over the piano?

For a few long seconds I stayed frozen, hesitating between the box and the piano. Eventually I ran to the back door, put the box on the porch, and went back to the basement stairs and yelled, "Mom! Your piano!"

I will never forget the expression on her face when she opened the basement door and saw the damage.

"It's my fault," she said.

She wasn't shouting anymore.

She grabbed all the cushions in the living room, still crying and swearing, and threw them on top of the piano, which was dripping onto the floor.

"It's my fault, I left the machine unsupervised. I went out to look for you. I was scared." She laughed as if disgusted with herself. "But you weren't even lost. You came back all by yourself. It's my fault."

She was saying "you," but she wasn't really talking to me. The pillows were quickly soaked through and my mother, her shoulders hunched, sat down on the piano bench and closed her eyes. She was crying. The water was still falling, but the force had lessened. It was now raining on the piano and my mother's hands. I looked at her from my frozen position in the door frame, not daring to make a sound.

Then my mother opened her eyes, slid the pillows to the floor, opened the piano lid, and attacked Clara Schumann's

Sonata in G Minor with a kind of resignation, not stopping if she made a mistake. Fine, here I am. What else can I do?

I listened to her in silence, right through to the end. She took her foot away from the pedal. She reclosed the lid. She put her palms on the surface. The water dripped from her hands, which had stopped moving, in rivulets that mixed with the grey water on the floor.

THE WEEKS THAT FOLLOWED WERE full of keywords uttered over and over by my parents—words that took on a slightly different meaning and a bit more weight each time they were repeated. Disaster experts, papers, insurance, loss of money, evaluations, sofa bed at Grandma's, return trips, gas, financial loss, papers, return trips, travel bags, fault. I could hear all these words being fired over my head like warning shots, like threats my parents were making, but deep down there were no more threats to make. The deed was done, the doers undone. Bad idea, your idea, piano, too late, lost, school, registration, market, real estate agents, financial loss, divorce, loss.

"You never played it anyway," my father said several times.

"I was waiting for the right moment," my mother said.

I WROTE THIS STORY ABOUT my childhood because there's something I don't understand. When I think about that little girl going beyond the pink ribbons, I feel love for her, I find that her journey through the woods has meaning. She is a whole child, capable of absorbing the magic and the immensity of the world because she hasn't yet learned to doubt. At the beginning of my life, I was that child. The kind of child who would normally turn into a self-confident adult, brave, accomplished. But now that I've reached adulthood, I find I've become a pretty mediocre adult.

I live everywhere, kind of, in the city, in the woods. At other people's places. In bedrooms that I never bother to decorate, in neighbourhoods that I never get to know. I kind of work everywhere too, doesn't matter how, a couple of months here, a hundred dollars there. The great constant in my life is that I'm often sad. I'm often awake all night, often in bed until noon. I wonder why I always have to start over. I have half ideas, desires for greatness that make me dizzy. I never finish my projects. I don't take care of myself properly. Every time I try to create something, some force takes hold of my hand and makes me write, "I am nothing, I am worth nothing." Something makes me close my notebooks, tear up my drawings, bury my pencils and pens at the bottom of a closet. A voice harasses me: What? Draw? You think you can draw? You're stupid, you don't know how to draw. And this same voice makes me think about art all night, all day.

One day I talked to my mother about it. She lives in a suburb of Ottawa with her second husband and is doing a bit better. She was mystified.

"I thought we did things right with you," she said. "Didn't we always say that you could do whatever you wanted? We encouraged you. We supported you in your unorthodox path."

"Unorthodox path." Not exactly the words I would have ... Okay, fine. Yes, it was true. It was all true. "Thank you," I said. "That's all true." I repeated to myself that everything was fine, that I had enough strength to get out of bed, to find a job, to create something, to fall asleep.

Now that I am an adult and I am writing this story about my childhood to get my ideas straight, I have the feeling I've lied somewhere. There is a lie somewhere in my memories. Some part of this story isn't true. But which part? What did I invent? Logic would say it was the dogs. It's the most implausible part. But it's also what I remember most clearly.

REDBIRD

MY FATHER CAME TO PICK me up from school in his Volkswagen Golf. He waited for me in the pickup zone. As I was about to get on the city bus, he stepped in front of me and said, "Here I am!" I exchanged glances with Céline and Sabrina. "See you tomorrow," they said.

My father was hopping about, his hands in the pockets of his beige chinos, a fixed smile on his face.

"Yeah, see you tomorrow."

My friends disappeared into the bus. My father tried to take my backpack, but I stopped him, even if it was heavy. We walked to the parking lot, where grade 12 students were tossing their backpacks in their trunks and unlocking their doors.

"I called her yesterday to say I'd come pick you up. Didn't she tell you I'd be here?"

Whenever my father wanted to talk about my mother, he never said "Anne" or "your mother," just "she." Initially,

I'd thought maybe it meant that he never stopped thinking about her and that there was a chance they could get back together one day. By now, I thought it was more likely he hated her too much to say her name.

"Uh, no?" I said, frowning, as if I didn't believe him, even though I knew there was a good chance my mother had just forgotten to give me the message.

We got in the car and buckled our seat belts. On the back seat were his briefcase and his recording device. His car smelled of coffee and cinnamon raisin bagels. My father picked his sunglasses up off the dashboard, put them on his nose, and started the car. He leaned his right arm on the headrest of my seat to reverse out of the parking spot. I noticed he'd dyed his hair.

"It's always the same with her. I *told* her I would come get you."

"Am I sleeping at your place?" I asked emotionlessly.

"Yes!" he said cheerfully. "And guess what I've rented?"

"What?"

Maybe *Requiem for a Dream,* a movie my mother would never let me rent.

"*Amélie,*" he said in a Parisian accent.

"Oh."

My father honked at the car in front, which was taking too long getting onto the St Patrick Bridge.

"*Oh?* What do you mean, *oh?* Isn't it your favourite movie?"

"It *was.*"

My father sighed. We had almost arrived at his house. He lived in a two-storey semi-detached in New Edinburgh.

"Do you have a lot of homework?"

He'd changed tone. Now he was being "my father."

"No, I did it at lunch."

"You can't have had much, then!"

"No, not much at all," I muttered. "It's easy."

"What are you saying? Please speak clearly."

"Not much at all! School's stupid, all we do is watch NFB films about addiction and draw right-angled triangles, it's super easy."

My father burst out laughing. I smiled too, in spite of myself. We were just pulling up to his house. He pressed the remote control button for the garage that was attached to the visor mirror.

"Do you watch these movies in French or English?" my father asked.

He picked up his briefcase and recorder with one hand and put my backpack on his shoulder. He unlocked the door with his other hand and threw everything down on the couch while he deactivated the alarm. I went in behind him and poured myself a glass of milk from the fridge. He didn't have a pitcher with milk bags like we always had, back when we all lived together. He bought cartons now.

"I dunno," I said.

"You don't know? You don't know if the movie you spent all day watching was in French or English?"

"No," I said, even though I was specifically thinking of Andrée Cazabon's *Enfer et contre tous*.

"Oh boy. This is bad."

My father was very attached to the French language and sometimes wrote about that very subject for his column in *Le Droit*. He often wrote using anecdotes, quoting people in his circle and letting their actions illustrate his ideas on a particular subject. "Isn't that cheating?" my late maternal grandmother once asked him accusingly. According to my father, she didn't understand that kind of thing because she was uneducated. Seeing that he was trying to get me to say things he could use in his next column ("French Public School Board of Eastern Ontario: Defending the French Language or Assimilating My Daughter?"), I said, "What's for dinner?"

"Haha. You really want to know?" my father said, anticipating my enjoyment of his culinary talents.

"Well, obviously. I haven't eaten since lunch."

With my father it was easy to find the words, to throw biting replies in his face. It was easy for me to let out the poison that had filled me for the past few years, and which, in my everyday life, the life where my father was nothing but a voice on the phone saying, "I'm really busy," like a parrot journalist, swelled my stomach and confused my mind. I was no more angry at him than I was at Barrie or my mother—I hated them all. But with my father it was possible to let off steam, because I knew that, whatever I did, I wouldn't really hurt him (I was afraid of hurting my mother) and I knew that he would never shut me in the closet (Barrie had shut me in the closet one day when he caught me taking money out of his wallet).

"Rigatoni," he announced.

"Wow. Congrats," I said, finishing up my milk.

I rinsed the glass, dried it, and put it back in the cupboard. My father's house was clean right down to the toaster slots, the tiles on the counter, and the floor behind the toilet. Since I hated hearing him say, "Looks like a little mouse has been to visit!", I was careful to remove all traces of my actions—except in my bedroom, where I'd stuck a drawing of mine on the door, of a purple monster in high heels smoking a cigarette and saying, "GO AWAY!"

I left right then, abandoning my father and his ego puffed up by Italian pasta. I closed the door, put my bag on my Ikea armchair in one corner, and inspected my hiding places and traps to make sure my father hadn't gone through my things while I was away. On the bedside table, the hair elastic was still covering the bird's eye on my matchbox. On the shelf, the corner of the yellow exercise book still extended a few centimetres past two black notebooks. The sock full of money I stole on a regular basis from Barrie and my father was still taped behind the headboard. Good, I thought.

I sat down on the bed and picked up my box of matches. I found that box's design very comforting: the picture of the bird with its wings spread; the number 250; the words "REDBIRD—Strike Anywhere Matches—*Allumettes qui s'allument partout.*" I emptied its contents on my navy, turquoise, and lime-green checked duvet. A dried rose from my grandmother's house. A cat's-eye marble and a Pog token with a yin-yang on it that I'd won in the schoolyard in elementary school. A shell from a trip to Maine we took when I was a baby. Obviously, I didn't remember it, but I had a bunch of photos, and my mother had chosen the shell especially for me because a dark line on its white surface looked like a *J* for Julie. A cigarette taken from a packet of my father's three years earlier, before he managed to quit smoking. A drawing signed "Julie, Céline and Sabrina," made playing the exquisite corpse game. An amethyst I'd stolen from a souvenir shop in Quebec on an end-of-year school trip we'd made the previous year. That was my favourite treasure: the only object that didn't remind me of anyone, that didn't have the power to make me sad when someone died or got mean or weird. An object that was me, that was just mine. Nothing particular had happened that day and none of the objects made me feel bad or good. I put them back in the box, and that's when I felt it.

I called it the feeling that isn't really a feeling, a kind of premonition that would come over me sometimes: I would be at the end of a TV program, or doing my homework, or looking at my treasures, and I suddenly knew that, for a while at least, I wouldn't want to do anything. It was like boredom, but it was much more than that. It was an abrupt change of colour and texture, a betrayal of my senses, which were suddenly totally uninterested in anything I liked—art, or swimming pools, or music or friends or TV or kittens. I couldn't do anything about it, it was like being paralyzed. It normally lasted until an adult showed up and made me do something, which I would be grateful to them for without saying anything about it, because as soon as I started to set the table or pack my bag for the next day, or wash my hair, the black hole closed up and I didn't think about it at all anymore, until the next time the sensation came. It happened quite often. I couldn't really say how much.

Sitting on my bed, I closed my eyes and listened to my father fussing in the kitchen. I thought about my Harry Potter books: no. Mint ice cream, which was always in the freezer: no. The blue dress my father had given me the previous month, which was hanging in the closet and which I could wear to school the next day: no. My folder on the computer in his office, with the Paint drawings I worked on when I was here: no. My new Broken Social Scene CD: no. I didn't care about anything.

"Come and find me," I begged my father in silence, unable to move.

I stayed like that for around an hour. Several times I held the matchbox in my hands. I even shook it, in case it put the magic back where it had been earlier—the bird looked dead to me, the words didn't mean anything anymore. I slipped under the covers and waited for it to pass.

"Julie! Dinner!" my father called at last.

The sound of his voice pulled me out of my lethargy. I even wanted to object, to stay in my room for a bit longer, since it was actually overflowing with games and interesting objects. But since I was pretty hungry, I went to wash my hands and joined him in the kitchen.

He'd set the table and made garlic bread to have with the rigatoni.

"So?" he asked after my first mouthful.

"It's good," I said.

I wanted to make peace.

My father talked extensively about his work. I listened to him as I chewed my pasta and garlic bread. "Everything's been different since 9/11," he said. "Everything's political, you can't write what you want anymore—otherwise you'll be accused of disloyalty! Am I the only one who remembers that just yesterday Canadians' favourite sport was hating the US?"

He shook his head, unable to get over the stupidity of people in general.

"But we're no better than the others: all those stories about Canada the peacekeeper, the tales of the blue berets, going off to protect all the little children in countries at war, you shouldn't believe all that! What do you think the Canadian Armed Forces did in Yugoslavia? They bombed it!"

He added Parmesan to his rigatoni, which was already well covered in cheese. I poured myself a glass of milk.

"And they didn't even hide it. People have short memories. The work of peacekeeping, they call it, but I call it protecting their interests. And whose interests really? American interests! Because their interests are our interests. People need to understand that!"

He emphasized certain words by separating out their syllables, as if he was talking to a five-year-old: "in-ter-ests," "A-me-ri-cans."

"And Mulroney's heirs are convinced that the Liberals are too wimpy to send troops to Iraq, but they're wrong."

For a second I wanted to interrupt his monologue, to tell my father I wasn't even sure who Mulroney was. I took a mouthful of rigatoni.

"The Liberals will do whatever the Americans ask them to do. They know, like everyone else, that the game changed after 9/11, and they want their slice of the pie too."

What's changed? I thought.

"They just want oil, but mark my words, they won't be out of Afghanistan for ten years, and it will be a complete disaster, I'm telling you, I'm telling you ... "

He took a huge forkful of rigatoni and ended his sentence with his mouth full, and I didn't catch his final words. He swallowed with difficulty and I lowered my eyes to my plate.

"But I can't write that, of course."

I didn't understand anything he was saying. I think my

father tended to forget I was his daughter and not one of his colleagues. He continued, going off at a tangent, and suddenly started talking to me about Martin Brodeur and Patrick Roy.

"I don't care about hockey," I said calmly.

He stopped talking, visibly hurt. It was always like that with him. He wanted to talk, but everything he said showed that we didn't know what to say to each other. It was unbearable. I didn't know why I could talk easily with my mother and Barrie, why there was never this kind of discomfort with them. Barrie and my mother never really talked to me. They just talked among themselves and only paused to say, "Eat your green beans." My father tried really hard to talk to me when he saw me, but we spent so little time together that it just made it all the more obvious that he barely knew me. Sabrina's father was weird, but at least they saw each other every weekend. Our friend Ange Niyomugabo hadn't seen her father for years, but he didn't even live in Canada. My father lived in the same city as me and I barely ever saw him. I couldn't ask to see him, I couldn't wait for him to keep his word. He came to see me when there was a gap in his schedule. He preferred journalism to his job as a father. Sometimes, he used his usual "I'm really busy" on me, and then a few minutes later would tell me that he'd been to a Senators game. He preferred hockey to his job as a father. I stared at my barely touched plate. My father looked at me, his lips pursed, uncomfortable.

"Listen, Julie, I know it's hard for you. I know we don't see each other much. But listen, maybe this summer we could go to Marineland? Hey, what do you think? Just the two of us."

"I've already been with school."

"This year? You didn't go with school this year."

I didn't answer. It was simply too late. I hadn't seen him at Christmas. He'd forgotten to call on my birthday. The previous summer, I was supposed to spend three weeks with him and he'd cancelled at the last minute. He'd become someone who always hurt me, and it didn't make me want to go to Marineland with him. But at the same time, my life with Barrie and my mother was too unsatisfactory for me to forget my father altogether. I wanted to cry, but I'd trained myself never to cry in front of him, because I hated the way he reacted: "Hohoho! What big tears! You're a big girl, Julie, stop crying."

"Can I be excused?"

"Yes, go on."

"Can I watch TV before I go to bed?" There was a TV in my room.

"Yes, if you want. But not too late. Not after nine."

"Okay."

I got up from the table and cleared my plate. I put the pasta back in the pot, washed my plate, and left it to dry. Then I went into my bedroom.

I lay down fully dressed on the bed, without turning any lights on. Tears were flowing down my cheeks. I stayed like that for a few minutes, motionless. Then I reached out my hand and touched the sock full of bills. I hadn't counted the money recently, but there had to be at least three hundred dollars. I'd started stealing money off them not long after my mother and Barrie got married. At the beginning, I told myself that when I had enough for two tickets, I'd escape along with my mother far away from Barrie, far away from my father. We would have gone back to the States, to Maine. Eventually, I understood that we'd need a lot more than the cost of two Greyhound tickets to survive without them—but it was more than just a question of money. My mother was no longer my accomplice. She hadn't even got mad when Barrie shut me in the closet. She didn't even seem capable of getting mad anymore, or laughing, or smiling, or crying. She slept and she cooked like a zombie, only talking to me about food or things to do with the house (clean your hair out of the bathtub—put the milk on the table—bring your laundry down—watch out, the toilet's blocked). When I asked my mother to go shopping or play a board game, she would say, "He'll be home soon, you can ask him." "He" was Barrie. Barrie got home from work around five, helped me with my homework, and willingly played with me, but I never relaxed because I knew he might explode at any moment.

All this was turning around in my head while my body was sinking into the duvet. I was falling asleep, but at the same time I was being bombarded with thoughts that spooled past at high speed like in a movie on fast-forward, with the grey bands, and the sound off. My thoughts dissolved into dreams, and in my dreams I shrank down to the size of a match and an enormous hand captured me and shut me up in a matchbox, and I was crying but nobody could hear me and I was having trouble breathing and suddenly I noticed a crack of light, the box was partly open, and I saw the red face of the bird from the match company looking me straight in the eyes. He said to me, "Don't forget, Julie. You're a strike-anywhere girl."

THE PORTRAIT

I'M NOT LIVING ANYMORE. THERE are no more days or weeks. No more "good days," no more "bad days." For me, everything is happening at the same time. I touch the fire, my shouts start, the pain, the coffee is ready, night, tears of rage, I remember a mistake, a regret, a bad memory, dawn, twilight, the toilet. I tiptoe from the TV to the fridge with my eyes turned inward, suspicious like someone who's been told that there's dust from steel wool all over the furniture and the floor, and who is barely breathing from the fear of swallowing some of it, even though she can't see the tiniest speck of metal anywhere. I've forgotten how to use my kitchen utensils, sleep is a drug I give in to again and again, I walk around the stains of everything I've dropped on the floor instead of cleaning up (I don't know where the sponges are).

"We all have our little habits," one of my old friends used to say to normalize his alcoholism. That was back when we were studying fine arts, we were all neurotic, egocentric, and obsessed with the idea of creating a new work, something that had never been done before, brainwashed by our professors, who hadn't sold a piece—nor even, in some cases, touched a paintbrush—since the dawn of time. This friend wasn't the only one who was constantly drinking; it was a general tendency. I didn't find it made much difference. With or without drugs, I was blocked, I was lost. It helped him to live. His name was Terrence. I haven't seen him for nearly ten years. "We all have our little habits." A habit's something you do without thinking about it, that fits the rhythm of your day. We all have our little habits. Well, not me. I suffer the consequences of the hours, one after another, without ever getting over my jet lag.

My only memory of that time is: what might have been. There was a time when I might have done something to avoid ending up here like this. But no longer. Everything starts without my permission. I've lost the privilege of choosing. I don't choose when to wake up. My alarm clock is an intruder that kisses me on the mouth. It stinks. "Come on, let's start all over again." I don't want to, I don't have a choice. Needs pile up. Peeing, drinking water, eating, washing. I don't know where to start. I don't have the authority to prioritize. I drink my coffee naked on the toilet seat. I pee in the shower, I cry in the shower, I fall asleep in the shower. I eat crumbs and hard-boiled eggs in front of my computer. I drop the shells everywhere. I look at my coat but don't put it on. I look at my swimsuit. The library opens and closes, the swimming pool opens and closes, the bus goes by, goes by, and then stops going by, and once again I've missed my chance to get out of the house. I waver between two chairs, two books. I stay standing up.

I think about the time I don't have anymore. About the period of my life when I always had too much or not enough of it, when I could quantify it and feel it passing. I took that as a given. Time. I thought that time was just a stupid human invention, I didn't wear a watch, I read at night. But I went to my classes. I remembered birthdays. I travelled during the summer. I visited my family at Christmas. I went out in the evenings. I whispered at night. In your ear.

I'm dizzy. I can hardly do anything now. I can close my eyes. I can go back under the hot water. That's about all.

MY MOTHER BRINGS ME TUPPERWARE full of spaghetti sauce. She puts one in the fridge and one in the freezer and empties one into a pot that she puts on the stove. She boils water for pasta. I sit at the table and watch her. I start explaining to her that I'm losing my sense of time. I don't need to explain it to her, she understands, she says. "Go and see a therapist. This one's good." She sticks Post-it Notes with the name and phone number in every room. She's brought me a new charger. She plugs in my cellphone. She calls me sweetie, honey, and rubs my shoulders. I can tell she's worried sick. She's scared, I'm scaring her. The words "I'm sorry" claw at my throat like the bones of a sick rooster. Just like every time my mother is here. I don't say them, otherwise it would be the finishing touch in ruining an already miserable day.

My mother sets a load of laundry going and gives me a plate of spaghetti. "What are you doing today?"

"I don't know. I could draw," I say bravely, stupidly.

A child's response in a woman's voice. Everything about my face is round, my cheeks, my eyes, I've always been told I look young. What nobody knows, because I'm blond and it doesn't show, is that I'm starting to get grey hair. I'm so ashamed.

But my mother, my mother, my mother doesn't attack me, she doesn't give me the slap I'm sure I deserve. She takes me into the living room, goes back to the kitchen for the cups of tea she's made, puts them on the coffee table. She French-braids my hair, ties it with elastic bands from the kitchen since I don't have any more hair elastics since I don't go to the pharmacy anymore.

"Yes, drawing, great idea. Do you want to start drawing again? What a great idea. I could bring you your charcoals, I kept them. Would you like that?"

"I don't know."

Saying I don't know hurts almost as much as saying I'm sorry, but I hold on. Physically. To the couch.

"Okay, forget the charcoals for now," my mother says, getting up.

She goes out of the room. I'm too tired to look where she's going. I can hear her rummaging in corners of the apartment I no longer go into. She comes back with a sketchbook and some wooden pencils. It's a year since I've drawn anything, longer still since I've used colour.

"Here you go, sweetie."

She puts the pencils and the notebook on a tray I use to eat in front of the TV and puts the tray on my lap.

"Now?"

"Why not?"

226

"I'm nervous."

She waves my words away with her hand. "All artists are nervous."

"I don't know what to draw."

She smiles. "Draw me."

She poses like a great lady, just for a laugh, lids half-closed over satisfied eyes, and a topsy-turvy smile. I imagine her made up and covered with jewels over her cardigan. I stretch my lips. To smile. I smile.

"Okay," I say.

I start with the colours. Her skin. Her grey hair. Her mauve cardigan. She doesn't move, but she isn't tense. She uses the time to look at me. It's hard to draw. It's been a long time. I want to go fast or stop. I try to focus on what I'm doing, on the way the pencil moves. I start sketching lines. One line. Two lines. A shadow. A curve. I'm strangely calm. It's good drawing in someone else's presence. I feel less crazy. I didn't invent all those hours spent learning pencil strokes. If anyone can confirm that, it's my mother.

I feel something else that resembles time. A subjective idea of time, like I used to have. Something other than an endless accumulation of seconds. I can see that this life I'm leading, where I never go out, never get dressed, barely eat, never have new ideas, this life has been mine for about a year. This year is the latest in a series of years making up my life. Before this year there were others where life was not like that. And those years weren't all alike. I've already changed. I've had good years before, I've had bad years followed by good years. I've done a lot of drawings. My mother probably has a box of them somewhere.

Right now, the colours are surrounded by the lines of my mother's face and shoulders. I stop drawing. My hand hurts. She's a good model. She doesn't fidget. I want to make this moment last, I want to keep us in this wordless conversation. She sees that I've stopped.

"You're not sure?"

"It's just ... I don't know how old to make you."

She laughs. "Don't worry about that, I've never been ashamed of how old I am. We get old, it's part of life. It's even kind of reassuring."

"I know. It's more for me. I don't know what age I want you to be in the picture."

My mother smiles, maybe because she understands, or maybe because she accepts it even if she doesn't. The smile makes crow's feet appear. She has beautiful cheekbones, lovely skin. Bronzed by the wind and the sun from all the canoe-camping trips she's been on with friends over the years. She actually goes canoe-camping, I realize. I'd never really thought about it before. How can she do that? Isn't she afraid of the lake, of the sunset, of ghosts, of bears? Isn't she afraid of getting lost or breaking her leg? She goes canoe-camping, and loads of other things that I would never dare do: she opened a foodie grocery store with a friend, she bikes there every morning, she takes history classes at the university, she goes to Europe for work, she rents a cottage on a lake and swims across the lake. And she plays the piano. She bought herself an electric piano and got all her music back out. She's done all this in the last five years, since leaving Barrie, and it's good for her. You can see it in her face. Behind all the sun and the smile wrinkles, I can see black bags under her eyes and lips turning down at the corners. I say behind, but actually the features are all mixed together. I can see myself in some of the darker features. I can also see the woman my mother used to be, when I was little, a woman who often didn't take her dressing gown off and who didn't turn the lights on during the day. A woman who always arrived late even though she wasn't busy. "Does your mother work late?" the children at the daycare would ask me. "No, she's just irresponsible," I sometimes said. As a teenager I'd come home from school and go through the house opening the curtains aggressively, then go back to the living room and stand in front of her with an accusing look.

"I saw you, Julie," she'd say without taking her eyes off the TV.

"You smell of cigarettes! You're addicted to cigarettes. You need to buy some nicotine patches," I would say angrily.

She smiled weakly, as if to say, "If only that was all."

When you see my mother today, you'd never guess she was once that woman who watched TV in her dressing gown all day long and didn't turn the lights on. But if you take your time to look at her, like I'm doing, you can see that the black circles stayed, the down-turned mouth is still there. I'm scared I won't be able to get the mixture of features across in my drawing. That's why I tell myself I could choose whether to make her young or old. I could draw her several times. I could draw her throughout her whole life. Her numerous lives.

"You have a complex face. I don't know if I'm good enough to draw it."

"We can take a break if you want. I can come back tomorrow."

Come back tomorrow? I want that, I want it more than anything, but I shrug my shoulders. "Only if you're not too busy. Whatever you want. It's just a drawing."

"No, Julie, whatever *you* want. I'd come and see you every single day. You know that."

Do I know that? No, I don't know that. I don't know what I know. It's true that my mother often calls and I don't pick up. Some days it's too disgusting to even hear the sound of my own voice.

"Well, come back tomorrow if you don't have anything else to do."

She comes back the next day.

I've got my easel out. I'm dressed. I'm wearing a pink shirt. My mother gives me a compliment: "You look beautiful."

She has something for me. She hands me a wicker bag that I recognize. Inside are charcoals, markers, paint.

"Hmm, it's been a long time," I say.

She seems to be in a good mood. I ask her to sit in the armchair that I've turned to be in the best light.

"I want to draw you several times," I explain.

"From different angles?" she asks.

"No, from the same angle. I want you to tell me about a period of your life. And while you're talking, I'll draw you. And if it's not too annoying, you can come back tomorrow and I'll draw you again, while you tell me about a different time."

I know I'm asking a lot, but I haven't wanted anything so badly for months. I've never asked her to talk to me about the past. Actually, I've always subconsciously believed that there was nothing to say, that I knew everything, because I was there.

But clearly, as I am realizing today, at the age of twenty-eight, that's not true. There must be things I don't know. Maybe some things that she'd prefer to keep buried.

"I would love that," my mother says.

She sits in the armchair. It's so easy. Why didn't I think of this before?

Because I didn't think of it before. Simple as that.

I sharpen my pencils. I don't pick up the charcoals right away. I liked the colours. I need colours.

It was a year ago that I started living like this, without living. It was a year ago that people stopped expecting to see me at events where they once would have expected to see me. I am always late even though I'm not busy, and the reason for that is simple: "ten o'clock" doesn't mean anything anymore. "Seven thirty" doesn't mean anything either. How can I explain to people that that's what I'm suffering from, that I miss ten o'clock and seven thirty terribly, that all I ask is to find the meaning of hours once again?

My mother understands, I don't need to explain it to her. But I need— I would need— I think I ought to say "I'm sorry," and those words would cut my throat like shards of glass from a light bulb I'd swallowed if I said them. I'm like you, I'm not like you. I'm mad at you, I'm not mad at you. I'm mad at myself, I know I shouldn't be mad at myself. I understand. I don't like living what I must live in order to understand, but I do understand now. I understand you.

"Where do you want to start?" she asks.

"Tell me about ... your first piano."

She starts talking. I draw. The more she talks, the more I draw. The more I draw, the more I draw. The world opens its hands and I am there to catch its light.

PART 4

It is still news to her that passion
could steer her wrong
though she went down, a thousand times
strung out
across railroad tracks, off bridges
under cars, or stiff
glass bottle still in hand, hair soft
on greasy pillows, still it is
news she cannot follow love (his
burning footsteps in blue crystal
snow) & still
come out all right.

—DIANE DI PRIMA, *Loba*

PREMONITION

SHE IS HERE AND I can't see anything anymore. I have to go and hold her hands covered in loose bandages. I have the urge to lay down my life. I already know that the memory I will keep of her will be immortal: her stomach knows how to read palms. Her hand is a wing, her arm is broken, I think it is she who will leave me with a scar lava red, organ red, sun imprinted behind my closed eyelids red, a scar that will go right through my soul and body and grow like a life. She is here and I know she can see me. I want to say: her dress is not the most beautiful thing; it is she.

ALL THE WOMEN I'VE KNOWN AND LOVED

JESS IS LIVING PROOF THAT beauty can bloom anywhere, even in sad, resigned families, even in a world of frozen foods, McJobs at Applebee's, surf shops, American flags in front of every house, and fun fairs where you can win stuffies. Even when the world is like that, even when the world is like nothing, it happens that someone like Jess opens their eyes and grows. Jess is proof that life doesn't stand still: it grows and it sheds its skin.

One day Jess ran away from his hometown and met people like him, runaways fleeing various godforsaken holes across the United States. We met by chance. Or maybe not. Jess couldn't live far from the sea, that's how Jess chose his destinations. There had to be a beach. I was just travelling. I hadn't burned anything behind me, I'd just taken a little side-step, just to see. They called Céline and me the Canadians. "Who's Stephen Harper?" they asked us.

"You're swimming in December?" I asked Jess one day when I saw him coming out of the house in a wetsuit. It was eight thirty in the morning and I was shivering underneath the wool blanket I'd wrapped myself up in to read on the balcony. Céline and I had sublet a room in the commune where Jess and fifteen other people lived. It was in a small town on the California coast where there was a famous university and a lot of freaks, activists, queers, and anarchists who travelled secretly in the goods trains and lived in the woods or shared dilapidated Victorian houses decorated with Tibetan prayer flags and played in folk-punk bands. Céline and I were planning on spending a month there then taking off again. I was reading *Zami: A New Spelling of My Name* while eating toast with nutritional yeast and drinking coffee.

"I surf every morning of the year," Jess said. "I haven't read that one. Is it good?"

"It's really good."

Jess crossed the street to where his little white car was parked. The back seat was lowered and Jess slid his surfboard in.

"Can I come with you?" I shouted suddenly.

A US Postal Service truck passed between us.

"Yes," Jess said when the truck had driven away.

That day, unable to read, I watched Jess moving between the waves, disappearing and reappearing for at least two hours, and I did not enjoy myself at all. I was watching him from a viewpoint at the top of a cliff, my fingers were gripping the handrail and my heart was clenched with terror that Jess would drown in the ocean or smash into the rocks. The waves were so high and his board was so small and his body was so fragile. It was so dangerous. In the car, I told him a bit about what I'd just been going through. I could laugh about it now that it was over and we were listening to a Breeders tape and smoking cigarettes, but my hands were still trembling.

"I'm not gonna die," Jess stated. His voice was firm, almost nasal, without any honey. "But if I died surfing, at least I'd die in the sea! It's not such a bad way to go."

I thought that was morbid and I said so. Jess explained where this casualness had come from. For Jess, death was a possibility, and one that had happened to his friends Hanna, Ryan, and Crystal. Too many drugs, living too fast, too much pain. The usual. I admitted that for me death was the terror I'd felt that day, the kind, I added, that makes little children scream when their mother leaves the room and they don't know if she even exists anymore when they can't see her. That's the punishment life threatened us with when we wanted something too much, to rebalance the accounts. Jess looked at me.

"He's the invisible man, catch him if you can," Kim Deal sang.

The next day, I saw Jess in the common room, dressed in black wool, his hair like little ears of corn standing up in rows of sun around his face that was all cheekbone, hollows, and arched eyebrows, reading *Zami: A New Spelling of My Name.*

"You inspired me."

I smiled, not flirtatiously, but like a child who's just been introduced to a perfect friend. I wanted to sit on his knee. Instead, I asked if he wanted a coffee and we spent the whole day talking, smoking, and telling jokes that were too twisted for our roommates. From that moment Jess floated in my head constantly. I noticed where Jess was going, where Jess was sitting, what Jess was reading. I invited him to the vegan café to eat fries. We laughed together at the whole culture—vegan cafés, communes, the one we lived in, the meetings that could last for hours, where we would discuss in turn the dishes, feelings, benefit concerts for such-and-such an activist group, the etiquette of all genders wearing a shirt during the shows, compost. We told each other fragments of our respective lives, amazed to see how funny or deep or meaningful these snippets could be when the other person was listening.

My visitor's visa would run out soon. The housemates had already agreed and selected by consensus the person who would move into the room Céline and I shared. They threw a party to say goodbye to us. I wasn't sad; on the contrary, I felt powerful, I was ready to dig, to make mistakes, to set off in someone's car, anyone's car, follow any revolutionary group to the middle of nowhere. Céline had decided to go back home and enrol at university in Montreal. Not me. I would carry on travelling for a few more months, I'd go to British Columbia, I'd go to Mexico, maybe I'd even go to Europe. I was ravenous. "Let's dance!" I said to Jess the night of the party. Jess squirmed. "I'd rather not," he said, then managed to slip away. He felt old even though he wasn't. We lost each other in the crowd. Jess watched me, his legs crossed, drinking beer, smoking joints, making everyone around him laugh, unable to dance in front of me.

A FEW DAYS BEFORE I left, we took bikes that didn't belong to us and pedalled to a park by the sea. We sat down under a tree, with nothing touching except our voices.

"What are you going to do now?" I asked.

"I'm going to find a job," Jess said. "You?"

"The wind will guide me," I said, laughing at myself, but believing it.

"You remind me of myself back when I was steady and fearless," Jess said.

"I have all the fears you don't have," I said.

JESS LIKED WEIRD PEOPLE AND gave off something that made homeless people who needed to tell someone their life story accost him regularly. He had relationships with old people, sick people, or people who were just vulnerable, he gave them things to eat, gave them gifts, made them laugh. He was an angel. But he was an angel inhabited by darkness. Because we felt the need to learn about each other quickly, we had decided to read each other our notebooks. His were full of thoughts about the disaster of the world and meditations on death, sadness, despair. So as not to succumb to his despair, Jess always needed to make lists of what was important, then devote himself body and soul to the tasks that made his life meaningful. His lists were made up of kind orders that Jess addressed to himself: Swim in the sea. Draw. Gather medicinal plants. Draw medicinal plants. Play guitar. Finish writing zine against the Iraq War. Make radio program. Read book about the Years of Lead.

In his bedroom there was a sheet of lined paper on the wall on which Jess had painted a red circle with a line

239

through it: the "no" symbol. Inside, Jess had written all the things he would no longer let himself do: Smoke, ask for smokes, buy smokes. Drink, stay inside all day. Let drama get to you. Despair. Jess didn't follow his rules to the letter but liked having the poster as a reminder.

The day before I left, I took the big paintbrush that was still soaking in water and plunged it into the green paint. I painted a dripping green circle.

"There," I said. "I've made you a shallow river."

"Perfect," Jess said. "Now I'll easily be able to see what's at the bottom."

At the centre of the circle, Jess wrote things he wanted to accomplish between now and our next meeting: paint, practise sports, have contact with other human beings, find a better job. Then we made a poster for me. Jess rinsed the brush well and dried it, then dipped it in the blue paint. On a sheet of white paper, he traced a perfect opaque circle.

"There," said Jess, "I've made you a very deep river. It's a magic river, turning and turning without ever flowing into the ocean."

I wrote down an unrealistic number of goals I wanted to achieve between now and the next time. We had decided, that day, that there would be a next time. His knee trembling like a caffeinated spring, Jess asked me straight out, "Can I sleep with you?" We hadn't slept together yet, nor even kissed. We'd built a promise, a conviction, just with our eyes and our words. I'd known right from the early weeks that I would love him for a long time. I remember that I'd teased him about being nervous, maybe to hide my own nerves. We lay down fully dressed on the mattress on the floor of his bedroom and whispered for a long time. Our voices echoed off the drums and cymbals of the old drum kit that was in his room.

"You play drums?" I asked.

"I used to play," Jess said.

Sex took its place between us that night, and I felt as though I'd taken another step toward my life, toward what was predicted for me.

In the darkness, Jess said, "I've spent all my life gripping my knife. I want to open my hands for you."

Over the next nine years, we made lists like that every time we parted.

"Oh!" Jess said again the next morning as he picked up my blue circle, which had dried overnight. "I forgot the waves."

Jess picked up a white chalk and drew movement in the water.

I looked at my blue circle, his green circle. It was all only just beginning.

"YOU ARE THE CULMINATION OF all the great people I've loved or lost," Jess wrote that night in the notebook I'd left in his room, while the music was still playing and he couldn't fall asleep.

LOVING SOMEONE THE WAY I'VE loved Jess is a strange mixture of abandon and resistance. For a few months after we met, I was travelling alone in western Canada and I would send him long, poetic emails at least once a week. I'd decided I'd go back and see him, but the border guard decided I wasn't allowed back into the US. "Come and live in Montreal," Céline wrote to me. "You can stay with us while you look for a job."

"This can't be happening," I said to myself, crying with rage, going back east by Greyhound and hitchhiking. I was determined, ready to do battle. But the battle was also in the form of submission: in order to be with Jess, I was ready to work full-time, to take the first job I could find that would pay for my plane ticket and give me some cash to show at customs; I was prepared to have my photograph and my fingerprints taken digitally; I was ready to be confident, blindly confident, in a love that would be lived long-distance or for a few months at a time.

CAN I SAY I KNEW him well? I think I can say I knew him very deeply. I also think he surprised me a lot. And that at one point I understood that I should always expect to be surprised by him.

Jess often changed his life and burned all his old bridges behind him, telling himself quite simply, "I won't need them anymore, I'm moving on to something else." He was someone who went deeper as he got older, not someone who climbed up the ranks.

"I don't want to work anymore and I don't want to pay rent anymore," Jess declared one day, and I knew I had to take those words seriously and that Jess would find a way not to have to do those things anymore.

His solution was to leave the commune and move into a squat in Oakland.

AT THE BEGINNING, IT WAS Jess and a few other punks. Then, as concerts, political meetings, and community events were organized there, the squat became famous, and over the course of a year hundreds of people passed through and lived there short- or long-term. Not everyone agreed on the best way to do things, not everyone pitched in to maintain and defend the space. Jess, who was there from the beginning, ended up taking on way more than his share of the responsibilities, even finding himself embroiled in an endless legal battle against a real estate promoter who'd bought the land from the bank, which had itself seized it from the former owners after a foreclosure. At the time of the sale, Jess and the others had been living on the piece of land and in the buildings for more than a year.

The promoter wanted to kick the squatters out, and the squatters were trying to prove that they lived on-site and had maintained it without concealing their presence for long enough that they could lay claim to legal ownership through something called adverse possession. Apart from Jess, two other people, Oliver and Jenna, defended the squat in court, but it was his name that was all over the papers. Nobody in the squat had the money to hire a lawyer. I went to court once with Jess and a dozen of the other squatters. He showed up dressed in a low-cut camisole and a suit jacket. He was wearing makeup and black nail polish. The walls of the courtroom were made of wood, the judge was aloof and cocky, like in a movie. The real estate promoter, who owned several lots in poor areas of Oakland where he was building condos, was white, bloated, and ugly. His lawyer had a pretty ugly mug too. We had to wait our turn for an hour, watching the other people appearing in court. Every single one, no exceptions, was Black. Jess drew their portraits in his notebook, then a repellent caricature of the judge, the promoter, and his lawyer, highlighting their size and their ugliness. The hearing only lasted a minute. The judge declared that a trial date would be fixed at the next session, a few months later. Jess came out in a fury. He waited for the promoter and the lawyer to leave the hearing room, he called out, "Hey!" and he scattered hundreds of documents on the steps of the courthouse, shouting, "Thought you could get rid of us, did you?" Then he poured coffee on the strewn documents. The promoter quickened his pace, avoiding his eyes, and went to complain to the security guard. The guard, an old Black guy, approached Jess cautiously. "Doesn't matter to me what you do with the papers, but be mindful of littering."

Jess, tense and depressed, drove too fast on the way back. He stopped to buy chips and candy. When he got back behind the wheel, he sighed. "I didn't get anything I wanted. We were massacred. That's what happens when you start believing in the law."

In the long term, a lot of stress and bitterness built up inside Jess. But the huge lot, the old Victorian house, and the decrepit apartment block had become his project, his life, his obsession, and Jess spent years defending the squat and becoming the numerous people who emerged from his former identities like snakes that have shed their skin.

I WAS LIVING IN MONTREAL, I invited him to our place in the summers, I went to visit him in winter, and I wrote to him in fall and spring. In a closet in my apartment on Rue

Saint-Denis, I had several blue rubber totes in which I kept not just my childhood photos but his childhood photos, old locks of his hair, all the letters Jess had written me, and even important papers that Jess didn't want to keep at the squat.

"All that seems so far away," Jess said, looking at the photos from his other lives when I insisted on getting them out of the boxes. "I don't like seeing myself like that."

"Why not? You were so hot."

After a year or two in Oakland, even surfing, which had been such a major part of his life, had lost all meaning. Jess was living in a city by the sea, but never even went to the beach.

"I was so stupid."

I laughed. I had loved him each year, I was sure I'd have loved him in the time before we met, even in that time when he was supposedly so stupid. I was fascinated by his face, which was undeniably the same in all the photos, even if the person behind it was changing his appearance dramatically every two or three years. It wasn't just a question of clothes. It was clear, even from the flat surface of the photos, that Jess was constantly changing on the inside. Every time Jess quit a version of Jess, it was by shedding certain parts from a former self and choosing others to keep; Jess was good at everything—drawing, music, sports, building, calculus, writing, comedy. Sometimes I was almost jealous, but as the years passed, I understood that talent doesn't really make people happy any more than beauty does. Jess, gifted and exquisite, was depressed all the time, without, however, ever stopping doing *something*, whether it be learning a new instrument, building a tree house, tending a vegetable garden, learning a new language, or writing a graphic novel with maniacal persistence. It was one of the traits that followed Jess from one version of Jess to another.

The old pictures of me were less interesting to look at. I never changed. I always had the same face, the same hair, the same tics, the same smile, and the same frown. And, I realized when I was looking through the photos again a few days ago, I always had a pen and a notebook or a book in my hands or on my knee.

He told me he loved me with letters, presents, flowers, drawings, dresses, postcards, and once a huge potted palm tree he'd found in the street. He told me he loved me with cakes, healing teas, lasagna, beef bourguignon. He told me he loved me with songs, dozens of songs, his own and other people's. He never stopped doing it, even when we started arguing. We never argued about the important things. We argued about the plan for the day or the groceries. I called him too often, he forgot to call me.

When the tension increased, we talked for hours and it never really helped. One of us would put on Bob Dylan's "All I Really Want to Do" to remind ourselves: "I ain't lookin' to compete with you, beat or cheat or mistreat you.

"Simplify you, classify you, deny, defy or crucify you.

"All I really want to do is, baby, be friends with you."

I WENT TO VISIT HIM in the winters. I stayed three months, never more, because I could never get a visa. I didn't have a career or a field of study, or anything else reassuring enough for the American authorities. I tried, I tried one year to enrol in the community college in San Francisco, but the truth was that it seemed too complicated and too depressing, the idea of studying full-time and living in a squat, in a city that Jess really loved but that didn't appeal to me enough to make me leave Montreal. Montreal had quietly become mine. I went to the orientation session for international students, then I wrote to the college to say I'd changed my mind.

I went back year after year, each time for a pretty long stay, but I could never get rid of the feeling that I was "Jess's guest." I went to jiu-jitsu dojos, community radio stations, Spanish classes, but it was all just something to do while I waited, it wasn't serious. I made friends, but there was always some awkwardness. Everyone knew I wouldn't be there for long. I went to their protests, but fearfully, since if I got arrested, I would never be able to go back to the US again. I read books pretty much all day long. I walked. I made love to Jess, but I wasn't making a life with Jess. That's how it was. I was taking root where life had planted me and it was out of my control. There was Montreal, and there was Jess, and me spreading myself between the two, me unable to choose, me unable to amputate half my body. Between us, there was a river that always brought us back to each other, an unpredictable love that always followed the same path, from one to the other. Before us there was simultaneously an endless ocean and a concrete wall, right there, and we couldn't get past it, the years added up, we knew it off by heart, and we were even used to it. The more time passed, the lower destroying the wall got on our list of things to do.

I WENT TO VISIT AT least once a year for nine years. My last winter there, the squatters were at loggerheads. It was a bit more than a year after Vincent had died. The fight against the promoter had got more complicated, more bitter, more

247

drawn-out, and the summonses to hearings had multiplied. Jess, obsessed, was always scribbling and muttering things like "Damned if you do, damned if you don't," or "I can't win," talking as much about the legal battle as about the quarrels among the squatters. His habit of making lists had more or less become a compulsion. Jess was trapped in a vicious circle: by default, the majority of the legal, hygienic, security, relational, and ethical responsibilities of the squat fell to him, and the other squatters took this sense of leadership as permission to do nothing themselves, or, worse still, thought it was a power trip. Jess was so worried that he hurt everywhere and hardly had any libido. That made me crazy with insecurity. I couldn't get past my disappointment to show him some compassion. In the mornings I would wake up and regret being there. I looked at his beautiful sleeping body, furious with desire and pain.

And then, knowing that Jess hated being woken up and that a bad wakeup often led to a bad day, I left the bedroom and went for a walk.

I always took more or less the same route. I went up Martin Luther King Street to a café run by Eritreans. This is what I went past: a bookstore named after Marcus Garvey; a garage where an old man sometimes sold watermelons; the MLK café, also run by Eritreans, on the ground floor of a new condo tower. I always passed a few homebums with whom I stopped to make small talk and who never missed a chance to ask for a dollar. One of these people was Dani, an old lady who lived in a trailer parked in the squat's yard. Sometimes I suspected, when she stopped me in the street to ask for a dollar, that she didn't recognize me, but, as if she was reading my mind at that exact moment, she always said, "A friend of Jess is a friend of mine. You got a dollar, sweetie?"

At the café, I ordered a medium filter coffee if Jess was with me, or a cappuccino if I was on my own. And then I chose the table at the back, near the toilets, the one Jess, Jenna, and Oliver had nicknamed "our table" because of its proximity to the toilets and outlets and the fact that it couldn't really be seen from the counter. I plugged in my phone and my computer, or if Jess was with me, I just plugged in my computer and Jess plugged in his phone. "Look at you!" Jess would say, seeing me absorbed in my things, overcaffeinated, reading the news, checking my emails, researching house foreclosures by American banks, and compulsively making notes in my notebook.

"Do you wanna check your emails?" I would ask him after a while.

"Yes!" Jess said, batting his lashes like a punkette doe. I passed him my old laptop and turned the page of my notebook, then started to tell the page how I was feeling again. Most of the time I felt pretty bad. If I was alone, things basically happened in the same order, except that everything took longer. I drank coffee and read the news. I went to take a shit and wash my hands, two things that I wouldn't have another chance to do until the next day. I carried on reading the news and ordered a second coffee. When it was time to talk about my feelings to my notebook, I would often see Oliver or Jenna arriving. If it was Oliver, he'd first of all buy himself a coffee, and then come and sit next to me and give me a high-five. He leaned his skateboard against the wall, asked me how I was in his hangman's tone, and got out his iPad. We read the news in silence. He cut off all my attempts to make conversation by saying, "Right on," and not asking any questions. Sometimes, having run out of ideas, I started to badmouth the squatters I knew he couldn't stand, and that would set him off for a few minutes. When Jess showed up, Oliver practically levitated out of his chair, straightened his spine, and started listing all the tasks related to defending the squat they needed to get done, ignoring me completely, and telling crude inside jokes that I didn't get. My research seemed pretty useless, abstract, trivial, something to occupy me while they were working—like the pots and utensils you give a child who wants to help with the cooking.

If Jenna was the first to show up, I was consumed with the desire to confide in her, to tell her that I was unhappy and that Jess didn't love me anymore. But she would sit down opposite me and take a long swallow of black coffee, and her inexpressive eyes immediately made me change my mind.

Jenna, Jess's co-conspirator and great friend, was one of those anarchists who led a double life. She could have worked as an architect if she'd wanted to, but she lived in a squat, rushed from riot to riot, and stole from high-end grocery stores. On her birthday, two weeks after I arrived, we went to play skittles in an abandoned parking lot with a big ball with three holes and some empty beer bottles, and then all ten of us crammed into Jess's hearse. We'd eaten pizza from dumpsters, drunk Pabst, and taken selfies with our iPhones. Jenna seemed hard to get to know, but I trusted her, and I told myself that as long as they didn't lose sight of each other, she and Jess would not become completely crazy. At the same time, I felt they encouraged each other to keep trying, perhaps uselessly, to "save" the squat that was wrecking their lives.

"How's it going," she said in a neutral voice as she replied to a text. The coffee never seemed to help her wake up that much. I was like a ball of energy in comparison with her. I told her I'd found some articles that might be useful in their legal battle. "Awesome," she said, without asking for any more information. I asked her in turn how she was. "Oh, you know," she said. Jenna hated all the squatters she lived with, with one single exception: Jess. She even hated Oliver, the third link of their legal defence triangle. "Fuckin' Oliver. He helps when he feels like it, and then doesn't warn anyone that he's going to Mexico for two months. We have to handle things without him." She stayed for two reasons: she didn't want to abandon Jess, and she was as stubborn as a mule. She wanted to win. "I'm so sick of it all," she said every day. I nodded.

"Maybe you should just drop everything," I hinted one day.

"Oh, I will," she said. "I'm about to."

But she'd been saying this for at least a year and she hadn't worked up the nerve.

Jess arrived. They talked squat, I wrote in my notebook. I offered theoretical, wannabe-journalist support. Maybe I could do an internship at the Berkeley Investigative Journalism Center, I thought, dreaming in Technicolor.

After coffee, my existential crisis started. Jess, Jenna, and Oliver said goodbye and headed off to the law library. Sometimes I stayed in the café, sometimes I took the BART, I wandered around Berkeley's streets, I struggled up mountains, and sometimes, if it wasn't too late, I went to San Francisco. I cried almost every day. I bent over my notebook and wrote things like:

"You spend days, months, years, thinking things are fine, moving along, loving your city. You make friends, toughen up, and forget how it was here, in the grime of the grey, in a body that barks basic orders: Move me. Feed me. Wash me. Shelter me.

"We are nothing more than our bodies. And it's up to our bodies to take care of our bodies. But our bodies don't know how. Our bodies forgot how years and years ago. Our bodies go to the store. They go to the bank to borrow money. Our bodies go online to pay off the credit card we used to buy fruit after waiting in line. Our bodies gave the credit card to the woman at the cash, the woman who also doesn't know how to grow fruit and vegetables, the woman who also has a backache from her job. Our bodies are rotting.

"My body is a soft little ball that just wants warmth and comfort. Its habits: going online, taking hot showers, eating shop-bought food.

"You start a new document.

"2014, 2015, 2016, they mean nothing, yesterday, the day before yesterday, today. Everything's constantly changing. One day you're in a horrendous mood. One day you don't want to write anymore. Another day you find you can give your life meaning through the possibility of writing. Another day everything is ugly, grey, too late. Too late. You've missed the train. Even if it's not true. Even if mathematically speaking you have the time to do everything, you don't have any time left. Even if nothing is broken, everything is broken.

Some days. You disappear under the weight of your love for someone who no longer wants sex, no longer has time, no longer has eyes for you, someone who is a prisoner in a house that isn't really a home, someone who can't promise anything. You disappear in his stories, his humour, his life. You are there to love, you don't know what love means. You don't know how to give when your body is crying and unable to take care of itself. It barely has any strength left, it doesn't know how to hammer a nail, screw a screw, plant, harvest. Your body is a ball in a line of people waiting to order a Vietnamese sandwich or a burrito, to have a hot shower, to check email. It wakes up simply because there is still coffee in the United States. It no longer likes to do anything except drive in cars, in an enormous grey hearse, a 1977 Cadillac bought for nine hundred dollars from a neighbour of the late Steve Jobs that drinks gallon after gallon of gas, and temporarily patches broken friendships back together.

"Everything is a game of chance, everything starts well and ends badly or starts badly and ends well before carrying on, before never really ending. Like this day, when first of all I took our clothes and sleeping bags to the laundromat, and watched the water turn grey, then black, then clear, as I mourned our sex life; when I met a man in the street who had just got out of prison that morning and who said to me, 'Life has no meaning, but I'm in love with the trees, bird-song, my daughter'; when I received one, two, three letters from Montreal, my subletter who had questions about the heating system and two friends who loved me, who told me about their days, who were thinking about me. My friends seemed like ants from up above. I didn't answer them."

"MY HEAD IS A COLD and hot block. I can't think. I feel. I smell. I desire. I wait. But I don't think. When I string words together and open my mouth, I don't even hear what comes out. When the others talk, it's the same thing. My love is constantly asking, 'Are you okay? You're sad. Are you okay? What's the matter?' And all I can say is, 'I'm fine,' or, 'I'm a bit down, but I'm fine.' And my love says, 'But you're on vacation. It can't be as bad as all that, you're on vacation.'

"I'm not on vacation. I can't even imagine leaving the city for a week, going outside the neighbourhood. But I'm useless here. I don't know how to hammer a nail, garden, fix a toilet, I don't know how to not be afraid. As if nothing had changed after all these years. I had accumulated a lot of strength before coming, but now all my resources are exhausted. I'm hoping I have reserves somewhere, but I don't have any way of knowing. Heavy. Everything is so heavy.

"I can't tell my love everything because our roles can't be reversed. I can't confide, I have to listen, I have to be a rock. I say: 'I've been strong up to now, right?' You say: 'You've been all sorts of things, you're a human being.' It's not the answer I wanted to hear. What I wanted to hear was, 'You've been an incredible rock.' I want all this to be over. I want to be congratulated."

"HOW TO BE
Stronger"

JESS USED TO WORK AT least an hour a day on the garden, vegetables, herbs for cooking and medicine, fruit bushes from which everyone helped themselves, but Jess was the only one who did any planting or watering, pruning or fertilizing. She read books on permaculture, she sang or talked in a low voice to the plants and flowers. Following her advice, I'd planted a few rows of beets. "You'll see, when you're the one planting them, you'll actually want to take care of them," she'd said, but this prediction turned out to be false and my beets never got past the dwarf leaves stage. To my great shame, gardening bored me. I had no interest in unravelling and repairing the tangled hoses, or staking out the tomatoes so that the fruit wouldn't hang on the ground, or weeding, or scattering sawdust around the Brussels sprouts to discourage weeds. I didn't like gardening, but I really wanted to like it. So I often ended up pretending to work in the garden, wandering between the plants, gazing at the bees, sometimes bending down to pick and eat a kale leaf or following on Jess's heels as she transplanted, watered, cooed, and pruned. She was so achingly beautiful and I wanted her to sometimes look at me the way she looked at her plants, even though I knew it was ridiculous and she would have been annoyed if I had talked about it. One day I made her jump (I think she hadn't noticed my presence in her shadow) by stretching my arm over her shoulder to pick a blackberry as I exclaimed, "I want one!" Jess lost her balance and toppled over into the prickly bushes.

"Jesus Christ, Sab!" she yelled.

I started crying and asked her if she was okay. Jess took me in her arms and comforted me for a few seconds, then went back to picking the beans. To punish myself, I stuck blackberry bramble into my arm and drew a circle around the wound with my blood, promising myself I'd help Jess with the garden more often.

A few weeks later, I had the chance to demonstrate my usefulness: On Craigslist, Jess had found someone who was getting rid of a ton of topsoil. We borrowed a pickup and went to Berkeley with shovels. On the way, it started raining. Even better, I thought. Jess was radiant. She had a passionate discussion about gardening with the woman who welcomed us. I didn't say anything, I didn't even stay long enough to find out why she was getting rid of all this soil. I pulled off the blue tarp that was over the enormous pile of humus, opened the box of the pickup truck, and started filling it, shovelful by shovelful. I was digging furiously, but the pile didn't seem to be getting any smaller. The earth was wet with rain, I was already getting blisters on my hands, my arms were hurting. Jess came over to join me. In a few seconds, she'd done more than I had in fifteen minutes. I stuck my shovel in the earth even harder without bending my knees, and I did something to my back. Jess sighed with irritation as she watched me twist in pain. I went to sit inside the truck while she finished up. I brought my knees up to my chest and closed my eyes, shivering, soaked, filthy, defeated.

AT NIGHTS, I SOMETIMES DREAMED that I was meeting Jess, that I was falling madly in love, and I had to work up the courage to tell my lover (who was also Jess) that I'd met someone else. When I finally made up my mind to do it, I set off to look for Jess, I walked for hours, but couldn't find her. Exhausted, I woke up. I could hear Jess breathing next to me, but I couldn't see her face. Panicked, I felt around in the dark for a lighter and lit the candle we used as a bedside lamp. I discovered her face, the most beautiful face I'd ever seen, and I blew on the candle, afraid that a drop of wax would fall on her eyes and she'd see me like this, hovering over her, like a thief, a ghost.

THERE WERE PILES OF GARBAGE everywhere in the squat's backyard (except for the garden, which Jess defended like a pit bull).

Whenever I felt alone, useless, or overwhelmed by events, I would go to the convenience store and buy a pair of dish-washing gloves and a dozen black garbage bags and go to work sorting the trash. I put a scarf over my hair, another one over my nose and mouth, and I set to it, often spending the whole day working. The urge came over me at least once a visit.

It came over me that day. Normally I got up before everyone else and sneaked out of the squat, tiptoeing past strangers sleeping in the corridors and dogs stretched out in patches of Californian sun, being careful not to let the chain squeak as I unlocked and relocked the big padlock of the fence around the squat. But that morning I didn't go out. That morning I could no longer ignore the disaster.

Carcasses, food scraps, computers and other broken machines, dog shit (and maybe human too), enormous num-bers of cigarette butts and all kinds of packaging, broken dishes, dirty diapers, puzzles, damp, mouldy clothes and books, filthy or broken toys, cardboard coffee cups, and enough beer bottles to fill thirty grocery carts. You can't let yourself think, Where should I start? You just have to dive in. So that's what I did.

Along one of the walls of the old garage that had been

converted into a free store, I set up several storage boxes and tried to organize them into a system for sorting.

In the first three containers, which I put under a tarp nailed to a wooden frame, I put all the bits that might be reusable: copper from electric wires in the first box, plastics that might be useful in the garden in the second, and anything that could be repaired and sold in the third.

In the next three boxes, I sorted out recyclable materials like paper, plastics, and metal. I didn't know if the city picked up recycling, or if you had to pay for it, or if you had to take the stuff somewhere to the official dumpsters. I'd think about that later.

Beside the containers there was an overturned wooden crate where I piled up dozens of flattened cardboard boxes. The boxes came from all over the place. We often found them at the side of the road, full of books, clothes and trinkets, vases and laminated frames. We sometimes got them in the mail, when Farid did some shopping with his fake credit cards. Jess used the boxes in the garden to keep the weeds down and make paths between the rows.

Finally, on the other side of the pile of boxes, there were three garbage cans provided by the city for any items that were beyond repair, and two grocery carts where I put the beer bottles and cans. The garbage cans were already pretty much overflowing and their lids had been off during a rainy night. Chicken carcasses, viscous cans of tuna, squished dog shit, and mouldy pastries swam in a stinky, bitter liquid that made me want to throw up.

The part of the yard that wasn't taken up by the garden was half asphalted. There was grass right behind the squat, but also a lot of earth that had been flattened by the comings and goings of thirty people. I walked around the fire-pit, picked up dirty plates and cutlery, crates of Pabst Blue Ribbon, ripped-open packets of cigarettes, two-by-fours with nails sticking out. I tipped out several crates, bowls, and kettles full of orange-brown rainwater into the grass and made a pile of dishes next to the coiled hose.

When I got tired of sorting, I started sweeping the dusty asphalt. Old receipts, blackened pennies, candy wrappers, sequoia needles and branches, hair clips, caps from pens and lipsticks, empty chip bags, and cigarette butts all ended up in my pile. I went to throw the heap in the trash, but then I stopped dead. The hearse was parked crossways, taking up most of the entrance. I was sure there was more junk hidden under the car.

I suddenly wondered if seeing me cleaning bothered some of the squatters. A few weeks earlier, some representatives of the neighbourhood association had come to tell them that the murals they'd painted on the squat walls were a blight, and that they were bound by municipal laws to rectify the situation. A long debate ensued among the squatters, trying to decide if the neighbourhood association was on the side of the gentrifying clan, Google employees and other tapas-eaters, or if the members of the association were speaking on behalf of "folks from the community," the delicate phrase the punks, anarchists, and other white radicals liked to use to talk about the Black people who lived in the area. I hadn't taken a position, since I always found it hard to understand the subtleties of the American context. There were so many tensions between the squatters that it would be good for them to unite against a common enemy, whether it was the neighbourhood association or the real estate promoter. Since there was no clear way of determining who lived in the squat and who didn't, the houses and the yard swarmed with quasi-enemy subgroups, divided along lines of identity and political positions: queer punks who drank beer, weren't very sociable, and distrusted white men; white men who exerted themselves in fields like plumbing, mechanics, political debates, and legal battles, who would take the tools out of your hand on the pretext of showing you how to change a bike tire and who never stopped bringing more white men along as potential squatters ("This guy's really cool!"); a small group of Black Nationalists inspired by Malcolm X, who were sometimes frankly homophobic; educated, tattooed, foodie anarchists who were leading double lives (cabinetmakers, university research assistants, or social workers by day, thieves, saboteurs, and propaganda distributors by night); druggies sleeping in the corridors (especially friends and clients of Farid, an ex-con who didn't use himself but didn't have many options for making a living); and finally five or six unclassifiable people, jokers who didn't take sides and were unpredictable in arguments or wars (those were the ones I liked best). The white squatters were, generally speaking, ashamed of being white and spent their time justifying their presence in the neighbourhood by talking about their working-class roots, their significant contribution to the fight against gentrification, their desire to settle down and develop "real relationships" with the community. They were also a little too quick to try to make friends with Black people they met in the streets, out of a desire to be seen with Black friends and thus bolster their credentials, which the homophobic Nationalists never missed a chance to comment on, denounce, ridicule, before publishing zines in which they announced a takeover of the squat by their group in the name of the People, which never really materialized because, for one thing, their tiny group wasn't influential enough in the neighbourhood and, for another, it was incredibly difficult to get rid of two dozen white crust punks and their dogs. I thought they were losing it, all of them, but I knew I wouldn't do any better myself.

I rested my broom against a wall of the free store and went off to look for Jess. I went to our bedroom, on the first floor of the ruined Victorian house. I got out my key ring (to which I'd also attached a little pink canister of pepper spray) and unlocked the two padlocks. Jess wasn't there. The bed was made, Jess had tidied her papers and tools. I heard the fence chain, voices, barking dogs, Oliver yelling, "Close the gate, ya fucking oogles!" I sat down on the bed for a moment, flipped through a practical zine about sabotaging capitalist flows and networks, then a brochure version of *What Is an Apparatus?* Then I left the bedroom.

In the hall, I saw Farid.

"Hey, good morning," he said.

"Hey, Farid. Did you sleep okay?"

"Hmmm … I didn't sleep much. Want a slice of pizza?"

He held out a Domino's Pizza box that was still warm. I took a slice. Farid ordered food at all hours of the day and night and paid with his fraudulent credit cards.

"He's playing with fire," Jess used to say.

Farid was a joker. He got on more or less with everyone. The year before, he used to cook a lot. Jess and I spent almost every evening with him, eating ramen noodles that he managed to dress up to taste like a gourmet meal. But this year he seemed depressed. He stayed in his room a lot, with his "colleagues," other hackers and crack dealers. He didn't mix with the punks too much.

"Thanks," I said.

"You're welcome. Listen, I haven't forgotten about our economics lesson. I'd love to explain the 2008 crash to you."

"Cool! Do you think I could record our conversation for the community radio station?"

"As long as I can be anonymous," Farid said, "why not?"

"No problem, you can choose any pseudonym you like."

"My girlfriend's coming from Richmond today to see me, but tomorrow I'm all yours."

I finished my pizza slice and said goodbye to Farid, then went back outside.

Half a dozen punks were lying on the grass, drinking coffee, huge cans of beer, and Arizona iced tea. "Have you seen Jess?" They hadn't seen her. I tried to talk to them normally, without letting them see that I was judging them. (Beer! It wasn't even eleven o'clock!) They looked at me with barely disguised irritation, as if I was a Greenpeace chugger accosting them in the street. I told myself that for them I was probably a poster child for the heterosexual hegemony, since I had long hair and just one tattoo. For me, they represented decadence and an intellectual void. I suddenly thought about my father, in his condo thousands of miles away, who would have thought the whole lot of us were not just crazy but disgusting.

I walked around the yard and then around the old building. I went in the back door of the house and ventured into the kitchen. I stepped over the pizza boxes, the dogs, the piles of clothes, the piles of tools, the broken furniture. No Jess. But Jess wouldn't have left the squat without telling me. I went back outside and looked at the sky. My eyes fell on the huge sequoia and I suddenly figured it out: she was in the tree house. Usually I avoided the tree house because I got vertigo. But that day I grabbed hold of my courage with both hands, gripped the ladder, and climbed up, one rung at a time, terrified.

I crawled into the tree house on all fours and found Jess lying down on a little camp bed, wearing a headlamp, deep into someone's personal diary she'd found at Goodwill.

"The author's talking about coming off heroin," Jess explained. "It's fascinating. I can't stop reading. What are you up to, pumpkin?"

I took off the scarf I was wearing around my head. I undid my bun and scratched my scalp. I sat down next to Jess on the camp bed. Jess turned off the headlamp.

"I was sorting the garbage."

"That's not your job."

"I don't know what else to do, and it's depressing seeing it every day."

"Well, it's very, very nice of you," said Jess, putting down the diary and starting to undress me.

I was so happy, I had tears in my eyes. I got up and locked the tree house door.

"Good thing there's a lock on this door," I said with a giggle.

I took off my dusty clothes and my muddy shoes. Jess took off her headlamp, her giant earrings, her studded jacket, lace camisole, jean shorts, black tights. We looked at each other, naked. I kissed her, I sat on her chest and suddenly felt a violent pleasure. I took her hands and guided her fingers over my hips.

I fucked Jess like I'd fucked her hundreds of times, my head empty, feeling waves of relief, recognition, happiness, melancholy, impatience, vertigo, and fragility wash over me. I was sure that the pleasure would last forever, and at the same time convinced that it would be over soon, too soon, from one second to the next. I cried like a body that allows itself to get sick only after a period of stress is over.

Jess pecked me on the lips several times, like a bird, then she looked at the time on her phone, an old pink flip phone still going from the first years of the millennium.

"I have to meet Jenna at the law library."

"Can you move the hearse?" I said, remembering why I'd come up to the tree house in the first place. "It's taking up all the room in the yard."

"I'm going to drive there. We'll probably be there all day. The next hearing's in two days. Then I'm going to come back and meet people for the protest tonight. Wanna come?"

"No."

"Are you sure? It's gonna be huge. You'll have FOMO again."

"I can't get arrested."

"Whatever you want, it's up to you."

"I want to come, but I can't. I'm too scared."

"You're gonna stay here by yourself?"

"I might go to a café."

"And pay four dollars for a latte?"

"A latte, a cappuccino, a macchiato, I haven't decided yet."

Jess shook her head, disapproving and loving. She put her clothes back on, then stood in front of a little broken mirror, got her eyeliner and mascara out of her pocket, and started putting her makeup on.

"I just want you to be okay here," Jess said distractedly.

"I'm fine. It's fine," I said, equally distracted. "I'm going to read and write emails at the café. I'm reading James Baldwin. It's crazy. Your country's history is completely crazy, Jess."

"Completely fucked," Jess said. "Do you want some makeup?"

"No thanks."

"You're so preppy."

I shrugged my shoulders, then fumbled under the bed for my scarf. "Do you need any help at the law library?"

"Pff, no. That's not your job. It might be nice if one of the hundred and twenty people who live here helped us, but where we're at now … I don't know. I feel like it's just a matter of time. It's just a question of shitting out the documents, finding the legal precedents. We just gotta milk them as much as possible until they realize we don't know what the fuck we're doing."

"You don't think you're gonna win?"

Jess sighed. "I guess anything's possible."

I nodded. "I'm going to carry on with the sorting for a while." I wanted to have a shower, but I didn't mention it. I kissed Jess and slowly climbed back down the ladder, holding my breath. If I didn't get vertigo so badly, I could do a lot more things I never do, I thought. Almost there, almost there … I touched the ground.

The punks who'd been sitting on the grass earlier were now in the driveway. They had dragged out a couch and chairs in front of the free store and were scarfing burritos and nachos, drinking growlers, and smoking cigarettes, throwing their garbage behind them as they went.

I looked sadly at my recycling containers. I was tired. I no longer knew what could be recycled, what I should keep, what should go in the trash. I no longer knew if it was worth sorting.

I DON'T LIKE THE 6 p.m. light, which drags on, when it's too bright to light candles and too dark to read or start something in the garden, this long, heartbreaking goodbye where Jess and I always end up in our bedroom with cigarettes and 7UP, sad, forced to admit that the day has got away from us without being spectacular. Or productive. Jess picks up a notebook and draws the garden from memory.

"There's so much to do," Jess says. "We have to make the most of the season."

"I can help you tomorrow if you want," I say.

"If *you* want," Jess says, without lifting her head.

Does she think I don't help enough in the garden? Is that it? I move closer, put my arms around her shoulders. "I don't know anything about gardening," I say.

She wriggles away. She adds a few exclamation marks and hearts to her drawing and then puts it aside. She goes over to the window. "I don't trust that guy," she says, watching a neighbour go by wearing a crumpled suit and black basketball shoes.

I don't ask why. It's the time, I think. That strange time between two lights that doesn't suit us. But we'll never leave each other. We'll love each other our whole lives. I go and sit on the bed.

I'm cold. I plug in the heat lamp we brought from the chicken coop a month ago, when a dog belonging to the punks ate all the chickens. I pull the dirty quilt up over my thighs.

"We have to wash this quilt," I say.

"Don't touch my quilt!" she says.

She moves away from the window and busies herself tidying her tools in the doll's house she uses for a chest. Nail by nail, bolt by bolt. I get into bed, pull the quilt, which is grey with grime, over my head, and start crying. I feel better in the damp, hot darkness than in the six o'clock light. I miss having my own bed. This one is made up of a simple mattress placed on a wooden teacher's desk, whose drawers store more tools, political texts, and a few unwashed sex toys. I don't want to do this anymore, I cry.

Suddenly she's beside me. She spoons me. The contact of her body reminds me of our history, draws a hot, deep line between all the selves Jess has been over the years. I can't tell her I miss the ones she decided to abandon. I turn toward her, wipe my tears in her hair, and kiss her neck.

The light has almost gone, I say to encourage myself.

THE DAY BEFORE YESTERDAY, WE were driving through the city in the hearse. At the corner of Adeline and Alcatraz, Jess burned through a red light and another driver came within a hair of crashing into us. He was driving fast. So were we. If the other guy hadn't braked in time, we'd be dead. We're not dead.

At least it would have been funny to die in a hearse, we told each other as we kissed.

LAST NIGHT, WHEN WE CAME out of the movie theatre, after yet another stupid argument, we sank into the front seat of the hearse and said, more or less at the same time, "We can't go on like this."

These words, the truth of these words, cut me in two, because I thought that if there was only one person in the world, it was Jess.

TONIGHT, YOU SAID TO ME, "You have to think of yourself. You always have these big ideas, but you never finish what you start."

Rolled up in a ball in the tangled sheets, I was crying as I swigged from a tall can of Miller High Life.

"I don't want to see you drinking in bed, Sab."

"I do what I can with the strength I have," I whined.

You were playing with the wax and the candle flames. "It scares me," you said. "I know it's better for both of us, but I can't imagine my life without you."

After several hours, I think you fell asleep. In any case, you stretched out and closed your eyes.

NOT FAR AWAY FROM HERE is a lake. You have to pay for access to its shores, but I know where there's a hole in the fence.

The water will be icy, but it will still be in a liquid state.

That's what I will do today. I will go through the hole in the fence and I'll dive into the icy water.

And then I'll go home.

PART 5

PART 5

We love life if we find a way to it.
And we plant, where we settle, some fast-growing
  plants, and harvest the dead.
We play the flute like the colour of the faraway, sketch
  over the dirt corridor a neigh.
We write our names one stone at a time, O lightning
  brighten the night.
We love life if we find a way to it
  —MAHMOUD DARWISH, *"And We Love Life"*

HORROR

IF I CARRY ON PUTTING myself in danger like this, scaring myself, terrifying myself with what I can so easily admit now that I've picked off the scab, now the fever's gone down, well, it's because the horror is better than the emptiness before it.

"Something's happening, but what?" I used to say to myself when all that (hypocrisy, bottomless violence, wanting to die) was simmering beneath my skin, beneath language. Now I know: it happens that we are always in danger, but also that the harm is already done, that we have swallowed and digested it and that it flows in our blood. That's the difference between dreamy eyes and fists up, between the fleeting glance and claws that hurt from growing so fast, between health and paranoia. Having the vague feeling that something's wrong is healthy. Being sure and convinced of rape is paranoia. It suits me. We paranoid people have our bearings, we are preparing our revenge.

I'm not asking you to like it. I'm not asking you to be my target audience. I'm going to target whomever I want. I'm going to shoot who I want.

It's scary; sure, it's scary. Everything's scary. I'm scared of being scared and even of making other people scared. But why would I make anyone scared? What is actually inadmissible? What would be more convincing if I had fantastic cleavage, what could be said better with a PhD, what would be easier to swallow in the dark, between young girls in flower, sitting around with a bowl of popcorn and a horror movie? He raped me and I think about it every time I try to touch myself? He raped me and I will never get better, even with "the man I love," he raped me and I am not sick, I am sickness? I am monstrous? I don't have a real face anymore?

That's it, that's almost it, but it's not quite it. That's it, and it's what's not said. It's what I refuse to give.

This is fine, but explain yourself, what exactly are you talking about?

Nothing. I'm talking about nothing. Let it go. If you don't get it, then forget it.

BREATHING

I SEE BEST IN THE dark, I breathe most powerfully then.

It was one morning when I woke up with a dark circle around my mouth. Insects had shat there, dogs had yelled there, children had lost their mothers' hands there. For a long time, this dark circle followed me everywhere and did everything for me, everything. It was a garden where I am still growing, the border between nothingness and skin, the line drawn between tiredness and the infinitely large, the one you can touch. It was the memento that was at first comforting, then insistent, then unceasing and strident, guilt-making, haunting: if I don't want to do this anymore, I can give myself death, I can make myself a gift of it.

In the dark, I am most certain, the night understands enough about mystery and deep breaths for me. When others dream and breathe, there is space for my colours and my luminescent eyes.

One morning I said to myself: if I want, I can live, and if I want to live, I can live how I want, and if I want to live, I will live with them, and whoever wants life can live at night.

I hear the voice that says: a gift is something you give away entirely.

Bring me back to the side of the living.

OTTAWA

MY MOTHER WAS HAPPY TO hear my voice on the phone.

"Where are you calling from?"

"Uh ... the Greyhound station on Catherine."

"What! Weren't you in California until January?"

I explained to her that I came back a month earlier than expected, that my room in Montreal was still sublet for another month. Could I stay with her? She said it would be no problem. And then, probably realizing that I was trying not to cry, she said she'd come and pick me up. I sat down on my bag and stared at the long line of people who'd bought tickets for Montreal. It was weird hearing French spoken.

My mother didn't ask any questions in the car. When we got to the house, she said she'd run me a bath. I put my bag down in my old bedroom, which my mother and her husband François had turned into an office, and then I went back downstairs and sat on the arm of the couch, staring vaguely at the stars and wooden figurines on the Christmas tree.

"A good hot bath will do you good," my mother said. "Then we'll talk."

François and my half-sister Lydia came back while I was in the bath. It's Friday, I thought, cleaning under my nails with a brush. On Fridays, François and Lydia go rock climbing. It's Friday, I'm in Ottawa, I'm back here, Jess and I...Jess and I. I listened to my mother telling them I was there. "I think things went badly with Jess," she added. I plunged my head under the water.

When I came out of the bathroom, I saw they were all standing by the door with sad smiles on their faces. I was happy to see them. They surrounded me with their six arms, my wet hair on their collars, my own arms gripping the towel around my body. Then I went into the office. Since all my clothes stank, I went into Lydia's room and took a polypropylene sweater, yoga pants, and a pair of Smartwool socks. When I went downstairs, François said, "Sabrina, what would you prefer? Pizza? St-Hubert? Or a nice big homemade spaghetti?"

I smiled. "A nice big homemade spaghetti, if it's not too much trouble."

"Of course not, we have meat sauce in the freezer, it's absolutely no trouble," my mother said, nodding her head several times to show that I was very welcome.

Lydia grabbed me around the waist and leaned her head on my shoulder. I burst into tears. Lydia held me in her arms for a long time while my mother and François, the perfect couple, made dinner.

I slept in the office, on the futon. I stocked up on beer, episodes of *Angels in America,* and an *Alias* graphic novel I'd found in François's bookcase, predicting that I wouldn't sleep. But I slept. I slept a heavy and even restorative sleep.

The next morning, Lydia and I went to the pond in the rich area of Manor Park, then walked along the Ottawa River to the ByWard Market. Lydia told me about her studies in international development at the University of Ottawa and her climbing gym. Her stories were soothing, I asked her questions and I wanted her to carry on talking. We stopped at Planet Coffee, which had once been one of my favourite places but now had been renovated and was teeming with screeching business people and couples wearing brand name sunglasses and Canada Goose coats decorated with ski passes.

"Shall we go?" I said. "I don't really want to be here after all."

I suggested walking to Elgin Street, maybe going to the Elgin Street Diner. She said she had things to do. She suggested I call the house when I was done, and she'd come and pick me up, or François or Mom would. We separated at the Rideau Centre.

I walked past chic hotels, boutiques, parliamentary buildings, and restaurants decorated for Christmas. Gone were the expanses of aloe, agave, and other succulent plants, the palm trees, the houses surrounded by wire fences, pit bulls, big cars, American accents, racial tensions visible in hunched shoulders and downcast glances. I was in Canada's national capital, and its bundled-up citizens were shopping.

I went into the Elgin Street Diner and chose a booth. I ordered coffee and I told the waiter I needed a bit more time to read the menu. I crossed my hands on the table. They were trembling.

I was sad. But I didn't regret anything. I contemplated my open wound knowing that it would one day close. I contemplated my new solitude. For a long time I'd been overwhelmed by an anticipatory loneliness. It doesn't matter to me, I used to say to myself about everything that hurt and everything that could do me good, because soon I will see Jess. Right now I was noticing a ton of details in the words and movements of the people in the restaurant, in the smells, the colours, the sounds, and I didn't have anyone to talk to about them. So I got out my notebook.

I no longer knew anyone in Ottawa and barely remembered who I'd been when I lived there. I was probably still the same person. And at each point of my life I would continue to change. The waiter brought me my coffee and I asked for a club sandwich.

I started writing. Writing down what had happened. What surprised me wasn't so much that Jess and I had separated. No. Nobody had been surprised when they heard the news, it was the right decision, there would be other people, life goes on. Rather, I was amazed when I thought: someone loved me. Someone loved me that much. It was like a fantasy, but it was reality. We could go back in time, pearl by pearl, and prove that it hadn't been a dream—at least, that it hadn't been one of those dreams that seem, once morning comes, incoherent and ridiculous. Jess had loved me in the world as it is. And now, I was going to carry on living.

"Sabrina?" I heard.

I looked up. It was Julie Grive.

A wave rolled through my stomach. I didn't say anything. I was too surprised. She was wearing a denim dress and a long black wool coat that trailed on the ground. Her hair was very short, like Jean Seberg's. The last time we'd seen each other, it had been blue. Now it was her natural colour, ash blond. She sat down opposite me.

"How are you?" she asked. "Are you ..."

"Yes. No, I'm good ... Well, I'm not that good, but ... I'm so surprised to see you, I never come to Ottawa, are you ..."

"Yeah. I came back a few years ago. After I finished studying in Vancouver. I ... a lot of stuff happened."

"Really?" I practically shouted, still in shock from seeing her. "Me too. I mean, a lot of stuff has happened to me too."

She nodded. I was overwhelmed by nostalgia and the feeling of being watched by my own past (but isn't that basically what nostalgia is, I wondered).

"Can I stay here and get a coffee with you?" she asked. She was pale and seemed tired, but calm. She looked me in the eyes.

"Yes, of course, sit down," I said, even though she was already sitting down.

She didn't mention the idiocy of my comment. With her delicate movements, she took off her coat. "I like your tattoo," she said, stroking my wrist. "Is it the only one you have?"

"Yes," I said. "I haven't had it long. It's for a friend."

She looked at me and widened her eyes, apparently understanding what I meant. "It's beautiful. The wings are very well done. I did one for Céline, like, forever ago. The snake on her arm. Actually, I think that was the last time I saw her. Do you still see each other?"

"Yes," I said, ashamed even though Julie didn't seem the least bit resentful. "We stayed close. She has a few tattoos now, but the snake is her favourite."

"Ah, it makes me happy to hear that," Julie said.

The waiter came to bring me my sandwich and take Julie's order. She asked again if she could stay there with me. I repeated that it was fine. She ordered a hot chocolate.

"Are you still doing it?" I asked.

"No. I sold my machine on a whim five years ago." She burst out with her waterfall laugh, and then she quietened down and looked me in the eyes. "How did your friend die? If you don't mind me asking."

I looked at the moth on my wrist. "He hanged himself," I said, feeling that it would be okay to talk to Julie about it, that she wouldn't react badly.

We looked at each other. She was very beautiful, with her apple cheeks, her freckles, even her chapped lips and black rings were beautiful. As a child I had loved Julie Grive so much. I didn't know what had happened, why we'd lost touch.

"I thought about that once," Julie said, in the flat, deep voice of those who've overcome ordeals and gone beyond coyness. "It was two or three years ago."

Her words made me dizzy, I was bombarded with very unpleasant images, and one part of me wanted to go and hide in the toilets or leave, but I could see in her eyes that she wasn't trying to hurt me.

"And what happened in the end?" I asked in a voice that was just as flat and deep as hers.

She hesitated for a moment and then shrugged her shoulders. "In the end I didn't kill myself."

We stayed together for another hour, talking about events without mentioning names, talking about pain without mentioning which city the wounds had been inflicted in, talking about ourselves without ever bringing up the fact that, ten years earlier, Céline and I had left together and she'd gone her own way all alone. I felt good with her and I could have carried on talking for another few hours, she didn't seem to be afraid of any emotion. But Julie got out her wallet and said she was really happy she'd bumped into me.

"You should come and see me in Montreal! I'll give you my email," I stammered.

She got a Sharpie with a very fine point out of her leather purse and handed me a little sketchbook. I didn't dare flick through it, but I made a wish that I would have the chance to do that soon. On a blank page, I wrote my name, my number, and my email address.

Julie paid at the cash and asked if I wanted a ride. She was going to her mother's in Vanier, "Not far from your mother, right?" I told her I needed to walk a bit more, to digest things. She headed for the door. But before she went out, she turned back to me. "Sab!"

I looked up.

"This is going to sound really strange, but I actually thought I was going to see you today." She shrugged her shoulders.

"Will you call me?" I said. My voice sounded like a supplication.

Julie put on her hat, an aviator cap lined with fur, it had started snowing outside, it was December 20 and I still had a lot of questions to ask her, but that was enough for today, she was leaving and I let her leave, she smiled and her smile gave me courage.

"Yes," she said. "I'll call you."

THE MUSIC GAME

"THREE SHADOWS ARE BENDING OVER each other around a table," Céline begins, "and the lanterns on the table and the walls reveal their attentive, focused faces. When one of the three speaks, the others listen and nod their heads. The old wooden floor stinks of beer, but a door is open to the black night and a healthy wind blows into the tavern. It's the beginning of summer. It's the country. It smells of hay and cool wind. A plot is being hatched somewhere. The shadows don't want to miss anything, or maybe they are the ones who have prepared everything. They are old, young, it doesn't matter. A hand moves and the number three blurs. Maybe there are actually four of them, or even more. A hand comes out of the shade, rests between the black coats. The glasses on the table are also lanterns. They don't touch them; they're too busy with plotting. Their faces are drawn with tiredness, you can read their intense concentration, a hopeful fury. A fist lands on the table: it's going to work. The plan is good. They set off."

Céline looks at the others. The others close their eyes, gaze at the ceiling, thinking. Tahar gets up from his armchair, crouches in front of the computer, and types something in YouTube's search bar.

"We Always Knew." The Black Heart Procession.

He sits back down in his chair. The others listen without speaking for five minutes twenty-six seconds.

"That could be it," Céline says. "That really could be it. Anyone else?"

"Yes," Sab says. "I have one."

She stands up and gives Tahar a falsely threatening glare, pointing two fingers at her eyes and then pointing the same fingers at him. She puts on a song in Russian called "The Letter" by Vladimir Vysotsky.

"Hmmm," Céline says. "Pretty good. Anyone else? No? Okay, you win, Sab."

"Yessss," Sab says. "My turn."

Sab gets another drink and offers Estella the bottle. Then she sits on the floor between Vincent's knees and says, "Our hero has just turned twenty. He's just left his native land after a massive fight with his parents. He won't inherit the farm, but it's even worse than that. He sinned and he was caught. His parents found him in the barn with a labourer. The shame. He had a happy childhood, he really loved his parents, his parents really loved him. But this morning, as he gets up at dawn, he knows he will never see them again. He leaves with his backpack, he takes the bus and hitchhikes to Montreal. This is in the eighties. He's scared, obviously, but now he's been pushed into a new life, he also thinks it's exciting. He ends up on Sainte-Catherine Street, staring at the drag queens, gay couples, the neon signs, and the junkies. Someone tries to steal his bag. He defends himself. He catches a young male prostitute's eyes. He looks for a place to sleep. His whole life is in front of him, he knows, he's scared, he's excited, but he has to start there: finding somewhere to sleep."

"Okay, okay," Vincent says, after a short silence. "Wait, wait, I have one … No, I don't know."

"I have one!" Céline says, laughing as she gets up. She puts on "Quand on arrive en ville" by Daniel Balavoine.

"Too easy," Tahar says.

"I still want to listen to it," Sab says with a laugh.

They drink and listen to the song. Then Estella says she can do better and puts on Grace Jones's "The Apple Stretching."

"No," Sab says.

"No," Vincent agrees. "It's not urgent enough. Too chill for our hero who's just turned twenty."

"Okay, I'll try again," Céline says. She puts on Marjo's "Illégal" and looks at Sabrina, nodding her head up and down as if to say, "See? It's this one, right?"

"Nah," Sab says.

"Settle down," Estella says.

Estella puts on "When Doves Cry" by Prince. "Admit it," she says to Sab.

"Okay, I admit it. You win."

The song lasts five minutes fifty-three seconds. They listen to it.

"I hope he doesn't get beaten up," Vincent says. "I hope he finds somewhere to sleep tonight."

Estella clears her throat. "My turn," she says. "It's 2053 and all the cities in the world are burning. The highways are jammed with people trying to escape to the countryside. There are bodies everywhere, bullets getting closer, militaries trying to control the crowds. Our hero lives between the fire and the forest, in a cabin under a bridge next to a river. Underneath the cabin, he's dug a deep tunnel that leads to a huge bunker. Over the last thirty years he was one of those people planning how to survive the end of the world. He spent his life preparing for this exact moment. His friends used to laugh at him, and he used to reply, 'You'll see, when the time comes, you'll be coming to me for help.' Out of love for them, he accepted the blows and mocking laughter, because the truth was, the only reason he had collected all this rice and lentils, the only reason he'd learnt to hunt squirrels and eat dandelions, was that he wanted to be a saviour. The thing he hadn't predicted was that all his friends would die in the cities before they even had the chance to make it to his bunker. The crowds have been filling the highways above him for months now and nobody's come to find him. He no longer has any reason to hope. His friends are dead, and now he regrets having wanted to save them, he regrets that he didn't stay and live with them. So he spent the day walking along the river. His clothes are in rags, he hasn't slept much, his backpack is almost empty. You can see him throwing stones into the river, but if you look more closely, you notice it's not stones but his own things, his clothes, his photos, his knife, that he's getting out of his bag and throwing, as if they were stones, as if it were a game, because he decided he won't need them anymore. Then we see him starting to dismantle the little cabin he built with branches, random two-by-fours, and sheets of plywood. He throws the branches, two-by-fours, and plywood into the river too. When he's finished destroying his house, he turns to his axe, his saw, his matches: he doesn't plan on having another fire. He throws it all into the river. Then he sits down and watches the water flow."

Estella stops talking and everyone looks at her. Everyone except Vincent, who doesn't dare, because he's afraid he won't be able to look away if he starts looking at her.

"What, that's all?" Sab says. "It's too sad, that can't be all."

"That's all," Estella says. "But anything could happen. The ending's open."

Nobody speaks.

"I have one," Vincent says after a moment.

He goes to the computer and plays "Orphan's Lament" by Robbie Basho. Nobody knows the song and nobody speaks while it plays for three minutes forty-three seconds. Céline doesn't cry often, but she wants to cry now. Sab has goosebumps. Estella wants to take Vincent in her arms. Tahar already wants to listen to the song over and over again. When the song comes to an end, Vincent lifts up his eyes, his ice-blue eyes, and looks at Estella.

"You win, Vincent," she says.

"Yes," the others say. "That's it. That's exactly it."

ABOUT THE TRANSLATOR

JC SUTCLIFFE IS A WRITER AND TRANSLATOR. Her most recent translations include *Worst Case, We Get Married* by Sophie Bienvenu and *Mama's Boy Behind Bars* by David Goudreault. She has lived in England, France, and Canada.